ORDEAL

ORDEAL

The Gordons

DOUBLEDAY & COMPANY, INC.
GARDEN CITY, NEW YORK
1976

Certain material that appeared in the Spring 1974 issue of *Tsá' Ászí'*
is used by permission of this quarterly which is written and edited
by Ramah, New Mexico, Navajo high school students with William L.
Rada serving as adviser.

Grateful acknowledgment is made to the following for permission to use
previously copyrighted material:

The American Museum of Natural History—"Prayer, Night Way" from
THE NIGHT CHANT, A NAVAHO CEREMONY, Memoirs of The
American Museum of Natural History Vol. 6, 1902.

Alfred A. Knopf, Inc.—"Twelfth Song of the Thunder, Mountaintop
Way" from DEATH COMES FOR THE ARCHBISHOP, copyright
1927 by Willa Cather and renewed 1955 by the Executors of the Estate
of Willa Cather. Reprinted by permission of Alfred A. Knopf, Inc.

Princeton University Press—BEAUTYWAY: A Navaho Ceremonial,
edited by Leland C. Wyman, Texts recorded by Father Berard Haile
and Maud Oakes, Bollingen Series LIII (copyright © 1957 by Bollingen
Foundation), reprinted by permission of Princeton University Press.

Library of Congress Cataloging in Publication Data
Gordon, Gordon.
Ordeal.
I. Gordon, Mildred, joint author. II. Title.
PZ4.G66260r [PS3557.0665] 813'.5'4
ISBN: 0-385-07806-4
Library of Congress Catalog Card Number 75–40726

For Henrietta Jelm, with
admiration and much love

1.

Slowly the realization that they were in jeopardy seeped into Sandy Wilcox's thinking. By now, the little Cessna 172 bobbed and tossed violently in the storm. The rain struck the windshield like a gusher shot from a gigantic hose, reducing visibility to near zero. About her, thunder boomed and cracked.

At the controls, she sat her seat as she would a saddle, tense, straight-backed, her body a little forward. She was twenty-four, tall and lean, with her hair tied in a pony tail and a loose plaid shirt tucked into a pair of faded Levi's. Beside her was a sixty-year-old man who looked very proper, in a stiff-backed way, in a pin-striped suit and dark tie. His thin mouth was puckered from a lifetime of wheeling and dealing.

The storm had caught her unexpectedly. One minute they were in the bright, harsh sunlight that marked this desert country of northern Arizona, then next in dark clouds slashed by lightning. The wind accelerated in minutes from a gust to hurricane intensity, and the rain fell as in a cloudburst.

Somewhere down there below them spread the Navajo nation, a land of mesas and canyons and mountains, 140,000 people, 16 million acres, bigger than some states or countries. It was as much an underdeveloped, sovereign land as any in Africa, a nation within a nation.

A gargantuan hand reached out, grabbed the plane, and shook it. "My God!" the man whispered to himself. Then he had to yell to be heard above the thunder. "Do we have a problem, miss?"

She nodded, her mind intent on rolling with the punches.

Keep the wings level . . . maintain a safe air speed . . . a safe altitude . . . outride this madness . . .

That was what her first instructor had drilled into her. *"You'll be scared to death. Everyone is."*

She was.

They had come up Canyon de Chelly, twenty-three miles long, its sandstone gorges a thousand feet deep in places. Shortly they would be over Hidden Canyon, which branched off from Canyon de Chelly. A few miles ahead was Highway 12, the road to Window Rock. If she could maneuver the plane that far, she would put down on it. If not, she might veer starboard and crash-land on sand dunes.

The man leaned over, with his girth tugging against the seat belt, to pick up a satchel at his feet. He was J. C. Berchtol ("Everybody back in New York calls me Mr. B."). Two days before he had arranged for the Page, Arizona, flying service, where she worked, to pilot him about the Navajo reservation. He was a buyer for a New York wholesale jewelry firm. Circumventing the trading posts, he bought directly from the Navajos for cash.

He carried the money—she estimated it at a half-million dollars, all in twenties, fifties, and hundreds—in the satchel. "Nothing like crisp new bills to get a man down on his price," he told her. "We've got so used to doing everything by checks and credit cards and computers that we've forgotten the wallop of hard, cold cash."

Each time he bargained, he opened the satchel wide, to put the money on display. She had begged him not to. He was going to get both of them killed. "It's not right to tempt people like that."

He smiled indulgently. "Thirty-three years I've been buying and selling and never lost a dollar. Little people steal little, not big."

"These people don't steal little or big, Mr. B.," she answered, "but if you're on drugs or liquor like some . . ."

Suddenly they were in an elevator that had fallen out of control. Their altitude dropped 400 feet. She pulled the plane out of it and into a steep climb. Except that it was not all that steep. No matter how much she increased the power, a downdraft held the Cessna to a dangerous minimum gain.

She had lost her bearings. She had no idea how far off course they were. On the reservation, there were no airports, only landing strips, and hence no control towers. It was a land that appalled some tourists, a vastness frightening by its very immensity, in places like the moon pictures the astronauts had sent back. In the canyons and up on the mesas, man was reduced to a flea looking at an elephant's wrinkle.

Yet she loved it, since she had been born to it. She saw the beauty of its changing colors and moods, its spectacular far reaches, the great white balloons that floated across turquoise skies, the clear, rousing air, and even the loneliness that gave one a chance to think and dream and come to know one's self and those close to one's heart. She was a trader's daughter who had had a lamb for a doll when she was four, and at five had cried when she learned she was white and not a Navajo like her little friends. No one had told her playmates, either, but the eventual disclosure was one of those strange adult puzzles they did not fathom and had slipped swiftly out of their minds. By eight, she owned half a horse, and her dearest friend, a Navajo girl, the other half.

"Bill," she whispered now. "Bill."

Mr. B. saw her lips moving. "What?" he yelled.

From his hogan on the rim of Hidden Canyon, Charlie Begay, who was fourteen and dreamed of running away to join the Air Force, stood in the doorway watching the plane pitch like a ship about to capsize. It was quite close and only a little above eye level. At a crack of thunder as sharp and startling as when his Anglo teacher clapped for attention, he took a step back.

He had first noticed the plane when gathering wood. By the time he returned to the log hogan—which was a low, octagonal, dome-shaped, earth-roofed home that faced east to catch the sun's first blessing and warmth—he was drenched. Watching the Cessna, he tuned his pocket radio into an Albuquerque station that was an altar to rock and roll.

Back of him he heard his mother chanting. He pushed up the radio's volume to blot her out. Who wanted to hear the Twelfth Song of the Thunder, Mountain Top Way?

> "The voice that beautifies the land;
> The voice above,
> The voice of the thunder
> Within the dark cloud
> Again and again it sounds,
> The voice that beautifies the land."

She called to him, "Turn it down. You hear me, son. Turn it down."

In the canyon below, on a rock shelf protected against the storm by a wide overhang, an old prospector also watched the plane. His heart thumped hard. Any second the aircraft would be sucked down. In a lifetime of roaming among a people tortured by hunger and sickness, he had seen much death, and even that of a stranger cut deeply.

He was called Shonto by the Navajos, from a place by that name near Inscription Rock where he had settled for a time. He was in his seventies, with bright, sharp eyes and wispy pink hair. He lay on the ground in a sleeping bag with his faithful companion, Sam, a mule, tethered a few feet away. For fifty years he had prospected over the West.

Tonight he was hungry. He often was these days. He lived mostly on handouts and desert plants. At one time he had been staked by friends who thought he would strike it rich, but they were all dead. Long ago he had given up on his dreams. Now he prospected only because there was nothing else to do.

Once he had been married. She had been a waitress in Flagstaff, a pretty little thing named Maggie. They had been eighteen and happy. They had a baby girl, and then at twenty his wife died, and her mother took the baby. As the years slipped by, he lost track of his daughter. He had always thought he would hire an investigator to find her if he ever hit a pay lode.

Once he should have. He had been up in the Lukachukai range the year before Willie Cisco found carnolite in Morrison Salt wash. The carnolite contained uranium, and Willie Cisco collected royalties on every ton taken out. It was an ore that was streaked with the yellow matter the Navajos had once used for war paint. But the year Shonto prospected in the wash, the Geiger counter, the "box that hears," had been deaf to what the "whispering mountains" were saying.

Now he had a small radio turned on, his only contact with a world he had not known since long ago.

The radio was on, too, in a motel room in the Navajo settlement of Chinle, not too many miles from Hidden Canyon. Vince Roberts, eighteen, sat on the bed cleaning his .38. He had it strung over the bedspread and used the spread to wipe the oil from his hands. He was a Los Angeles street-gang leader, tense, sullen, calculating, far older than his years. He had killed, and killed with no more feeling than if he had stepped on a spider.

He was quietly proud of it. "What's one more?" he asked Jigger Hardin, a year younger, sitting by the window reading a pornographic magazine. Jigger wore steel-rimmed glasses that encircled a perpetually amused look. He was always at ease. For the last year, he and Vince had been inseparable.

Vince continued, "You been reading the papers? Not enough food to go around. We're helping out."

Jigger grinned. "You're fantastic." When he was around Vince, fantastic was his favorite word.

He didn't do much talking, Vince didn't. He was quiet,

well mannered, and a little old-fashioned. He said "yes,
ma'am" and "yes, sir" to older people. They loaned him
money, and when he failed to pay it back, he was so contrite
they seldom minded. They felt good about helping out a fine
boy like Vince.

But when he was knocking over a service station with
Jigger, he was another person. He didn't raise his voice much
but Jigger swore he sounded as if he were about to kill everyone within sight.

Jigger himself came from a good, middle-class family. His
father managed a movie theater and his mother was a substitute
teacher. He had had all the attention and love parents could
give a child.

Vince, on the other hand, had scarcely known his father
who had been a carpet salesman covering four states. Five
months ago he had died—of a heart attack, according to the
obituary notice. Vince said that was a lie, and then clammed
up. Although Jigger could scarcely contain his curiosity, he
hadn't pried. Vince had a thing about questions. You never
asked him what he was doing tonight, or where he was going
tomorrow, or what he was thinking. Vince talked little about
his parents although Jigger knew that his mother was an alco-
holic who spent most of her evenings at a neighborhood bar
and, when she was home, was a hellcat.

"You're weak, Jigger," Vince once had told him. "Nothing
against you. It's how you're born. The genes. You can't help it.
I got the right genes. But don't let it bother you. Nothing you
can do about it."

Goggle-eyed, Jigger followed Vince everywhere. He
couldn't believe there could be a guy like Vince.

Like a few nights ago in Los Angeles. High on amphetamines and liquor, they had been cruising around at dusk, and
on a dare, Vince had killed a six-year-old boy running along
the sidewalk. He wanted to prove to himself he could hit a
moving target at two hundred feet. They had fled then to

Gallup, New Mexico, and subsequently, to the Navajo reservation.

As Jigger said, Vince was always thinking, and he figured if they had to hole up, they would need a woman. So they had taken along a girl friend, Penny Thompson, fifteen, whose father had disappeared and whose stepmother hated her. Penny was ready to run off anywhere with anyone who was kind to her.

Now she came out of the bathroom in bra and briefs. She hated wearing clothes, and liked the attention she got when she didn't. The guys said she was pretty. Nobody had ever told her she was pretty. She didn't really think she was. She had a run-of-the-mill face, looked like anybody's daughter, just another high school girl. She had soft eyes and lips and flesh. She was a little overweight and well filled out, and liked herself that way.

She grabbed the magazine out of Jigger's hand and threw it across the room. "What you reading those dirty old magazines for when you got me?"

Jigger laughed and pulled her down on his lap.

The radio continued to spout forth a smattering of music and news and commercials, unheard, unappreciated. Neither Jigger nor Penny dared to turn it off. Vince needed the security of continuous sound.

2.

Only a few hours before, Sandy had squatted on her booted heels, Navajo fashion, behind Mr. B., who was encircled by a crowd. He placed the satchel wide open on the ground near him and topped it with crisp, new hundred-dollar bills. In a big city he would have been elbowed and shouldered by the curious, but here at Chinle, in the heart of the Navajo nation, they showed a man consideration. They stared at all of that money but stayed a respectful distance.

Although it was late in the day, past five, the sun still

burned the withered Arizona land. Man and animal moved
with effort through the enervating August heat. Neither
sweated, for the air was an antiperspirant, absorbing moisture.
Only the pickup trucks, which every family owned that could
possibly afford a down payment, shot about recklessly. Off the
main street, they stirred up dust devils that whirled through the
little town.

It was a busy community consisting of a couple of supermarkets, a post office with a bulletin board advertising classes
in English and Navajo, Garcia's Trading Post, which accepted
BankAmericard and Master Charge, a boarding school, a hospital, and a tribal headquarters housing the police and tribal
courts. At the far end of the settlement, in a clump of cottonwoods nestled Justin's Thunderbird lodge. From here tourists
took off on dry days in World War II ammo carriers to explore
one of the West's wildest and most spectacular regions, Canyon
de Chelly. It was the last stronghold of the Navajos before Kit
Carson and his soldiers in 1864 burned and sacked their country and starved them into submission.

In the big, sprawling parking lot before the Imperial
Market, Mr. B. began his trading. Nearby, girls in jeans and
curlers were washing a new pickup. A teen-age boy passed in a
tank shirt with an Indian in a G-string imprinted on the back.
The Indian held a battle shield that read: Drink Coca-Cola.
And wherever there were Navajos, there were dogs. One could
tell how The Dineh (The People) were doing by their dogs.
This year they were sleek and well fed. Some years their bones
showed.

"The trader at Teec Nos Pos says he'll give a thousand
dollars," said a stocky young Navajo speaking for his dried-up
grandmother standing by him. He wore a black Stetson, work
shirt, Levi's, and a black belt with an enormous silver buckle.
"One thousand." He held out a squash-blossom necklace in
turquoise and silver.

Sandy's attention was diverted by a teen-age Anglo who

stood over her staring at the money. He was neatly dressed in jeans and a Hawaiian shirt. The latter was out of place in this country. She glanced at his hands. Soft. He had to be a tourist.

"That for real, ma'am?" He indicated the hundred-dollar bills.

She tensed. He was attractive except for the eyes. They were small and calculating. "Looks like the ones on top are."

"Window dressing, huh?" He drifted away.

Mr. B. squinted his tightly set little eyes to inspect the necklace. The demand for Navajo jewelry that had swept the fashion capitals of the United States, Canada, Great Britain, and Europe had upped the price drastically. In recent years it had doubled and trebled. A financial journal had listed turquoise along with diamonds as a good investment in the jewelry field.

However, the best silversmiths were under contract to the trading posts, and the finest turquoise was difficult to come by. Only 10 per cent mined was considered good quality and much of that was controlled by a very few parties. Two copper-mining companies had given the right to paw over their waste dumps, in search of turquoise, to individuals. So Mr. B. had come up with the idea of buying old pieces from the Navajos themselves. In the last two days he had purchased mostly squash-blossom necklaces in turquoise and silver for prices ranging from a few hundred to eight thousand dollars. He had paid five thousand dollars for a collection of beads, nuggets and chunks that included Lone Mountain spider web and Bisbee blue. He had paid twenty thousand dollars for a rug that had eighty threads to the inch.

While Mr. B. studied the squash blossom, Sandy's gaze roamed about the crowd. She recognized the winner of the fried-bread contest at the last Window Rock fair, smiled at a teen-ager with a baby in a cradleboard on her back, nodded to the instructor in Navajo history and culture at the Navajo Community College, the first college founded and operated by an Indian people, and waved to a teacher who was collecting soft-drink bottle caps for her math classes "so the kids can see and 'feel' and count numbers."

Her gaze was drawn magnetlike to the Anglo in the Hawaiian shirt, who had returned. He had her under scrutiny. Even lifting the Pepsi bottle from which he was drinking, he kept his eyes on her. He was joined shortly by a nice-looking high school girl, also an Anglo.

Mr. B. handed the necklace to Sandy. He wanted confirmation of his judgment. Her eyes danced. "It's Morenci. Very fine Morenci. And old."

"Eight hundred," Mr. B. told the young man, who shook his head and took the necklace back. Except for a few, they did not bargain, these Navajos.

"Nine." The young man started away with his grandmother. "Eleven."

The young man handed the necklace over, and Mr. B. made a ceremony of fishing eleven one-hundred-dollar bills out of the satchel. "You guys always win."

The Navajo let out a laugh. Mr. B. smiled. Two weeks ago when he left New York he had expected to deal with a stoic people. And they were until they knew you, then, hell, they were as much fun as his cronies. They had a great sense of humor, though you would never know it from the long, solemn faces moving about the trading posts. ("See that big rock up there? It's called Poison Rock. One drop can kill you.")

A friend from the Rough Rock Demonstration School called out to Sandy. "Hey," he said, "you want to become a medicine man? We've got a good course now. Six medicine men are teaching it."

A swaggering guy just out of his teens proffered a necklace of chunks and nuggets. "It's a hundred years old. Was my grandmother's and her mother's."

Sandy smiled. "I didn't know they were 'treating' turquoise so long ago." Quality turquoise was easy to fake. Low-grade mineral could be colored, stabilized or compacted. Even the experts found it difficult to spot treated turquoise. A town in Germany, Idar-Oberstein, specialized in hardening chalk turquoise —that is, stabilizing it—and shipping it to the United States. The worst fakes were the plastic pieces. They could be spotted by placing them to the teeth. They "felt" plastic.

The guy was surly. "The white lady is mistaken."

Sandy smiled. "Oh, come off it now." He broke into a slow grin and disappeared.

Mr. B. looked about. "Still got lots of money." His gaze stopped on a young woman in traditional dress. He could scarcely believe his eyes. She was wearing very fine, old, dark blue Burnham spider web. It must weigh, he estimated, seven hundred or eight hundred carats, and be worth in excess of ten thousand dollars. The silverwork was fluted and tapered. "What about that piece?" he asked. She looked shyly away, a young doe about to run.

Sandy rose and stepped forward. Repeatedly, she had told Mr. B. never to take the direct approach. They considered it bad manners.

"Has she been to a trader?" Mr. B. asked Sandy, recognizing the girl spoke no English. "I'll give her a couple thousand more than her best offer." A London or New York shop could easily sell it for thirty-five thousand dollars, possibly more.

She spoke softly in Navajo to the girl, then turned to Mr. B. "She needs it. Some day she may get sick and then what will she do if she has nothing to pawn?"

Pawn was still big business on the reservation. It was a Navajo way of life. Even the more sophisticated kept their silver and turquoise pieces against the day they might need a loan. The trader charged 2 per cent a month interest and held the piece one year. If any payment was made, he was required to hold it one more. Most of the honest traders—and some were not—held the pawn indefinitely if the party indicated he would eventually redeem it.

Sandy continued, "Besides, it was given to her—and you don't sell gifts, not even in hunger."

He shrugged in resignation. "In New York she'd be mugged."

He liked these people but did not understand them. What was wrong with putting the money in the bank and letting it draw interest, against the day one might be ill?

"They wear it and are proud of it and it is something of beauty to enjoy," Sandy told him. "But interest, where's the beauty in that?" She smiled. "They're the only people I know who wear their bank account and enjoy it."

He would be glad when he got back to New York, where people had a healthy respect for money.

He snapped the satchel shut and tossed it in the back seat of a car Sandy had borrowed. She retrieved it and locked it in the trunk. She was exasperated. "How many times have I told you, Mr. B.—I don't mean to be disrespectful but there are Anglos around, too, you know. There was this kid . . . I didn't like his looks . . ."

"Hi," said a low voice behind her, and Sandy turned to find a beautiful young woman in a nurse's uniform, her figure as trim as a model's. Her jet hair cascaded to her shoulders.

"Rinni!" Sandy cried, and they went into each other's arms. They had been eight when they met at boarding school.

"Grandmama wants to see you. Got time?"

Sandy told Mr. B. she would meet him at the airstrip in an hour. Jess, an old Navajo friend who had offered to drive them about, would arrange with Garcia's Trading Post to ship the rug.

Rinni resided in a small trailer a short distance outside of Chinle. Close by the trailer was a traditional forked-roof hogan where her grandmother lived. Her grandmother liked the old ways best and had refused to move. Even if she had, Rinni would have kept the hogan. If one of them were ill, they would need it for the medicine man to conduct the sing that would entreat the gods to cure them. Rinni might shop at the Fed Mart in Window Rock for miniskirts, but she was not about to desert

Begochiddy, the Great God who had created the world, or
Changing Woman or the other Holy People.

Once Rinni had laughed and said, "We've had women's lib
all the time and didn't know it. You don't have a female god.
Your whole religion is male dominated. But we've got Changing Woman."

Inside the dirt-floor hogan, it was dark. Where once had
been an oil drum, a modern stove now stood. Pots, pans, and
food jars and tins were arranged neatly on a shelf along the
wall. From the beams hung herbs, clothing, a sheepskin, blan-
kets, and an old-fashioned light bulb. An ancient trunk with
rusting bands sat at the foot of a neatly made bed. The trunk
was used for storage. There was no refrigerator and no running
water.

Sandy called out, "Grandmother!" which was what she
had called her as a child.

She was very old. No one, including herself, knew how
old. Nor did she know her birth date. Her mother had told her
that she was born "when the grass was beginning to grow."
That would have been in March.

She was feeble and spoke slowly. She had a face that
looked sculptured, a patrician face. She had poise and dignity,
yet had spent her life rearing eight children and herding sheep.

The three alternated between English and Navajo. They
would use one but switch when something could be expressed
better in the other language.

When Sandy rose to go, the old lady said quietly, "With
beauty all around me I walk. In old age wandering on a trail of
beauty . . . It is finished in beauty. Soon."

She had quoted from a prayer in The Night Way. To her,
the word, beauty, had meaning beyond that in English. Beauty
was peace and calm and above all, harmony with nature.

"There are still many moons to go, Grandmother," Sandy
said.

On the way to the car, Sandy said to Rinni, "She's always
walked the corn-pollen way. I hope I can."

The corn-pollen way. A life lived in beauty.

"Me too," Rinni answered. "When's the wedding?"

The pause was significant. "Oh, I thought I heard . . ." Rinni began.

"You did—but it's off."

3.

Sandy turned off the main road, and bounced in Rinni's car, which she had borrowed, over a narrow, rutted trail, drove around a school, and passed through a rusty two-inch pipe gate. Ahead was the dirt strip where sat the Cessna and a green-and-tan-striped Piper Cherokee 6 with an insignia on the side that read: "Air couriers for the Great Southwest Bank." Distances were so great that the bank ferried money and checks by plane between its branches.

Leaving the car, she sagged for a moment. Her eyelids were heavy with the heat and her feet swollen. Her hearing still replayed the hail-like noise of rocks hitting the car's underpinnings.

No one was about, and a sudden fear slipped a shroud over her. She had stressed to Mr. B.'s driver that under no circumstances should he leave the car. Mr. B., though, was demanding and might have ordered the driver to run an errand. The fact there was a half-million dollars left unguarded in the trunk would not faze Mr. B. She was all the more concerned, too, since Mr. B. had been most anxious to reach Two Gray Hill on the other side of the Chuska Mountains, and knew she would not put down after dark on the improvised, unlighted strip near Two Gray Hill. Unless Mr. B. appeared within the next fifteen minutes, she would cancel the flight.

She set about to check out the Cessna. She was as meticulous as a 747 captain. The exterior flight controls: aileron, rudder, elevator. The tires, landing gear. The engine oil, fuel and running lights.

As she worked, a deep, great hurt surfaced inside her.

Eight nights ago she and Bill Delaney had quarreled, and she had returned his engagement ring. Out here on the lonely, windswept runway, it all seemed so unreal. There had been no bitter words, only a very quiet statement of position by each.

Late in the afternoon, they had gone on a picnic to the Elephant Feet, two giant sandstone monoliths rising from the desert floor. There had been the usual tourists about, but she had seen no one except the big, handsome blond she had been engaged to for two months.

Seven months before, she had met him at a little get-together in Kayenta. He had been on the reservation only a few months. He was a junior executive in charge of personnel for a strip coal-mining company working the country a few miles to the west. He had instant physical appeal. He stood six feet three, with broad shoulders and a body that tapered to the waist. His friendly blue eyes flickered lightly over her and returned to rest on hers. She was struck by his tremendous vitality. He was constantly in motion. To put him in a small room, she thought, would be to endanger even the pictures on the wall. He was in cowpuncher boots and dark blue jeans, and the only man at the party to wear a tie. He took a ribbing about that. "My New England heritage," he explained.

She acknowledged the introduction and brushed him off. She considered strip mining debauchery of the land. She was irked that the girl giving the party, who clerked in the curio shop at the Holiday Inn, would invite him. The Holiday Inn catered mostly to Anglo business executives and tourists. The latter could scarcely believe their sight when they found this symbol of the white man's civilization dumped down in the heart of the Navajo nation. If they had come from Window Rock, though, they would have been conditioned. Colonel Sanders had invaded the Navajo capital with his Kentucky Fried Chicken.

Toward the end of the evening, he managed to sit by her. "I've got to do some shopping in Gallup Saturday. How about coming with me? We could have dinner and—"

"No, thanks," she said coldly.

"That's the fastest no thanks I've ever gotten."

"Nothing personal."

He studied her. "Look, I'm not married, never spent a night in jail, love my father and mother, vote the straight Republican and Democratic tickets, gargle Listerine every day, and use a deodorant twice as powerful as the next one."

She laughed. She couldn't help herself. And soon, she didn't want to.

So come Saturday she was in his dusty Mustang bound for the off-reservation town of Gallup. He was easy to be around and within minutes was an old friend. He drew her out, and listened to her talk about her work, and she loved him for that. Most men were interested only in their own careers. They laughed and shopped and strolled noisy streets crowded with Navajos who had come in pickup trucks by the hundreds for a big Saturday.

She bought records (Beverly Sills and Les McCann), a Gwen Bristow novel, and a new pair of Levi's. She helped him pick out two shirts, a pair of boots, and a watch.

"She can't compare to Joan Sutherland," he said.

"Who can't?"

"Sills."

"You trying to start a fight?"

"Yeah."

"You got one."

That night they had a Mexican dinner—enchiladas, tacos, rellenos, even sopaipillas—and danced to a mariachi orchestra. He complained about the hot food. "It's no good," she said, "if you can talk the next day."

It was a glorious trip, marred only by her knowledge that he was helping to desecrate this land she loved. Not knowing how she felt, he talked about the strip-mining operation and what he did. With effort, she contained her thoughts. In doing so, she experienced guilt, as if she were consorting with the enemy.

She had met few men, if any, who had the confidence he
had. He knew what he wanted and where he was going. Later,
she was to think that a little uncertainty in a man might be a
good thing. Uncertainty was thinking about the people around
you, and the country you live in, and considering the way of
beauty.

At the click of a car door, she turned quickly. From the
pilot's seat, she saw a bright orange Porsche with California license plates parked at the beginning of the runway. The young
Anglo in the Hawaiian shirt emerged from the driver's seat,
was joined by a boy about his age, and then the girl. The guy in
the Hawaiian shirt lit the girl's cigarette and patted her on the
fanny. She laughed.

They would have seen her if they had looked toward the
Cessna. They were interested, however, in the Piper. They
walked about it, talking quietly, then returned to the Porsche.

After they had gone, she sat in puzzled thought, debating
whether she should talk with the Tribal Police. She had nothing, though, to support her uneasiness, and it would be unfair
to stop three teen-agers for questioning who were only cruising
around, exploring the country, having a good time.

In the months that followed the Gallup trip, she and Bill
had been inseparable. He soon learned why the people called
her Ye'-Nil-Bah, the girl who makes things happen. He went
with her to Window Rock to plead for a college scholarship for
a boy, to Phoenix to transport a seriously ill Korean War veteran to a veterans hospital, to hogans to help old friends, and
once to Flagstaff to find a market for piñon nuts gathered by
people she had known as a child. She even conned him into
serving as umpire for a girls' softball team she had organized.
He did all of this good-naturedly with something akin to worship in his light blue eyes.

One weekend they drove to the Far Mountain Trading
Post, up in the Rainbow Bridge country, where she had grown

up. It lay in charred ruins. Her parents had never recovered
from the fire. Within a few months, her father died, and only
recently, her mother. Sandy could still see her mother bandag-
ing up a boy's torn leg or a little girl's shoulder. She could hear
her mother getting up in the middle of the night, following hard
knocking at the door, and setting forth to serve as midwife. Her
mother had written thousands of letters in English and
translated more thousands into Navajo. Her father had gone
out into blizzards to take food to the old and sick, and to rescue sheep near freezing. He had interceded with the police,
served as judge and jury in quarrels, and many times buried the
dead. Her parents, constantly defending "our people," had
been a bridge with the white world.

"They had an awful time getting me to speak English when
I was little, before I went to school," she recalled. "I was stubborn about it. I couldn't see why I should. None of the other
kids did. I remember one night at dinner when I was rattling
away in Navajo my mother said, no English, no food."

Bill was fascinated. His background had been in sharp
contrast. His home was Chestnut Hill, Massachusetts. His father owned an advertising agency in Boston. He himself was a
graduate in business administration from Boston University. "If
anybody had told me a year ago I'd have three hundred
Navajos working for me, I would've said he was crazy. I didn't
even know where they lived. They were just Indians to me.
Primitives. You know how it is when you catalogue people
without thinking about it."

Her eyes lit up. "It makes me so mad. Just because they
speak another language, and many run sheep, and they have a
different culture—that doesn't make them primitives. You
don't call a cattle rancher a primitive because he's in the cow
business.

"And then, too, everybody thinks all Indians are the same
when the tribes are as different as white Americans are from
the Arabs. The Navajos aren't the same as the Ogala Sioux you
read so much about. The Navajo leaders are businessmen.

They think they can outdeal the Anglos at their own game—
and they've been doing a pretty fair job."

The two recognized they were poles apart. It bothered her
that he was the hard-driving type, worked long hours, and was
ambitious. She had no desire burning inside her for money or
status.

"You're too Navajo," he said.

"Is that bad?" she countered. "I want love and a husband.
Not a pay check. I can get a pay check on my own." She
added, "And two children. I don't want to increase the population, just replace ourselves."

Another time he said, "You sit around in college in these
rap sessions with the guys and talk about girls. Serious talk, I
mean, about the kind of a wife you want, and we'd all agree
that if you're going anyplace you've got to have a girl who'll
help you in your career. You know, someone who's smart and
poised and knows what to say and can handle people. You're
all of that, Sandy, and more. My boss thinks you're a knockout."

She was pleased and disturbed. "You wouldn't marry for
love alone? If a girl didn't match up to all that you said . . . ?"

He laughed. "That's entrapment. A theoretical question. I
don't have to answer it because I don't have to worry about it.
I've got you."

From the beginning, he was honest. The night they returned from Gallup, he told her he was engaged to marry a
childhood sweetheart back in Boston. When he proposed to
Sandy, which was at a sing, he said he was writing the girl to
break the engagement. Sandy protested that it would be cruel
to write. He should telephone.

He never got around to phoning. He was always going to
do it next Sunday. He would be certain to find her home Sunday. Sandy never brought up the subject. She feared that pressure might be an irritant that would erode their love. Nonethe-
less, she worried. She would battle to hold him. She was
one-quarter Irish. The Irish had never surfaced in her parents

but it had in her. She admitted she was determined and even pugilistic when she wanted something.

Early, he met her two great loves and approved. One was Glamorous, a scrawny, nondescript dog that welcomed one and all. She explained the name. "You've got to do all you can for a nothing dog."

The other was Skeet. She didn't know how Bill would take to Skeet, who was six and a Navajo. "My boy," she said proudly in introducing him.

Two years before she had found Skeet sitting on her doorstep. He was in shock and his feet were raw from having walked miles. She tried talking to him in English, then Navajo, but he couldn't or wouldn't tell her where he belonged. She had called the Window Rock police headquarters but they had no report on a missing boy. Months after he arrived, he told her his name was Skeet. That was all, just Skeet. Skeet was a last name in the Navajo country and she checked with some Skeets she knew over at Rough Rock.

Last fall he had gone to school, and given his name as Skeet Wilcox, and his mother as Miss Sandra Wilcox. She was touched, and her worst nightmare now was that someone would claim him.

"You marry me," she told Bill, "and you've got a built-in son."

"Yeah, and the people back home will think I bedded down with a Navajo, and if you've ever been to Chestnut Hill . . ."

He liked Skeet. He would like anyone or anything I did, she thought. He's that kind of a man. Driving and ambitious, yes, but gentle and thoughtful and kind.

Sitting in the old, beaten-up Cessna, which long ago had overflown the junk heap where it should have landed, she could not explain what had happened that night on the way back from Elephant Feet.

4.

Restless, she walked the short runway, scuffing up red earth with her boots. The land was still, without breath. The weeds along the airstrip drooped, listless and parched. Big white clouds hung low against a deep blue sky. They looked like cardboard cutouts for a high school play. On her right was a deserted Quonset-type hangar and a low, small structure. No one was about. Another might have felt lonely but this was a country where one was often alone.

She was hot and dirty, longed for a shower, had to wash her hair that night, and somehow must get her boots half-soled. She was thirsty for a Coke. She had been five, she recalled, when she had first tasted the "jumping water." She had run out of the house screaming because of the unexpected sting.

What had happened to Mr. B.? She would give him ten minutes more, then leave a note on the plane. She would spend the night with Rinni.

At the end of the strip, she turned, then stopped. The bright orange Porsche was parked alongside the Piper. The three teen-agers sat inside the car talking. The driver pointed to something about the plane and the other two nodded. There was none of the levity of their previous visit.

It was odd they should return. She could understand the first time. They had wanted to see the "airport."

The Porsche rolled slowly toward her, and quietly except for the crunch of tires. The driver—the boy in the Hawaiian shirt—waved at her, then with a burning of tires, swung the car about in a wild, careening movement, and shot at high speed back toward the main road.

She sagged, then picked up her feet and headed for the Cessna. She was tired, and when she was tired, her imagination took over.

She would phone Skeet the first chance she got. She missed him terribly. He had become very much a part of her life. He even accompanied her to a community church service each Sunday. She had not asked him to go, but one Sunday he was dressed and waiting for her. She would rear him a Christian as she would one day her own children. Since he was Navajo, though, he should know the legends of The People. The Navajos had no faith in the sense that the Anglos knew faith. They had many Holy People, and most of them, except Changing Woman, were to be feared for the curses they could put on one. ("They don't worship them exactly," Sandy had explained one day to Bill. "The gods are just around everywhere, and like the old-time school master, will whack you one if you don't behave.")

Changing Woman, however, loved the Earth People. She was a vibrant, beautiful young woman, a virgin who had given birth to the Hero Twins. The Sun, who had got her pregnant with his rays, was their father. When they grew up, the Hero Twins set forth to visit their father, and along the way, had to battle many monsters whose blood spilled over the land and could still be seen. The Anglos called it lava, but anyone could tell it was dried blood. The Hero Twins embodied the finest virtues, and for generations had been boyhood idols.

Yes, Skeet must know about the Hero Twins. Anglo society, which wrecked every pedestal it could find, offered few heroes or heroines.

She was finishing a note to Skeet when Mr. B.'s driver pulled the car alongside the plane. Mr. B. looked haggard. "They told me at the Park Service about a needlepoint, and we had a devil of a time finding the hogan." He handed her a turquoise and silver bracelet that was true needlepoint with each turquoise stone set in a bezeled silver compartment.

Her eyes brightened, then she glanced uneasily toward the main road. "We'd better hurry. We've just got time to make it before dark."

Mr. B. was not to be rushed. He was a precise, deliberate man. He handed her the attaché case containing the jewelry he had purchased that afternoon, worth possibly seventy thousand dollars. Then he wanted to count the bills in the satchel.

She was alarmed. "Do it after we get there—in your motel room."

"Take only a few minutes."

"Please, Mr. B. I've got my reasons. We're out here alone. Nobody could hear us if we shouted."

Her apprehension swayed him. Grumbling, he boarded the plane with satchel in hand. "I must determine if I have sufficient funds to last out the trip. I've bought more than I had anticipated."

"Yes, Mr. B." She was warming the engine. The driver handed Mr. B. his two regular cases. "Thank you, Jess," Sandy said. "Phone Rinni, will you, and tell her I won't be staying? Thank her for the car."

Canyon de Chelly spread below them, its sheer walls of sculptured sandstone softly tinted at this hour in pastel oranges, pinks, and purples. It was deeper than the canyon of any great city, and at this point, wide as a city block. In other parts, though, it narrowed to as little as thirty feet. In places, Navajo "tears" had splashed across the walls—dark manganese and oxide stains that formed lovely old tapestry designs.

No matter how exhausted she was, she never flew this country without coming alive. She remembered that at boarding school in Tuba City she would run to the window at the sound of an occasional plane. Up there was adventure, a whole new world. As long ago as that, she had decided she would become a pilot and fly over this land she loved. When she was sixteen, her father's closest friend, who operated a flying service out of Page, taught her. At seventeen she had a private pilot's license. The day she was graduated from the University of Colorado was the happiest of her life. The Monday after that she would start part-time work as a professional pilot.

She pointed out to Mr. B. the river bed far below, the Rio

de Chelly. It was dry now, but when the rains came, raging waters would roar down from the Chuska Mountains. Russian olives, cottonwoods, and tamarisks lined the bed. In the autumn the cottonwoods looked like the work of an artist fond of yellows and golds. He was the same artist who in spring went slaphappy with his palette.

Car and wagon tracks snaked crazily across the canyon floor. "That's because of quicksand and soft sand. You have to know the floor to drive it."

In the summer, Navajo guides shepherded thousands of tourists in ancient weapons carriers that accommodated sixteen —if the visitors were not too broad of beam.

"What do you think of it?" she asked, indicating the canyon.

"I'll be glad when I get back to New York. Don't tell me people are fool enough to live down there?"

Near the trails were occasional hogans. "Summer residences," she said, laughing. She explained that quite a few Navajos, who had permanent homes up on the rim, farmed the canyon during the summer months. They had apple, peach and pear trees, truck gardens, sheep and goats. The women wove rugs and posed for pictures. "They make more money some months from what the tourists give them for posing than they do from the rugs."

The canyon was wide enough, and the farmers were sufficiently distant from the river bed, to escape the occasional summer torrents. "But even if you know the land," she said, "it can be treacherous." A few Navajos and Anglos had died in flood waters or perished in the quicksand.

"Looks like we're in for some rain." She nodded ahead. Dark storm clouds were moving toward them.

"The name *de Chelly* comes from a Navajo word, *Tsegi*," she continued. "You say it like a cat spitting, and the Spanish who were in here thought it sounded like *day shay-yee,* which in Spanish would be spelled de Chelly, and then we come along and corrupt it some more, and now it's *d'Shay*. Weird, isn't it?"

"Are we going into that storm?"

"Want to turn back?"

"No, no, I can't lose any time."

"We may get some turbulence, but it's probably only local. The weather report didn't mention it."

Still, it was a half-shrouded world ahead, all the way across the horizon. The black clouds were shattered every few minutes by lightning strokes. At the time, though, there seemed no reason to return to Chinle. She had flown through countless thundershowers. They were a part of a desert pilot's work. The turbulence would jostle the plane around a little, and if Mr. B. was susceptible to air sickness . . .

"See that condominium?" She indicated a prehistoric cliff house, high above the canyon floor. It perched on a ledge under a wide overhang. "That's where the Anasazis lived long before the Navajos. They came and went and no one knows why. They left a lot of pictographs on the walls, and some of them are good."

"Almost got killed once in a storm over the Catskills," Mr. B. said. He was sitting bolt upright, his hands in a tight grip.

Talking might help. She continued, "The Navajos call them the Swallow People because they were like the swallows that build adobe nests under rock formations. How'd you like to climb up there every night? Or come down mornings before you had your coffee?"

"Almost got killed in the Catskills," Mr. B. reiterated. "Nothing to worry about, I don't suppose."

"Nothing at all, Mr. B." Nevertheless, she tightened up her thoughts and muscles to brace for the storm.

"I haven't got a will. Always intended—"

"Forget it."

She thought she detected a change in the engine noise, a coarser pitch.

"Any place to put down near here?"

"Road to Window Rock's up ahead."

One second they were in the smelter-red glow of a sun

about to set. The next they were alone in a pitch-black world punctuated by zigzags and exclamation marks of lightning that seemed to hunt them down. The lightning thrusts had tributaries running off from the main trunk, giving the effect of white skeleton trees set against a velvet background. Sometimes two bolts would flash simultaneously, and the thunder would roll and boom and crack.

The furious wind buffeted them one way, then another. She tried climbing, then turning, but found herself kicked about by the whims of the storm. Her heart was a pounding piston. Turbulence in itself, sufficiently violent, could render a plane uncontrollable.

She got the tower at Gallup on the radio. "Gallup tower, this is Cessna five-seven-six-foxtrot. Over."

Scarcely could she hear herself. The thunder was like massed kettle drums beating in her hearing.

"Cessna five-seven-six-foxtrot, Gallup tower. I read you weak but readable."

The voice lifted her spirits. "Roger. Gallup tower, this is Sandra Wilcox, Cessna five-seven-six-foxtrot over Hidden Canyon, approximately twenty-five miles east of Chinle requesting the Gallup weather."

"Roger. Cessna five-seven-six-foxtrot. Gallup weather is eight hundred broken, two thousand overcast, visibility one to two miles in heavy rain, wind zero six zero degrees, twenty-five gusting to thirty-five, altimeter two niner eight three. How did you copy?"

She could never reach Gallup or nearby Window Rock. That had been a sixty-second hope. She was in a true thunderstorm, a cell unto itself, which was growing ferociously turbulent. Normally she would have flown around the storm, but its intensity had taken her unaware.

"Cessna five-seven-six-foxtrot has you loud and clear. Do you have weather information for Chuska Mountains?"

As if slapped savagely, her head snapped from side to side.

"Roger. Cessna five-seven-six-foxtrot. We've had report of severe thunderstorm activity around Toadlena."

Her voice was strained. "Roger. Cessna five-seven-six-foxtrot. I'm in severe turbulence and losing altitude, I'm . . ."

The cloudburst hit. It was as if they were under Niagara Falls.

The radio went dead.

At the Gallup airport, modeled after an Indian pueblo, an anxious, weary but alert controller stared out into the thick night porridge. He could see little of the big, garish motel signs along Highway 66, and the car headlights had no more thrust than weak flashlights.

He sounded monotonous, but his breath came a little quicker with the passing of each minute. "Cessna five-seven-six-foxtrot. Say your location . . . Cessna five-seven-six-foxtrot. Say your location . . . Cessna five-seven-six-foxtrot. Do you read me?"

When there was no response, he said, "This is Gallup tower on one two one point five."

That was the emergency frequency.

"Does any aircraft read Cessna five-seven-six-foxtrot?"

5.

Window Rock, the capital of the Navajo nation, sprawled over miles of bleak and usually sun-drenched desert. The scattered businesses included a Fed Mart, which was a supermarket offering everything from groceries to clothes, a mall featuring a hay-and-grain feed store and laundry, a modern, attractive, tribal-owned motel, and all the other shops indigenous to small-town America.

The capital took its name from a large, circular hole in a cliff that most days framed a picture postcard view of turquoise sky and lazy white clouds. Near the "window" was a pueblo-type building, in the soft, pastel tan of the desert, where the

Tribal Council sat, a one-body congress or parliament. Behind it, and seemingly a part of it, towered two enormous fat brown loaves of stone. The bare earth about the pueblo looked as if it were swept every morning.

A short distance down a winding, desert road was the police headquarters, a large, modern building of blocks and squares and planes, and much glass. From here orders went out to five divisions, forty-three subdivisions and more than two hundred officers scattered over a territory as big as West Virginia. Some areas, reached only over twisting trails faintly marked, were the most isolated in the United States. The action of the movies' Old West was long gone, but the topography in a few far places remained the same.

The call from the Gallup tower came into the police communications center at 7:56 P.M. Mary Burnsides, a college graduate who was fluent in both English and Navajo but spoke only English over the air, sat before a small radio panel talking with officers on duty. She noted their calls on a ruled sheet, set forth the location of each cruise car, and forwarded instructions. She had a code sheet before her to which she constantly referred.

Gallup said, "I took a call a few minutes ago from a pilot who identified herself as Sandra Wilcox and the plane as a Cessna. She said she was in a storm over Hidden Canyon and losing altitude. Contact was broken and . . ."

The controller advised he had notified the Air Route Traffic Control Center of the Federal Aviation Administration at Albuquerque. The Center would report a possible crash to the Air Force Search and Rescue Center at Scott Air Force base, Belleville, Illinois, which would co-ordinate rescue work if the Air Force and other agencies were needed. The National Transportation Safety Board in Washington, D.C., delegated by Congress to investigate all accidents in which fatalities were involved, was alerted. The New Mexico and Arizona Civil Air Patrols, too, were advised, although they would not be called in if the pilot, Sandra Wilcox, was correct in stating her position over Hidden Canyon. The patrols would be used only if a search was necessary for locating the plane. Since it was mandatory that civilian aircraft be equipped with an ELT (emergency location transmitter), the beep from the aircraft, if it had crashed, would be picked up on one of the emergency frequencies. That is, unless the ELT was malfunctioning.

Working swiftly, Miss Burnsides notified the Chinle police division and the U.S. and Tribal park services. Then she dialed the home of Major Paul Tonalea, head of the Navajo Police Academy, who had established a reputation for directing rescue missions. A year ago, all local agencies that had jurisdiction of one kind or another over catastrophes on Navajo territory had agreed that when one developed he should take immediate charge.

He and his wife had been watching television, together with a teen-age daughter who looked like a fashion model and a teen-age son whose one ambition was to play college football. Now in his forties, Tonalea was himself a graduate of the University of Arizona. But college would be different for his children. He remembered he had hitchhiked to Tucson carrying an old, battered suitcase. He had slept in a culvert the night before he arrived and looked like a bum. Too scared to ask directions, he had walked miles looking for the university. When he came across a young woman in white, he thought she was a nurse and stopped her. Frightened, she ran from him. On the reservation, all women who wore white were nurses and helped people. He had tried using a telephone, but the device was too complicated.

That was a long time ago. Now he moved easily back and forth between two worlds, liked by his own people and the Anglos. He was outgoing, quick with a smile and a joke, but objective and a firm disciplinarian in his work, a brilliant investigator whose police academy had much the same courses, high standards, and standing as the FBI one at Quantico, Virginia.

Hanging up, he turned to his wife. "Looks like we've got a plane down in Hidden Canyon." He searched in a closet for his rain gear. "Dammit, I know I put it in here. I may not be back tonight."

She located his raincoat and boots. "I don't know how you ever find a criminal. Pure luck, I guess. You'll call me soon as you know?"

Sheepishly, he took the coat. "Sure."

Outside the rain stung his face and the wind hit him a boxer's punch. He almost went down. He gained his balance and made his way to a Volkswagen. He couldn't remember a storm as violent as this one.

At headquarters, he learned that Miss Burnsides had taken a call from the division center at Chinle, an hour's drive away.

One Charles Begay, fourteen, had telephoned Chinle from the Big Rock Trading Post to report he had seen a plane fall into Hidden Canyon. Begay lived on the rim. He promised to wait at the post until an officer arrived. Using binoculars, the officer would look over the rim at the point where Begay had seen the craft disappear. The lightning might pick up a reflection of metal, the plane might have burst into flames, or a survivor might be signaling with some type of light. Otherwise, Captain Chee Yazzie, who commanded the Chinle division, doubted if the officer could spot the aircraft. The dark was too impenetrable, the night too wild. Still, it was a routine lead that must be followed.

Over the radio, Major Tonalea discussed with Yazzie details of the rescue work. "Her name's Sandra Wilcox and the plane's a Cessna. That's all we've got."

"Anyone with her?"

"We don't know that or where the flight originated. We're asking all the divisions to run a check on their airstrips. Someone may have seen her take off—that is, if the flight originated on the reservation."

They agreed Chinle would dispatch officers, rangers, and a paramedic by jeep immediately into Canyon de Chelly in co-operation with the U.S. and Tribal park services. They could reach Hidden Canyon, which branched off from Canyon de Chelly, only by going through de Chelly.

The party would take in standard rescue equipment. In addition to first aid, the matériel would include ropes and tackle to use in reaching the plane if it had landed on a ledge, stretchers, and pneumatic jacks to lift wreckage if a person should be pinned down. They would also carry bags for removing bodies.

The first step in covering a catastrophe of this kind was to determine if there were survivors. Until this was learned, time was of the essence.

"How far can you get a jeep into de Chelly?" Tonalea asked.

"About seventeen miles, Major. The last six are impassable by vehicle. Narrow and lots of boulders. We'll have to truck horses down there and pack in."

Tonalea studied a detailed map of the region. "Can you make it on a night like this?"

"If we don't find too much water down there. We'll have to ford the river a time or two to get to Hidden Canyon."

"See what you can do. I'll get a helicopter to stand by, but I don't know when we can take off. May be hours. What about trails into Hidden Canyon from up on the rim?"

"Let me check that out. But I don't see how we could get a man down in this blow with equipment. He could find out if there are survivors, of course—if he could get down without breaking his neck."

"Which he just might," Tonalea said. "Offhand, I think it's a good way to get one of our men killed. But we might give it a try at daybreak if we don't get through tonight."

"Hold it a second, Major." Tonalea could hear talking in the background. Yazzie came back over the radio hookup. "One of our officers knows Miss Wilcox. She flies out of Page for an outfit up there. Has had a buyer out of New York in tow, a man about sixty. We don't know his name. He pays cash for jewelry and rugs, and bypasses the trading posts. He was buying on a parking lot here this afternoon up until four-thirty or five. The talk is that he carries a fortune in cash with him. I think it's a safe assumption that he was with her when she took off."

"Anyone see her take off?"

"Some kids may have. One party remembers seeing a Porsche with teen-agers in it going toward the airstrip."

"I want a report every half hour."

"Yes, Major."

Finished talking, Tonalea sat thinking. Sandra Wilcox. There had been a Tom Wilcox who ran a trading post up at Far Mountain. Probably no relation.

The radio droned on, a noisy, forgotten child. Penny snuggled up in Vince's lap, a cat too big for her basket. Her stomach bulged over her briefs and her breasts, above her bra. Falling down over the bra was a squash-blossom necklace.

Jigger sat across the room, manicuring his nails. Occasionally he glanced up. He was glad Vince had thought to bring Penny along. Sometimes when Vince wanted a woman, they would cruise around until they found a girl they could pick up. Vince would then rape her. Jigger had never taken part in anything like that. He couldn't help but feel sorry for the girl. Once he had offered the girl his handkerchief when they put her out of the car and she sat on the curb crying. Vince said he was "weak." He was, he knew. He wished he could be a guy like Vince.

"Say it again," Penny said to Vince. "I'm beautiful."

"Beautiful. But bad."

"Bad?"

"Going to have to punish you. Told you when I got you something and you didn't thank me—"

"You stole it when Jigger and I got the clerk off to one side. I don't have to thank you when you steal something."

"You wanted it."

She fingered the necklace. "Only jewelry I ever had was a pin Papa gave me."

He grabbed her to turn her over his knees and met with instant resistance. She was laughing. She loved to wrestle with Vince. She had had a cat once that like to wrestle. Never seen anything like it. She wished she had a cat with her.

Overpowering her, Vince got her across his lap, pulled the briefs down, and spanked her hard.

Jigger said quietly, "It's my night."

Vince stopped. "Just warming her up for you."

"It's my night," Jigger repeated.

Vince shrugged and let her up. A newscaster interrupted the rock and roll. Vince looked out the window. "I don't figure he'll take off at six even if he is a bank runner with a schedule. Not if this keeps up. But we'll be on hand if he does."

Jigger started to comment but Vince, indicating the radio, shushed him. "A light plane carrying two persons has crashed in a storm into Hidden Canyon. The plane was piloted by Sandra Wilcox of the Page Flying Service and had taken off shortly before from Chinle. The craft carried a New York jewelry buyer whose identity is unknown. He is believed to be carrying a half-million dollars in cash and jewelry. The Chinle police and rangers will pack in to locate the plane and determine if there are survivors. We will bring you further reports . . ."

Vince pushed Penny aside. At a bedside table, he rummaged through papers and came up with a map. He spread the map out on the bed and studied it. "Hot damn!" he said. "Hot damn!"

A long time after he turned off the radio, Shonto lay thinking. He was warm and dry in his old sleeping bag. Outside, the storm raged unabated, thunder, lightning, and a violent beating of rain such as he had never known. The gods were angry tonight and with good reason. The world was going to hell, and fast. He almost never read a newspaper, but times when he did, to find out how Snuffy Smith was doing, he saw Armageddon was not far off.

It would be a fight to get on his feet. Only yesterday he had explained how it was to the Big Rock trader. "When I sit down, I can't get up. When I get up, I can't sit down. I need a new hinge."

He worried about what would become of him. Funny about people. Take the tourists. They thought old prospectors were born that way, never had a childhood like other people, never the same ambitions and hungers. They came the way they were at sixty or seventy. They never got sick or died, either. They went on plodding into the sunset alongside their mules. They were picturesque. Picturesque, my foot. They were losers, most of them. True, they were lucky losers. In the cities they'd be down on skid row. Winos, probably. He was glad he was a loser in the wide-open spaces.

If he could summon the courage to get up, he might strike gold. It'd be on the ground, not in it, but he wasn't particular. After fifty years, he'd take it wherever he found it. If he struck gold, he might get into one of the Leisure Worlds he had read about. And he would see his daughter. By now she would be nearing sixty. He couldn't imagine her that old. He remembered her as the rather pretty, shy girl of twenty he had talked with once for a couple of hours. He had met her by pre-arrangement at a bus station in Albuquerque. She was headed for San Francisco to find a job. He hadn't kissed her and she hadn't called him Father. They were strangers meeting but strangers who wanted to like each other. She looked like her mother when he had married Maggie. Exactly like Maggie, whose picture he still carried. It was as tattered as the old wallet he kept it in, the Mexican one imprinted with the Aztec calendar.

A thunderclap hit his hearing with the force of an explosion. He could swear the lightning that preceded it plunged like a dagger right past him. Sam was nervous as a bobcat at bay. He kept shifting and stomping.

But no matter how fierce the storm, fifty years of living with a vision moved Shonto to shed the sleeping bag. He emerged completely dressed, in an old gray shirt and frayed pants that he had bought for two dollars at a thrift shop in Holbrook. Long ago, he had concluded that a man wasted too much effort and time dressing and undressing.

Painfully, he managed to get to his hands and knees and work his way to the rough sandstone wall. Finding a projection to hold to, he dragged himself up by painful stages. Once erect, he shut his eyes and set his lips to adjust to the grinding of joints. Then he made it to Sam, who watched him with a growing suspicion that he was up to no good.

After saddling him, Shonto tied on his bedroll. All the while he talked to Sam, even though he realized it was useless. No man had ever conned a mule into doing anything. Talking, however, bucked up Shonto's own courage. A man needed a stiff drink on a night such as this and Shonto took a long draw from a bottle of tequila he had saved for an emergency. It was the first drink he had had in weeks. Time was when he headed once a month for a town off the reservation to get roaring drunk on his welfare check. No longer, though, could the old body take it. Times, too, had changed. Instead of good-natured Navajos, the bars were jammed with a new breed of Navajo: cat skinners, hoistmen, mule drivers and drillers from the uranium mines. They drove like madmen, gambled wildly, and consumed more liquor in an hour than a reasonable man would in a couple of days. They didn't know how to drink and, worse yet, spent most of their time shacking up with women. Indian, Mexican, or Anglo, it didn't matter.

He pulled on Sam's reins, then got behind him and shoved. He didn't want to get rough because he and Sam had a love born of two creatures needing each other. Finally, however, he kneed Sam hard in the ribs. He didn't know whether the kneeing hurt him or Sam the most. Sam moved a foot, got another kneeing, moved another foot, and after repeated pressure of this nature, found himself out in the storm.

Shonto hurried. Taking Sam by the reins, he headed down a slippery, muddy, washed-out trail with only the lightning baring the crevices and fallen rocks. More sure-footed, Sam lurched along, resigned to his fate.

Shonto began whistling. Dark as it was, he could see the rainbow.

6.

How long she had wandered about the wreckage she would never know. There were some things so violent that the memory never taped them.

When she came to, she was slipping in soft, waterlogged sand alongside the cabin. A warning signal flashed: Beware of quicksand. Once she had seen a dog run into it and still could hear his pitiful cries as he was sucked down.

The wind and rain whipped her fully conscious, and the thunder and lightning stirred terror within her. In one flash of lightning, she saw the cabin, sheered of its motor, a toy an angry child had smashed with a hammer. It tilted crazily, half sunk in the sand. In the next flash, she discovered one side had been whacked off, the side where Mr. B. had sat. She had had to climb out his side and jump down. Surely, she had been aware that he was not there. She had, though, no recollection.

Where was Mr. B.? She looked frantically about. She had to find Mr. B. He might be injured; he might desperately need her.

Carefully feeling her way with her boots, she took a step, then another. Each time she sank a few inches, but it was not quicksand. She could determine that by the feel. She fell over a hard object, probably a rock, and sat where she had fallen. Her thoughts wandered. How beautiful the lightning was, slashing across the sky in one geometric design after another. The lightning was a flash gun permitting her to take pictures of the broken cottonwoods and tamarisks and willows. In crashing, the cabin had clipped and stripped them.

I'm in shock, she told herself. I've got to shake myself out of it. I've got to get organized. I've got to find Mr. B. He may be injured. Somewhere out there he could be dying.

Something was running down her face, something thicker than rain. Blood was oozing from a forehead cut. It seemed to the touch wide and deep. Her right arm grew excruciatingly painful. Why hadn't she been aware of it before? Then suddenly she doubled up. An intense burn flared through her abdomen. More than anything else, it brought her sharply, agonizingly alive.

Mr. B. He must be injured. Probably he was calling her this minute. Her mind refused to consider the possibility that he was dead.

Her shirt was torn and covered with blood. The small silver cross her mother had given her on her sixteenth birthday was gone. The ring! Her engagement ring was missing! Then she remembered. She and Bill had quarreled and the next day she had put the ring in the mail. But what had they quarreled about? What was it?

Oh, God, don't let Mr. B. die.

She discovered she was sobbing. Ridiculous. She never had given in to her feelings, not even when she was little. Her mother had taught her the Navajo way. If you fall down, pick yourself up and go on playing.

I must get organized. I've been in a plane crash. I've survived.

Once on her feet, she forced the pain out of mind. I can will myself to do anything. Anything.

She staggered a step or two. Partly it was the wind buffeting her, the smarting of rain on her torn flesh, the treacherous underfooting of sand.

She called loudly, "Mr. B.!"

Unless he was a few feet away, he could not hear her. With each bolt of lightning, she advanced a few feet. Not far from the mangled cabin, she spotted the prehistoric cliff house—only it wasn't a cliff house since it was on the ground—rising in an

enormous cavelike recess of the perpendicular canyon wall.
Built of stone by the Anasazis, it sat there defying the elements.
For centuries, it had stood up under the battering of countless
rainstorms and the sand blasting of high, hot winds.

Something brushed her legs and she jumped. Instinctively,
she kicked out to fight off whatever it was, then saw the tum-
bleweed go rolling away from her. When the flash floods came,
the river ran with tumbleweeds that had gathered in the
parched bed during the dry seasons.

He could have been tossed out and fallen a considerable
distance away. If he had, he was dead. Quickly she shut the
possibility out of her mind. He was alive. She was, wasn't she?
Miracles did happen.

She would walk around the cabin in ever widening circles.
She must not lose sight of it or she would lessen the chance she
would be found. At dawn a helicopter would come over looking for the wreckage. The controller at Gallup would notify
someone. She and Mr. B. must be standing by the cabin waving. She would take off her shirt or he would his. Even then the
pilot might have difficulty spotting them. There were too many
trees, too much foliage.

Still stunned, her body crying out in pain, she completed
one circle around the cabin. The thunder now was quite low,
rolling up and down the canyon. Like something haunted, its
echo followed. In between, she heard the roar of water, the
tributary that spilled into the Rio de Chelly.

The second time around, she encountered a footing of
hard sandstone, great whorls shaped like cow dung. Twice she
passed hunks of wreckage—a slice of the fuselage and a stripping of metal skin.

Bill. Oh, God, I wish you were here. I don't know why I
got so upset. I was tired, I guess. When I'm tired, I'm always
saying things I don't mean. Even when I mean them, I don't
put them right.

Now that she had a better reckoning of the land, she

moved a little faster, pushing a foot out at a time, feeling her way. That was how she located the attaché case. She was about a hundred feet from the cabin. Lifting it, she felt the weight of the jewelry. Deciding it was too heavy to carry, she put it upright on the hard sandstone. She waited for the scene to be lit again, then fixed its position in relation to the cabin. She noted, too, that a sacred datura plant, used as a medicine and a narcotic, was only a foot away.

She was starting her third circle when she stumbled over the satchel. A quick flash of lightning showed a hand, half buried in the sand, reaching.

Mr. B. lay sprawled face down, his head caved in. She tightened her fists to hold herself under control.

Some distance away, she found a rock to sit on, and there with the wind whipping her savagely, she debated what to do.

She couldn't put his crushed face out of mind. Not in all the years ahead would she be able to. She had seen death before but not catastrophic death. She knew only that death which comes when a body runs out of its allotted time.

She had been eight when a little friend's mother died. She and her own mother went to the sing. Over and over, all that night, the medicine man chanted the complicated but beautiful rituals that asked one or more of the Holy People to grant renewed life.

The medicine man was wrinkled in face and his hair wispy. He was humble and kind. His low chanting, though, sent shudders along her spine. She knew the Holy People through her playmates and that night she stayed in the shadows for fear the Holy People might see her and punish her for an offense she did not know she had committed.

Weeks before, the family had taken the mother to a hospital, and a doctor had examined her and prescribed treatment. That was all right with the medicine men, who did not consider the Anglo physicians in competition with them. The white doctor was a diagnostician and an herbalist when he prescribed

medicines. But only a medicine man could intercede with the
Holy People. Only a medicine man knew the haunting rituals,
handed down by mouth from one generation to another.

Toward morning of that long night, her little friend's
mother died. The Holy People had decided it should be thus. It
was not the fault of the medicine man. He had asked and been
refused. Still, as a practical matter, if he lost too many patients,
people might think his influence with the gods had waned, and
they would look for another.

A short time before the woman died, Sandy and her friend
were ushered away from the hogan. The medicine man left,
too, and most of the woman's relatives. If they had remained,
they would have had to undergo a lengthy cleansing ritual. It
was difficult to explain to Anglos the Navajo attitude toward
death. A dead body was to be shunned and feared. Sometimes
the dead came back, and wandered around, and haunted people. They were called *chindis,* which, loosely translated, meant
ghosts of the dead. The greatest favor a white man could grant
a Navajo was to bury his dead.

Now soaked to the skin, her hair a rat's tail, she sat in a
stupor. Eventually she forced herself to a decision. The helicopter would not be over until morning, and not then if the
storm persisted. As long as the rain fell, there was little chance
of anyone reaching her by foot or horse. Yet she could not
spend the night here and perhaps tomorrow.

Bill. She wanted Bill.

Mr. B.'s body. The crushed face. The Navajos deserted a
hogan when someone died. They never went back. She had to
get away. She couldn't sit here. Even as a child, she had had a
compulsion to act, to be doing something. She must get out of
the canyon. There was a trail leading to the rim she had seen
many times from the air. The Navajos said the ancient ones,
the Anasazis, had used it.

She set forth for the cabin. For minutes, she studied the
partly sunken plane, tilted on its side. She considered whether

she could work her way up over the slick outside of the body to the opening and concluded she would probably slide off. Instead, she took a running leap, landed on the body, felt her boot slipping but, propelling herself with the other foot, threw herself far enough to grab the framework about the opening. She was wracked with such pain she thought she would black out.

Pulling herself up, she dropped inside. Once she had in hand the old blanket she sat on while flying, which was soaking wet and heavy, she hoisted it up and threw it out. Only momentarily did she pause before dropping several feet to the soft sand.

Slinging the soggy blanket over one shoulder, she reconnoitered. Minutes later, she found a piece of metal. She had no idea what part of the plane it had come from. It was roughly a foot wide, twisted as one might a newspaper used for kindling a fire, and a foot and a half long. It was heavier than she had expected.

Steeling herself, she worked her way to Mr. B.'s body, and quickly spread the blanket over him. She fell to digging a trench alongside the body. She had to cover him to protect him from the coyotes. She dug in fast strokes, driven by a frenzy that demanded she excavate the grave with all haste. But even though the sand was soft, it was heavy with water, and the going was frustrating. Only when exhausted did she stop to slow the heartbeat and breath. When she did pause, she was conscious of frightful pains in her arm and abdomen.

She forced her thinking away from what she was doing. Skeet. He would be asleep by now. She had left him with Navajo neighbors. This was no life for him. She was gone too much. She had always mothered something or someone. A lamb when she was a child, a younger girl when she was in boarding school; and in college, she had worked in a day nursery.

When she had the grave about two feet deep, she stopped. She stared at the blanket-covered body. From somewhere deep within her, she dug up a courage she never knew she had. Lifting his head, she wrapped the blanket carefully about it. She wanted no sand to touch the face. Finished, she felt his blood on her hands, and washed them in the rain.

Getting on the other side, she pushed against him to roll him into the trench. To her horror, she failed to budge him. He was too encased in the sand. After repeated tries, she got her make-do shovel, and using it as a lever, rolled him over. Before dropping him into the grave, she adjusted the blanket again to assure herself he was protected.

"Oh, God," she said, "I guess I should pray or say something, but I don't know what to say."

Once she had buried him, she smoothed out the sand, and covered the grave with rocks to hold the earth in place and thwart the digging of animals. Lugging the rocks was a painful process. Soon the rain would blot out all evidence that the ground had been disturbed.

Some twenty feet away, she dug a hole for the attaché case and the split satchel which she held together until she had it well packed in the earth. To mark the location, she stacked a few rocks into a little pile, to resemble a prayer cairn for travelers. She started away, then turned back. Picking up a twig with a few leaves on it, she placed it on the cairn with a rock to hold it down. She mumbled a few words in Navajo. Now she was assured of a safe journey out of the canyon.

How many years had it been since, with other children lost on a mesa one day, she had done that?

Next she scouted around until she found a piece of a tree trunk that would serve as a club. She took a firm grip on it and set off. Besides coyotes, there were seldom seen foxes and brown bears in the canyon. None would probably harm her unless she inadvertently surprised one and he thought he was trapped.

Desperately she wanted Bill. She needed his gentleness to calm the agony of mind and body.

7.

Vince pulled the car up before the Big Rock Trading Post. In doing so, he struck a boulder.

"Damn wipers. Can you imagine a guy with a Porsche too cheap to buy new wipers? Crazy."

They rushed to get into their raincoats, zipping them up and poking elbows into each other. "I don't want to go down," Penny said petulantly.

"You don't have to."

"I don't want to see dead people."

Vince handed her a Saturday Night Special. To Jigger, he said, "Didja ever think we'd be pulling two big jobs the same night?"

"Never did."

"Put it in your purse, sweetheart," he told Penny, then said to Jigger, "We've got to be back by four at the latest."

"I've never fired a gun," Penny said, slipping the weapon into a little blue denim bag.

"No big thing. Point and pull the trigger. Leave the purse open and keep your hand wrapped around the gun, so you can come out firing."

"You said—"

"Don't worry, nothing's going to happen." He pushed his .38 a little deeper down inside his belt, and Jigger, who had an identical weapon, followed suit.

Jigger felt high. He had taken a couple of amphetamines. They would help him overcome his weakness.

"Do what I told you, sweetheart. Okay?"

"Gives me the creeps feeling it."

"I'll buy you a candy bar."

"Big deal."

Vince pushed through the door first. Jigger followed, and then Penny, who stayed by the entrance. They had to take precautions. After fleeing Los Angeles, they had holed up in Gallup. They had been afraid to knock over service stations, and so Penny had worked the bars and streets, shaking down drunks. Then one night they heard a police officer asking about them at the motel office. While he was still talking with the manager, they took off for Chinle.

The post, which resembled a general store at the turn of the century, was lighted only by a lone bulb dangling over the counter. On one side were groceries lined up on shelves along the wall. Near them were Stetson hats stacked high, men's Levi's, work shirts, wide belts, saddles, and cowpuncher boots. On the opposite wall were women's clothes: velveteen blouses, long skirts, miniskirts, pantsuits, and shoes and boots.

The trader, tall and thin, was counting the day's receipts. He looked up, said nothing. Strangers were to be assayed warily. Vince unzipped his raincoat and let it hang loose. His hand stayed near the .38.

"Evening, sir," he said pleasantly. "I got a sister down in the canyon in a plane crackup and—"

"Just heard about it over the radio."

"I was told there was a trail out here somewhere."

Two days before they had been fooling around, exploring the country, and had talked with several Navajos their own age. The three had thought it would be a lark to pack into the canyon. The Navajos said there was an old trail up ahead that the ancient ones had used. At the time Penny felt ill and they decided to return another day.

"I don't know as you could call it a trail," the trader said, putting the money and checks into a bank bag. "Nobody's been on it for years, far as I know. No reason to. Nothing down there."

A voice rose from behind the Levi's. "I've been down. Twice." Charlie Begay emerged from the shadows. He had gone with the officer to the rim but they had been unable to spot the plane, and he had returned to buy flour for his mother.

"How was it?" Vince asked. Penny remained by the door. The stiff, awkward way she held her hand inside the purse suggested she might have a weapon. Jigger looked over the boots.

"One place you have to jump ten feet. Also, you have to slide down gravel and if you don't stop . . ." He indicated a plunge off a precipice.

"Supposing you could take us down?"

"I gotta get home."

"We'd pay you."

"You couldn't make it tonight," the trader said. He stooped down to put the money bag inside a small safe under the counter. "You'd just be asking for it."

"She may be injured, dying. I've got to get to her. We've always been very close."

Jigger stifled a laugh. That Vince, what an actor.

"You'd be better off packing in," the trader continued. "Go back to Chinle and ask at Justin's Thunderbird. They can outfit you and get you a guide."

Vince turned back to Charlie. "We'd make it worth your while."

Charlie hesitated. There were the Rock Monster That Kicks People Off, and Tracking Bear, and other ogres. There were the chindis, the ghosts of the dead. On a night such as this, they would all be out. Not that Charlie believed such stories. Only the old ones believed them.

"Also, got homework to do."

"What would you say to fifty dollars?"

The monsters didn't seem nearly as foreboding. It was a fortune. It would mean a lot to his mother, who was on welfare. She was ill and needed medicines she could not afford.

"Cash?" By not even the blink of an eyelash did Charlie indicate that he considered the sum exorbitant.

Vince nodded.

"Also, I run home and tell my mother. Good-by." He was out the door before Vince could yell to him to hurry.

Vince indicated to Penny that she could leave her vigil at the door. Vince bought four of the best flashlights the trader had, batteries, and a pocket radio. Penny shopped for salami, bologna, cheese, crackers, bread, instant coffee, and a burner. "Don't forget matches," Jigger put in. The three tried on boots and got the most expensive, and replaced their rain gear with more durable wear. Getting a small sack, Vince filled it with chocolate bars and handed it to Penny, who kissed him.

The trader toted up the bill. "Two hundred and fourteen dollars and thirty-seven cents."

Vince offered an American Express card they had taken during a mugging. The trader asked to see his driver's license.

Vince's hand went to his rear pocket and the strangest expression surfaced. "Guess I left my wallet in the motel, sir. I've never done that before."

The trader frowned. Jigger sauntered to the right of Vince but remained behind him. He had an easy, unobstructed shot. He was no more than twelve feet distant. Penny drifted to the entrance. She never took her eyes from Vince.

"I'll bring it in tomorrow, sir."

"It isn't like you was one of my regular customers and I knew you," the trader said.

Vince's right hand sneaked its way along his midriff. The trader studied the card, a deep frown settling in. He was seconds away from death.

"Got any identification at all?"

Vince shook his head. "You could call the American Express, sir. I'll pay for it." His hand slipped under his belt and around the weapon. He would pull, firing. The bastard probably had a revolver stashed under the counter.

The trader relaxed. "Okay. You're a nice-looking bunch of kids. Not like some we get in here. And any brother who'd go down in this weather to help his sister . . . what'd you say her name was?"

"Sandy Wilcox. My half sister, actually. We're very close."
The name on the credit card was Rudolph Circassian.

The trader ran the card through the imprint machine.
"Used to be a trader named Wilcox up at Far Mountain."

"We're from L.A."

The trader handed the statement slip for Vince to sign.
Vince faked the signature that was on the card. The trader
glanced casually and was satisfied. "Name sounds familiar.
Sandy Wilcox. Guess I'm getting to an age when all names
sound familiar. Heard so many of 'em."

Outside, Penny kissed Vince and said, "I'm glad there
wasn't any trouble."

"Didja forget something?"

She giggled. "Thanks for the candy."

8.

Bill Delaney would have been the first to admit that he had
a single-track, narrow-gauge brain. He prided himself on his
concentration. It had been primarily responsible, he thought,
for his rapid rise in the Stanbury Coal Mining Company. Only
four years out of Boston University, and he was personnel
manager for one of Stanbury's major projects.

Tonight he was barely aware that a storm raged outside,
even though the wind did occasionally shake the small frame
office building. It sat high on a rise overlooking the earth
movers which were lined up to start the next day's excavation.
They were "the beasts that eat the earth," modern dinosaurs
that dug out one deep, vast trench after another. The giant
green-and-yellow stripping shovels—or draglines—weighed
three million pounds and "walked" along slashing into the
earth. Each time they took a bite, they gobbled fourteen to
thirty-six cubic yards. Usually they worked the clock around to
produce 13 million tons of coal annually. Tonight, because of
the storm, they were quiet.

The project was a fantastic one. Once the earth had been stripped, great crushers cracked up the aggregate, and a processing plant mixed it with water and dumped it into giant pipelines that carried it almost three hundred miles. There the coal was used to operate power plants that served about 4 million people in the Southwest—but few Navajos. However, Stanbury paid millions in royalties to the Tribal Council.

While the storm failed to disturb his concentration, Sandy Wilcox did. She kept getting in the way of the monthly report he was drafting. These last few nights he had slept little. He alternately berated himself, then held her to blame. He vowed he would return to Lucy in Boston, who knew nothing about Sandy. He would pick up where he had left off. Lucy was a great gal, a little too serious, too much her mother's daughter, too quick to tell him what he should do. But beautiful, poised, sophisticated. Definitely she would be an asset to his career. He had loved her once. He could again. Probably it was all a matter of proximity.

The figures showed the lowest rate of absenteeism yet. He could thank Sandy for that. During his first months on the job, he had dismissed scores of workers who had taken off for as much as a week to attend a sing. Sings were held for children reaching puberty (a sort of Navajo bar mitzvah), approaching marriages, expectant mothers, people off on trips, and for those suffering from illnesses. They were conducted to assure peace with the Holy People, and hence, personal well-being. They were partly ceremonials and partly social affairs, much like an Irish wake or the Anglo funerals of another era when people got together to see old friends and gossip. Someone was always having a sing. It gave a family prestige and blessed them with a good feeling.

One night, in this very office, Sandy and he had talked until long past midnight. They had been to the tribal museum at Window Rock to see a collection of paintings and had stopped by to pick up mail he had forgot to post. By chance, he mentioned his problem. She dropped into the chair across from him and talked quietly. He could see her now in the dark blue pantsuit and feminine shirt open at the collar.

"I know how they feel," she said softly, referring to the workers. "I know because I'm a product myself of two worlds. Except for my father and mother, I was close to few white people until I went to college. I grew up thinking Navajo. And I had as hard a time adapting as a Navajo.

"The white man fails to realize that other people don't have the same work ethic that he does." She laughed. "Now I'm talking as if I were Navajo. But people in non-industrial countries—and that goes for Zaire and Malaysia and half the world as well as for the Navajos—may work only when there's a need to do so. Usually the need is for basics—food and clothes and shelter. They don't have this crazy compulsion to make money for the sake of making it—to store it up. And they are seldom conscious of time.

"But we live by the clock in the industrial western world. We live by a code of stern personal discipline. We get up every day to go to work, we're there on the dot, and we work hard to produce as much as possible."

"So what?" he asked. "I'm not paying anyone a thousand dollars a month to goof off."

"I've got a suggestion—and I don't like women to tell their husbands"—she laughed—"I'm a little ahead of myself there, but if you'd explain to them that there is this difference in cultures and that you've got a problem, and point out to them that it's important to feed their families and educate their children, and if they want a pickup truck, that is how they get one.

"And then be reasonable. You must let the men off for a sing if someone in their family is seriously ill or dying. Another thing, ask one of the tribal leaders to talk with them. The Tribal Council knows that the Navajos have to compete in the white man's world, since they're engulfed by it, and they're trying their best to persuade their people to see that they can compete and still not give up their culture. I'm sure one of them would be glad to talk with the men."

The next day he had followed her suggestion, and week by week the absentee rate dropped. The Navajos were an amazingly adaptable people. For centuries, they had been quick to latch onto new ideas. From their next-door neighbors, the Pueblo people, they had borrowed sheep raising and weaving, and much later, working in silver and turquoise. From the Spaniards they had stolen and bartered for horses and weapons. From the wives of U.S. army officers had come the hoop skirt, still worn with the hoop removed. Recently, they had acquired pickup trucks and pocket calculators.

Only a decade ago, the Anglos were saying they would never fit into the industrial world. Yet near Shiprock, Fairchild once had an electronics plant where several hundred worked over microscopes to wire miniaturized circuits for use in satellites. In time Bill realized there was nothing the Navajo could not do.

More and more he went to Sandy for her insight into the thinking of The People. The workers developed a fondness and respect for him unusual in strip-mining operations. He had a quiet manner and they liked that. They themselves were a quiet people. They liked him, too, because he treated them the same as the Anglos. He came to know their wives and kids; he and Sandy helped with their problems; he went to bat for them with the company.

He gave Sandy full credit. When first he had heard about her, he had expected a freak in buckskin pants. Instead she was as feminine and sexually appealing as any girl he had ever met, yet firm, at times stubborn, with a quick, perceptive mind and quick decisions. She was always "into something." She painted, designed cloth she marketed to Saks and other specialty houses in New York, and collected crafts. She played the guitar, and nights the kids would crowd around to hear old Navajo songs that she had adapted to the Anglo scale.

It was her care for people, which was a strong emotional

and intellectual part of her, that had first touched him, and later puzzled, confounded, and angered him.

"None of us can do a great deal to change the world," she said one night, "but if each of us would help someone close we would effect a change greater than the industrial revolution. If we would only care about what happens to people."

He kissed her, and with his body pressed tightly against hers, felt the fast beat of her heart. A strange, emotional mixture of love and idealism swept through him.

And then, unreasonably and illogically, she had gone off on a crazy tangent and applied that kind of thinking to strip mining. Not by any interpretation of fundamental concepts could it possibly apply. As his father would have said, "She's off her rocker."

He heard a car pull up outside and a door slam. Someone stamped his feet repeatedly on the door mat. His Navajo assistant, Ralph Yellowhorse, entered, shaking himself dog style.

"What're you doing around this time of night?" Bill asked.

Ralph ran a big brown paw up over his wet hair.

"Well?" Bill asked.

"You haven't had the radio on?"

Bill shook his head.

"Miss Wilcox crashed in Hidden Canyon about an hour ago."

Bill stared. "Oh, my God!"

"They're getting up a rescue party at Chinle."

Bill got into his rain gear.

"Wait," Ralph said. "Nobody's going to get to her tonight."

"The hell you say!" He was halfway out the door when he turned back. "Get the lights and lock up."

Heading east over Highway 160, he gunned the car to eighty miles an hour. He had trouble seeing. The windshield wipers failed to keep up with the torrential rain. He felt the tires skid on oil dropped by the gargantuan trucks that served this country. The night was dark. He passed no settlements, no hogans, only a very few cars. He could have been in a capsule shot into space.

9.

In the cloudburst, the Navajo tribal government building in Chinle wavered like a surrealist painting. It was a low, concrete block structure with a pillared porch across the front, a white fascia, thirsty-looking trees in a bare yard, and a low fence. Out by the highway hung a black-and-yellow sign supported by impressive brick pillars: NAVAJO POLICE DEPARTMENT, CHINLE DISTRICT, CHINLE, ARIZONA. In the dry season, meandering wagon tracks bisected automobile ones on the dirt approach to the paved parking lot.

As they sloshed through deep water, the police officers and rangers loading the jeeps and horse carriers looked more like New England whalers than desert inhabitants. They had to shout to be heard above the storm, and brace themselves against the wildest wind anyone could recall.

Inside, Sergeant Art Tachee, who was heading the rescue party, checked details. He was in his forties, short, chunky, square-headed, and endowed with tremendous drive. He wore his holster low, barely under a pot belly he made no effort to hold in. His shirt tail appeared on the verge of crawling out. He had a silver belt buckle the size of a saucer. He took pride in his belly, shirt tail, and buckle. They were symbols. They defied authority.

An eighteen-year police veteran, he would have headed the division if he could have moderated his dislike of the white man. He was one of the few Navajos in a responsible job who openly expressed such views. He blamed the government for ruining his father by its stock-reduction program, which limited the number of sheep a man could have. He himself spoke no

English when he was carted off to boarding school, and suffered a traumatic experience when he was ridiculed by an Anglo teacher and had his head shaved and washed with kerosene to kill the lice. He thought the government clinic where his sister died of typhoid fever was guilty of negligence. From high school, he went to Los Angeles and found employment on a warehouse dock. Five days later the Immigration Service picked him up and almost deported him to Mexico as an alien. With it all, however, he managed to maintain an innate sense of humor.

To the men and women gathered for final orders, he said, "It breaks down this way. We've got six male police officers, one female, two Tribal park rangers, one paramedic from the hospital, and we're allowing two U.S. park rangers to join us—courtesy of the Navajo nation. All right?"

"Nation?" taunted one of the U.S. rangers.

"I don't want any trouble out of you foreigners. All right?"

"When're you going to get the United Nations to hear your case?"

"Don't worry, wait till I tell the United Nations how you foreigners have subjugated a poor people and denied them their sovereign rights as guaranteed by the Treaty of 1868."

He added, "Didja see that report a few days ago?"

The U. S. Commission on Civil Rights had described the reservation as an American colony beset by shocking and disgraceful economic, educational, and health problems. In the overcrowded clinics and hospitals, the report maintained, Navajos died because there were not sufficient nurses and doctors.

Along with a few others, Tachee had proposed that the Tribal Council present a case against the United States and demand full independence. He had one point going for him. Most Navajos thought of themselves as a nation by reason of culture, tradition, language, and domain over the land long before the white man arrived. A tribal road sign posted outside

Window Rock read: YOU ARE NOW ENTERING THE NAVAJO NA-
TION.

Other Navajos campaigned for a separate state. They had
visions of their country becoming the fifty-first state of the
Union. Their plan had encountered stiff opposition from three
states—Arizona, New Mexico, and Utah—since those states
would be whittled down.

Many Navajos, including some tribal leaders, hoped eventually to gain independence through a commonwealth status.
They would handle their own affairs but be aligned with the
United States. They would be Navajos and Americans, and
enjoy a dual loyalty.

For economic reasons, some wanted the present reservation arrangement continued. If they achieved independence by
statehood or commonwealth, they feared they might lose the
millions that Washington sent out each year. For a people un-
dernourished for the most part, with unemployment ranging
from 40 to 70 per cent, such a loss was horrible to contemplate.

Tachee continued, "If we were in Africa, we'd be an inde-
pendent country and have our own airline. Air Navajo, the
flagship of the Americas."

The room quieted. Captain Chee Yazzie, a commanding
figure, tall and straight, had entered. He had served in World
War II, one of the Navajo Marines who had used their language as a "code" in radio communications between military
units. It was a "code" the Japanese never broke.

He enjoyed quietly boasting that the Navajos had won the
Pacific war. "The Japanese broke every code the military tried,
and it wasn't until we started talking that our troops began win-
ning the war."

He belonged to the Navajo Code Talker Association, and
marched in parades carrying the association's flag which bore a
symbol of the sacred prayer stick that Talking God had given
the Hero Twins. The prayer stick had bestowed on them the
mystical power to choose the right way. Yazzie had often

thought: Wouldn't the Japanese have been surprised to learn they couldn't break the code because Talking God would not permit it!

Yazzie motioned Tachee into his office where a tall, uniformed young officer paced about, head down, deep in thought. He was Frank Ramah. He and Tachee exchanged nods. Ramah didn't care for Tachee but never showed it. A man never got promotions bad-mouthing his boss.

"Frank's volunteered to go down into the canyon by an old trail up near Big Rock Trading Post," Yazzie informed the Sergeant. "We got an okay from Major Tonalea provided Frank doesn't pack in equipment. He'll take a radio, of course, and keep in touch with us here at headquarters and with you— if the storm permits. I've told Frank . . ."

He had instructed Ramah to proceed with caution and to return if he considered the trail overly hazardous. Once at the scene of the crash, he was to report immediately if there were survivors. If there were none, he was to remain until Sergeant Tachee's party arrived. "Don't touch anything," Yazzie ordered. "We want it exactly as it is for the NTSB and FAA people when they get here."

Ramah nodded. He was of a new generation who could meet the Anglos on their own terms any time, anywhere. He had had no bitter experiences. The son of a tribal leader, he had studied at Northern Arizona University, and, summers, worked as a car mechanic. He had a sister who was established as an artist. Both were second-generation Christians.

To Tachee, Yazzie continued, "Until we hear from Frank, we must assume that we have survivors down there, which means we must move fast. If we get word from Frank, though, that both are dead, we'll call a halt until the weather clears and the waters recede. No sense then in taking risks. Okay, Frank, get started. But remember, you're not to get your neck broken. Hold back on the gung-ho business. Sometimes I think you've seen too many movies."

Ramah smiled. "I'll watch it, Captain." His words had a jauntiness that stirred doubt about their sincerity.

Yazzie shrugged in resignation. "Ask Officer Davis to come in."

When he had gone, Yazzie said in a quiet, tough tone, "Sergeant, how many times do I have to tell you I will not tolerate discussion of political matters in my division?"

"I apologize—to you, not to the damned Yankees."

"I've never yet asked for the dismissal of an officer but I will if I hear you mention the United Nations or statehood or anything of that nature."

"Yes, Captain."

Yazzie turned to find Officer Ramona Davis about to retreat. In her late twenties, she was very dark, slender, and tall, with sad, thoughtful eyes.

"Come in, Ramona—and forget anything you overheard. As you know, the sergeant heads up the rescue party but he tells me he feels in need of assistance and has asked for you to share the responsibility with him." Yazzie smiled wickedly. "Isn't that right, Sergeant?"

Art Tachee squirmed. He had not requested assistance. The captain was a clever one. He was punishing Tachee for his remarks by forcing him to share command with one below his rank.

"I—I—" Tachee stuttered.

"So you will be equally in command with Sergeant Tachee. He will discuss all decisions with you before making them. That's what you wanted, wasn't it, Sergeant?"

"I suppose so."

"You mean—?" Ramona Davis asked.

"Do I have to repeat it?"

"No, sir."

"Well, Sergeant, you have everything you requested. So let's move."

Officer Ramona Davis was one of a score of women in the department. They were assigned to all types of cases, working them indiscriminately with the men.

She had been graduated from the Academy first in her class. She was considered a model officer. In time she would work her way into the top echelon.

She would, that is, if she could solve a personal situation that could endanger her career.

No one knew that she carried in her conscience the knowledge she had committed—and was committing—a terrible sin. Some nights she would awaken thrashing at the bedclothes as if she wanted to escape the nightmares that she often suffered. Then for hours after awakening, her thoughts would walk chained to a treadmill that turned and turned and never let them off.

She was of the Bitter Water clan (her mother's), born for the Red House clan (her father's). In the matter of sexual relationships, no crime was held by the Navajo people more immoral and despicable than the marriage or co-habitation of a man and woman who belonged to the same clan. This was incest, although the relationship might be as remote as forty-second cousins. No girl who loved her parents and The Dineh would even dance with a boy from either her mother's or father's clans. There were sixty-four clans in the nation, which averaged out to better than two thousand members each. In the beginning The Dineh had had four clans, but as the birth rate soared and the population increased, new ones came into being.

She had fallen in love with a young schoolteacher, Larry Etcitty, who belonged to her mother's clan. Secretly they met in towns off the reservation. They sneaked about like Victorian lovers. If they had dated openly, they would have brought shame on her mother and his parents, and on friends and relatives. They would have been pointed out as breakers of the old moral laws. The people in their clans would have ostracized them. In effect, they would have had no clan to help them when they were ill, in need of jobs, and no clan to gather at their sings and pray for them.

Many young people defied the old teaching. They dated within their clans and danced and went to movies together, and sometimes married. Like some youth in every culture, they were in rebellion. They scoffed at the medicine men and the Holy People. Most loved their parents, since this was an agrarian society where respect for parents was inbred, but refused to accept their counsel.

Ramona was not rebellious and never had been. If one close to her was ill, she would send for a medicine man. Always she walked the corn-pollen way.

Larry did too. They thought much the same. He was on the rolypoly side with a kind, rounded face, dark eyes, and a gentleness she had never known in a man. He invariably wore a plaid Pendleton-type shirt, Levi's, and a high-crown Stetson. He looked more like a cowpuncher than a teacher. He was one of some two hundred Navajo teachers out of three thousand. The others were Anglos. It was in the schools that the two cultures clashed decisively. The Navajo child was often torn apart emotionally. At school he was likely instructed in the "American" way: rugged individualism, competition with each other, and a final goal of success at any cost. At home, however, he was taught that competition was evil. It hurt others. He must co-operate; he must work in harmony with his fellow man. It was better for all to be successful rather than for one.

This was Larry's creed. "We must teach our children the Navajo way of beauty. The Anglo's way may be all right for his children but not for ours."

Now the time had come when she had to decide between different loves: love of a man, a mother, a clan. Either she had to bring her love for Larry into the open or spend her life in a situation the Anglo would call a "back street wife."

If she chose the former, she would destroy her mother. At her mother's age, it would be a disgrace from which she would never recover.

If the latter, Ramona would live furtively, never have a home to which she could invite friends, never a hogan for a sing, never have children by choice, and if accidentally, would have to rear them as outcasts, members of no clan.

But she would have Larry and his love.

She could not continue to drift. The years were going by too rapidly. She was twenty-eight.

No amount of thinking ever changed the problem: no matter what her decision was, she would ruin lives. Larry's and hers, or her mother's and his parents'.

10.

The going was slow. The thunder had lessened, the lightning was seldom, and hence, the night darker. With the aid of the club she carried, Sandy struggled for higher ground, but the roar of Hidden Canyon wash, now a raging river, was ever louder. The canyon had narrowed and she was forced closer to the swirling cascade. The sandstone merged into soft sand and fear mounted. Testing for quicksand, she took one step at a time. With every movement, pain stabbed her in the arm and abdomen. Yet pain could not still her fanatical compulsion to escape the canyon.

The cottonwoods broke the steady fall of rain but signaled she was near the river. The cottonwoods and willows and Russian olives and reeds. She stopped to reconnoiter, and the second time the lightning flashed, she spotted a strata of rock high up that looked like a ledge.

She climbed and slipped and stumbled. A prickly pear clawed her, and she cringed, and cried out. She had suffered too much. She had been reduced to a hurt child.

Reaching the ledge, she sat in the downpour and regrouped her resources. *You've got the stamina to make it. Soon you'll be up on the rim.*

I killed Mr. B. I killed him. Don't be ridiculous. You flew into the eye of a hurricane. You did the best you could. Don't give me that old guilt complex.

She had to put his crushed face out of mind. She thought of Bill and Skeet and an old chant. *"Today I will walk out.*

Today everything evil will leave me. I will be as I was before. I will have a cool breeze over my body. I will have a light body."

A cool breeze. A light body.

The thunder. Skeet. "If you throw the egg of a night hawk up in the air, it will bring great thunder." And: "One should never follow a bear trail until you want to meet a bear." That Skeet. "If a stink bug gets all muddy it means rain." Silly.

Bill. "I love you, Sandy." How long ago? Two months. The happy days.

I've got to mail him back his ring. I guess I did. Didn't I? His ring.

From up here, every time the gods turned on the lightning, she could see the turbulent wash below. Lit up but a second, it was a clear, sharp picture.

She moved faster. The ledge was solid, no danger of quicksand. There was one peril, walking off it, falling, her body mangled by jagged outcroppings. Most of the way, she was under overhangs, protected from the rain. She wrung herself out but her shirt clung. Her boots were a load to lift.

Then a detonation from a distance thundered in her hearing and swelled until it was the roar of Niagara and Iguassu and Victoria Falls combined. At first she thought another cloudburst in the Chuska Mountains had sent more waters raging down the canyon. Quickly, her hearing corrected her. The din, increasing in intensity until it was literally deafening, was from above.

Panic strengthened her legs which had been steadily weakening. Flouting danger of a fall, she hurried along the ledge. She took refuge in a cave seconds before the avalanche fell before her, a roaring, plunging torrent of rocks and boulders. The ground shook violently, she staggered and dropped. No lightning flashed. She was encapsulated in a dark, shaking, shattering, deafening world.

Within thirty seconds, the worst of the avalanche had thundered its way to the canyon floor. As had happened a thousand times in aeons past, a slice of the gorge's walls had split off, eaten away by the termites of wind, water, and sand. Long after the last of the spill had fallen, she sat immobilized by shock. For the first time, her body shook beyond control.

She quieted her nerves and muscles. Lighted up for a second, barely inside the cave, was a pictograph of a man and a woman. An Anasazi artist had painted it. It looked as if it had been done only yesterday. So others had lived and loved here.

Bill.

They had driven a short way out of Kayenta. Parked near a desert trail, they had the world to themselves. The small cry of a bird disturbed in his sleep came over, and an animal padding softly through the brush. A full moon provided a dream quality.

They kissed and talked softly. His hands ran over her, hands stirred by longing.

The heat of the day had not yet broken, and they left the hot, airless car. Arms about each other's waist, they climbed a little rise, scuffing up dust as they went. They had to skirt desert growth but never let go of their half embrace. They staggered and laughed and staggered some more.

At the top, they looked toward Kayenta. There were only faint pinpoints of light except for the Holiday Inn which was ablaze.

"Somebody ought to burn it down," she said.

He laughed. "I'm going to report you to the police as a potential arsonist."

He took her into his arms. Slipping one arm behind her neck, he placed the other at the small of her back. Against her soft lips, his kiss was rough and hard. Aroused, she pressed back, powered with all the longing inside her. She felt the quickening beat of his heart, the tremble that coursed through his body. Her own body pounded in rhythm to his. Kayenta's lights went out, and the Holiday Inn's, and the stars'. Matter was no longer matter, time was not time. She was suspended in both space and time, the world blacked out except for his eyes.

He was the first to break the bond. He was breathing hard. "Why aren't we married?" he whispered.

"Not my fault," she murmured.

"Not mine, either."

"Skeet keeps asking."

"We've got to make him legitimate."

She held him as if never to let go. "For Skeet's sake, we've got to get married."

"It's those dinosaurs. Digging, digging. I've got to watch them—but next week . . ."

"Do they work on Sundays? The dinosaurs?"

"Sunday. It's a deal."

She looked up at him. "I love a man who sets his wedding day and calls it a deal."

Not Sunday or the Sunday after. Another girl he had loved stood off stage. To Sandy, a ghost woman.

"What's she like?" she had asked.

He shrugged. "Just another girl."

"Look, Bill, I don't like devious people who don't answer questions and people who're casual when they should be concerned."

His eyes glinted. "You're jealous."

"Sure I am."

"Sandy," he said quietly, "there would've been no Lucy if I'd met you first."

But it wasn't a ghost woman who came between them.

The break came that evening returning to Kayenta from the picnic at Elephant Feet. The sun was low, but the August heat had not yet broken. They were both hot and sweaty but with that comfortable feeling that a dinner outdoors and good companionship induces. That was why, looking backward, it seemed incomprehensible that the talk should have drifted in the direction it did. That was the key word, drifted, Sandy was to think. One should never let conversation wander idly about, not even between friends or lovers.

Bill said, "How about dropping in on me tomorrow? I've got something I want to show you."

"Like what?"

"A mechanical tree planter. You've never seen anything like it. Goes along, discs the soil, and drops the trees in. We're going to give the Navajos back a forest instead of bare land."

Strip mining. It was a subject that instantly produced a violent, tailored reaction. Most of the time, they skirted around it, each knowing how the other felt. He had made a point a few nights ago, though, of reporting on the restoration of the land. The earth had been shoved back into place and topsoil spread. Either pine and hardwoods would be planted or alfalfa, sweet clover, and Russian rye.

"It's a dead land," she said, her voice tense.

"How can you say that, Sandy? We're spending a fortune—"

"A dead land. The first rains will wash everything out, and it's like bad fill in the back yard. It'll sink."

He shook his head. "Sometimes I don't understand you."

"You don't understand me! I don't understand you. You can't go around tearing up mountains and entire countrysides. The Navajos are right historically when they say you have to live in harmony with nature. That's the very heart of their faith. And every civilization that's abused the earth, wrecked its soil, is gone, forgotten. The Navajos say the earth gives us our life, we can't live without it, and if you've got a sick earth, you've got a hungry and sick people."

"I agree with you, but—"

"What's more, it was sacrilegious to tear up Black Mesa. The People believe it's the body of a Holy Person. It's like wrecking Calvary or the Wailing Wall."

He raised his voice, "Listen, Sandy. Just a minute. In the first place, we're mining only about twenty-five square miles. That's not even one per cent of Black Mesa. And in the second, a medicine man came up and said somebody was buried there, one of the Holy People, so I said, point out the spot and we won't touch it, and he waves his hand and says it's the whole damn mesa, which is pretty ridiculous. You know yourself that every mesa, mountain and canyon in this country is sacred, and has some legend connected with it. Instead of a reservation, Washington ought to declare this a religious monument."

"Don't be funny."

He hurried on. "I think you'd embalm this country. Keep it for posterity. A pretty picture postcard to look at. Well, there are some hungry and desperate people around here who want more than a picture postcard. They'd—"

"Please, Bill, let's don't argue. It's too beautiful a night. I just want to lie back and feel the warm air on my face and listen to the tires humming."

The sun was about to set. The car was chasing its shadow. A fence pole slanted twelve feet tall and an Indian boy by the side of the road was a giant. Suddenly the lowliest of things had gained in stature, and become, no doubt, the size they thought they were.

"Okay, but let me say this. I think land is more than just for people to look at. It's for people to work in. It's for feeding people and putting clothes on their backs. What if the first guy to see the Hudson had said, 'Let's don't touch it.' "

She sat up, ramrod stiff, in the stance she unconsciously took for battle. "You trying to tell me New York's a credit to mankind? All right, all right, I'll admit we've got to have big cities. Those that are here, I mean, but don't let's build any new ones. We've got to control the population."

"You tell that to these people," Bill retorted. "Haven't you heard what the Navajos themselves say? We make love, not war. They haven't anything else to do nights. Why, when the 1868 treaty was signed, there were only 15,000. Now, 140,000."

She said quietly, "They're doing something about it. They're getting birth control clinics started. They know they've got to limit their people and they will. They're adaptable."

"What you mean to say is they'd limit their families if they could afford contraceptives. And that's what it's all about, jobs that bring in money. Now be reasonable. They don't have the money for contraceptives, do they?"

"What are we talking about, pollution or birth control? Don't change the subject. Every time I fly over Four Corners, I see the stacks belching out the pollution. Three hundred and fifty tons of it a day. More than thrown up by New York and Los Angeles combined."

Four Corners was where Arizona, New Mexico, Colorado, and Utah met. A complex of coal-fired electrical generating plants operated there. Government planners estimated that they would one day serve 7 million people.

"And Page—" she continued.

"I know, I know, but the companies are spending millions to clean it up. Give them a little time."

"That's what they said in Los Angeles thirty years ago. Give us a little time."

Darkness had fallen. On the peripheral vision of their headlights, eerie shapes rose and fell. At night the desert assumed another planet look. The Navajo legends about monsters took on reality. Darkness, too, separated them. No longer could they see each other. They were two disembodied voices floating in the blackness. In replaying the tape, as she was to do a hundred times, she blamed the darkness. Voices lacked the communication of a glance.

"Let me say this and then I'll keep quiet," Bill said. "Some figures were shoved across my desk a couple days ago. Twenty times as much alcoholism on the reservation as in the rest of the nation, partly the result of unemployment. Tuberculosis, fifteen times more. One in ten homes has electricity. Four out of five, no indoor plumbing. No public transportation. No emergency medical care. No ambulances. Don't tell me it isn't economics. We're hiring thousands—Stanbury and the other companies—and we're pouring millions of dollars a year out in salaries, royalties, taxes. Yes, we're making profits, good profits, but at the same time we're doing something for people.

I get so tired of these damn bleeding-heart liberals acting as if a business—just because it is a business—is a gang of blood-suckers. The Navajos need but one thing—money. They're sinking in quicksand."

She took a good hold of herself. She said in a teacher's tone, "What happens when you finish ripping up this country and there's no more coal and you go home and there's no more money? And anyway, right now, what good is money when you're dying from pollution, and your stock is, and the land is? Don't you see what's happening? The extermination of a people by another people. The Anglos don't care what happens as long as they take care of their own. We don't have gas chambers today but—"

"Gas chambers! My God, Sandy! If you believe that—"

He slowed down. His mood had accelerated the speed. "We shouldn't be talking like this. It isn't that important. Nothing is."

"The rape of the country? The murder of its people?"

"You've got a closed mind. If someone so much as touches your damn desert—"

"I'll fight them till hell freezes over."

"So I invite the boss home for dinner some night and you accuse him of being an assassin."

"If you believe I'd do that . . ."

He brought the car to a sudden stop before her mobile home. She prayed Skeet was asleep.

"Sandy," he said softly.

She brushed her hair back, stood very straight. Other nights he had got out and they had talked for moments precious to each. "I'm sorry, Bill. But some things mean a lot to me—and this is one."

"More than us?"

"I've got to live it as I see it. There's no use pretending and later having it all come out."

"I suppose so, but—"

"You've got a job, a career. Like me, you've got to believe

in what you're doing . . . Well, that's about it, Bill. Thanks for all the good times."

"Let's see each other now and then."

"Sure. Night now."

"Sleep tight."

11.

The narrow, winding trail through the dark forest of piñon and ponderosa pines was hard-packed but dotted with water-filled pot holes. Charlie Begay led the way. The flashlight Vince had given him opened up the dark for only a few feet. The blinding rain barely permitted light to filter through. Charlie, however, could have walked the path blindfolded. As a child, he had played in the forest, and each fall had come with his mother to gather the piñon nuts which were a cash crop readily salable. They were packaged like peanuts for the nation's supermarkets. Many a winter the income had meant the difference between hunger and a little food.

Stumbling, cursing, Vince followed. Seemingly, he put a foot into every pot hole. City bred, he hated this alien land. Until their flight from Los Angeles, he had never set foot off concrete, except in the postage stamp yards of his neighborhood. To him, the open spaces alone were frightening. They exposed a man. In the city, he could outdistance any police car. He knew the streets, alleys, and hideouts, and he could time each move. Here a man was engulfed by miles of nothing and time had no meaning. Tonight was a nightmare. No matter how uncomfortable, though, he kept doggedly at it.

Behind him came Jigger who had doubts about this mad, impulsive adventure. He would have settled for the dawn attack on the bank courier at the Chinle landing strip. They had no need of two coups the same night. Cuddled up with Penny, he could have waited until an hour before sunrise to leave his warm bed.

Penny trailed, the flashlight in one hand, the sack of chocolate bars in the other, her denim bag slung over a shoulder. She was more cautious than her lovers, and found herself far behind. Frightened, she yelled for them to wait, and Charlie called a halt. She liked him. He treated her like a lady, and was concerned about her.

"Go on back to the motel," Vince told her. "You can't keep up."

"I can, too."

"Get lost."

"She's my sister, too!"

Charlie had wondered about the relationship. So Vince and the girl were brother and sister. Where did this guy they called Jigger fit in? Charlie wanted to ask but that would be rude.

Penny continued to tag along, and a few minutes later, Charlie announced they had arrived at the rim. They stared intently but could make out nothing in the blackness beyond the beam of the flashlights.

"God, I hope sis is okay," Vince said. "What's your name, kid?"

Charlie paced slowly along the edge, searching for the trail down. "Got many names. Charlie Begay. Also, my nickname, Son of Tall Man. Also, Charlie Mud. That is my clan, Mud. Also, got nine Social Security cards."

"Nine!" said Jigger, then to Vince, "Think what you could do with nine cards."

"Got a sister, Charlie?" Vince asked.

"No, sir. No sister. Only my mother. Also, my father dead."

His mother would be worried about him, Charlie knew. She never went to bed until he was home. She was old-fashioned. She sprinkled pollen every morning before they had breakfast, and again after the evening meal. Nights, when finished, she sang from the Blessing Way rite. In her rugs, she left an outlet for the spirits, a few dark threads that ran beyond the design and were lost in the outer edge. Constantly, she beseeched the Holy People to look after Charlie who had his doubts about the Holy People but never expressed them. He loved his mother and would never say anything that would cause her sadness. Some day when she was gone, he would go to the mission and talk with the father. He liked what he had heard about Jesus, what Jesus had said. He was good and kindly. Charlie thought most of the Holy People were out to get his scalp.

"Just your mother and you?" Vince asked.

"Yes, sir."

Charlie dropped to a ledge three feet below. "We start down here." The others followed. "Also, be most careful. If you slip . . ." He let out a whoosh to indicate what would happen.

Charlie scrambled down, and landed on another ledge. The others slid after him, ripping raincoats and hacking up their legs.

"Is it like this all the way down?" Vince asked, puffing.

"Worse. Also, why do you carry a gun, mister?" Vince's .38, anchored in his belt, stuck out through a vent in the raincoat.

Vince covered it. "Thought there might be animals down here."

Charlie stared in disbelief. Brazen kid, Vince thought. Stupid. He would overlook Charlie's shortcomings. An overman had to. Charlie was one more peasant. Vince had read as much of Nietzsche as necessary to learn about the overmen—the supermen—and the inferiors, the masses.

Patiently, he had explained these truths to Jigger, a very intent pupil. Jigger recognized that he was an inferior. Penny was, too, but Vince had not told her. She would not have understood, and he would not have wanted her to. Such knowledge might have ruined her. She served the order of things with her body—and did it very well. She and Jigger were good inferiors. There were bad ones who had to be dispatched when they got in one's way.

In the matter of the so-called virtues, he had explained to Jigger their evil effects. "They're good for the masses—such things as kindness and gentleness and patience and all that rot —because they keep them in their place, but they're a drag if you ever hope to get to the top. Don't ever forget, Jigger, that if you listen to all this goodness crap, you're going to end up working yourself to death and getting crushed by the take-it guys."

Jigger believed him, although on rare occasions he would retrogress. Like the time he gave his handkerchief to the raped girl sitting crying on the curb. "You take what you want when you want it and walk off. So somebody gets hurt. Lots of people get hurt. That's their business, not yours."

Charlie said, "We jump here. To over there."

"I don't see anything out there," Jigger said.

"How far?" asked Vince.

"I'll jump and you can see me. Also, I'll hold up my hand and wave."

"I'm not going," Penny said.

Charlie backed up a few feet, took a couple of steps, and leaped. He called back, "Come on."

"I never was good at jumping," Jigger said.

"I'm not doing it," Penny repeated.

Vince was irritated. "Don't hassle us. Go on, you're first. If you don't make it, Jigger and I'll send flowers. Won't we, Jigger?"

Penny began crying.

"You know something, Penny," Vince said. "You're beautiful even in the rain."

She copied the moves taken by Charlie. Leaping, she was a misty blur. The two could scarcely see her when she screamed. It was one long, horrendous cry.

"Oh, my God!" Jigger shouted. Vince stood in shock.

Charlie called out, "She is okay. Also, come on, next one, please."

They leaped without difficulty. Vince had to restrain himself from socking Penny. She had screamed when she dropped her bag of chocolate bars.

This time the ledge was smooth and level, and they traveled it easily. Charlie sang low to himself.

Vince asked, "Where'd you learn that, kid?"

"I read it in *Tsá' Ászi'*. Also, made up music."

"Now you know," Jigger said.

When they came to a slight drop, Charlie explained they would navigate the next hundred yards on their hands and knees. "It is very narrow. Also, a shelf about two feet wide. Some places, one foot. Also, nothing below. We crawl and go slow. You understand? Slow. Are you all right, miss? . . ."

"Penny."

"The name of a coin. Most interesting."

"I'm okay."

Again taking the lead, Charlie kept them advised on the lay of the ground. At one point, soft sand, at another, a dip. Once he stopped to clear a rock slide. He felt with his hands, exploring a foot or so ahead before he moved. It was good, he thought, that the three behind him could not see far in the storm. The drop was sheer, several hundred feet.

When at last they could straighten up, they walked slowly through a forest of scrub pine which protected them somewhat from the hard beat of the rain. They had not gone far before they stood staring down at a rock slide. As Charlie played his flashlight over it, the others instinctively backed up a step. The slide, composed of sizable rocks, pebbles, and sand, dropped at a gradual slant about fifty feet and as far as they could see through the downpour, ended in space.

"You cannot see from here," Charlie said, "but there is a place where you land. Also, you must slow down when you get halfway down or you will go too fast and keep going."

"Into the canyon?" Vince asked.

Charlie nodded. "Also, I will go first and grab each one if you do not go too fast."

"I'm so scared now looking at it I'll die going down it," Penny said. "Don't ask me to go, Vince. Don't ask me."

Vince wrapped an arm about her. "We'll go together."

"No money's worth it," Jigger said.

"What money?" Charlie asked.

"Shut your fool trap," Vince warned Jigger, "and get ready. Hell, it's nothing more than another slide in an amusement park. All for free."

"It's okay if you go with me, Vince," Penny said, struggling to act brave.

Charlie said, "Also, you act like you sit but you do not sit down. Understand?"

"Go on, kid," Vince told him, "let's get started."

Carefully feeling his way, Charlie stepped into the slide. When his feet gave way, he squatted and rode down. They followed him with their flashlights. When he stood up, he was only a blurred object. He looked as if he were out in space.

Jigger followed. Losing his balance, he tumbled down. Charlie grabbed him by an arm, but Jigger's momentum was such that he pulled Charlie almost to the edge.

Penny held Vince's arm in a death grip. He managed to keep them on a straight course. As instructed, he braked his speed and shouted to Penny to do likewise. When they landed on their feet, Charlie was screaming at them. They had stirred up the slide, and a small avalanche was descending in their wake. Charlie shoved them ahead of him to safety. Seconds later they would have been swept into the canyon. It was as if someone above had emptied several truckloads of aggregate. The slide now poured over into the canyon.

Penny gasped in horror. "How're we going to get back?"

"Not this way," Charlie said.

"How?" Vince asked.

"Through Canyon de Chelly to Chinle after storm is finished."

"No other trail?"

"No, sir."

"What'll we do?" Jigger asked Vince.

"I'll think of something."

"You always do."

For a few minutes, they stood regaining their composure and taking stock. Their clothes were ripped and torn, and their arms and legs badly cut. They discarded the shredded raincoats and cleaned the cuts as best they could. Penny accepted it more stoically than Vince had expected. After that first outburst, she had decided she could take it as well as her men. Jigger was more shaken. He could not stand the sight of blood, and his right arm, below the elbow, was bleeding profusely. Charlie plastered it with mud, put a broad leaf over it, and told Jigger to hold it on. "It will heal very good. Mud is good for a wound."

Jigger doubted that. After a short walk, they reached a ledge that widened until it was a shelf a hundred feet broad. Charlie hastened his pace, and Vince called out to him to slow it.

Charlie kept going. Back in a gigantic recess of the sandstone wall was a cliff house. The chindi, the ghosts of the ancient ones, prowled back in those rooms. He could hear them talking. Very low. He couldn't distinguish the words, and didn't want to. Once a ghost had chased him, and he had barely escaped. He had heard of a boy who had been jumped on and the ghost had torn his clothing before the boy got away.

Vince shouted, "What the hell's the rush?"

The ghosts of the dead ones were talking louder now. Several of them. At least three. Charlie started running. He had had another thought. They might not be ghosts at all. They might be wolves, or witches, actually, who wore wolf and coyote skins. If they disliked you, you would fall ill with a horrible disease. If they hated you, you would die. All you could do was to take gall medicine, an emetic that would eliminate the wolves' poisoning. Fortunately, when he was leaving home, his mother had insisted that he take her little pouch of gall medicine. She said he might need it in guiding strangers. They might be wolves in disguise.

The shelf ran out and there was another trail, this time a steep one. Taking flying steps, he plunged down it and didn't stop until he had put considerable distance between him and the cliff house. He stilled his heavy breathing to listen. Then satisfied he heard no talking, he collapsed on the ground.

Ten minutes later, the three found him squatting Navajo fashion, leaning against a scrub tree. His breath was still labored.

Vince was angry. "What'd ya run out on us for?"

"Wolves," Charlie said.

Jigger froze. "Wolves?"

"Why you dirty little creep," Vince said without raising his voice, "you left us to be eaten by wolves." He pulled the .38.

"No!" Penny cried. "No!"

"Not now," Jigger said, very low. "We don't know the way down."

Vince hesitated, staring, then squeezed the trigger. The explosion was muted by the storm. Charlie fell over backward, Penny screamed, and Jigger stood paralyzed.

Vince wiped the moisture from the gun with a handkerchief, and pushed it back under his belt.

"Next time," he said to Charlie who was getting up, "I won't shoot over your head."

12.

At Window Rock, Major Tonalea listened intently to the clear, crisp voice of Officer Ramona Davis coming over the radio. He remembered well the day she took off to study at the University of New Mexico. A shy, frightened girl who returned four years later a mature, poised, intelligent young woman. When he had recommended her to the Tribal Police, he had bet on her judgment and he had been justified. The only woman in a class of forty-six, she had excelled the men in most of the eighty-odd courses the Academy offered. In accord with the Navajo tradition of working in harmony with one another, they had shown neither male chauvinism nor a patronizing attitude. On the contrary, they had helped her in courses difficult for her, such as tearing apart and reassembling a submachine gun in Firearms.

Tonalea recalled that in the field with the Search and Rescue class, she had been the only one to determine how to reach a child on a canyon ledge. He wondered if Yazzie had known of this when he chose her to co-lead the rescue party.

If he could have faulted her on any score, he would have on her impersonal approach to a problem. It was as if she were a computer she had programed and knew what the read-out would be. She was equally as impersonal in her private life. Clearly she got the message across: "Don't ask me questions."

Tonalea fully intended to do just that. Obviously, she had a problem. He was very fond of her, both as a superior and as a father would be. She was too good an officer and too fine a woman . . . well, he must call her in when this was over and find out what was bothering her. He followed through on his graduates. They were "his officers." He wanted each one to be a credit to the Academy.

She said, "This is Officer Davis reporting in for Sergeant Tachee and the rescue mission. We're passing the junction with Canyon del Muerto. The river is running high and we're making slow progress. We've had to dig two jeeps out of soft sand and clear the trail once of fallen rocks . . ."

Tonalea checked the map of the Navajo nation spread across the wall opposite his desk. The rescue party was following a twisting trail that stayed at some points well away from the river and at others, ran quite close. Wherever the map showed large areas of quicksand, the trail wound at least fifty that Officer Davis mentioned was a large one branching to the left. In 1804, Lieutenant Antonio Narbona and his Spanish horsemen killed 115 Navajos and took 33 prisoners at a place feet distant. The Canyon del Muerto (Canyon of the Dead)

known today as Massacre Cave. His men cut off the warriors'
ears and dispatched 84 pairs as trophies to the Spanish gover-
nor at Santa Fe. Narbona offered his personal apologies for
failing to send all the ears, but unfortunately some had been
lost or stolen.

Tonalea returned to a highly polished, glossy desk which
was bare except for a picture of his family, a speech, and a letter.

The letter read: "Dear Officer Kirk and Officer Denny—
Thank you for coming to our school. We liked the whistle, gun
and bracelet, and the siren was LOUD. Yours truly, Fort
Defiance Co-operative Pre-school."

On the wall behind him was a blown up photograph of the
Navajo police shoulder patch. In the center was a blind lady of
justice with the figures 1868, the year when the United States
signed the peace treaty granting The People sovereignty. Underneath the figure of justice was the motto: TO PROTECT AND
TO SERVE. Around the figure were fifty arrows to signify the
states. NAVAJO POLICE was in green to indicate the green pas-
tures needed for the sheep and cattle, and a yellow background
denoted the corn pollen, symbol of wisdom, power, and
healing. A green circle stood for the rainbow, significant in
Navajo religion.

From time to time reporters from the media telephoned.
He gave what information he had, and pointedly added,
"Somebody put out a story that there's a half million in cash on
that plane. We don't know where they got that. It's something
we don't know anything about and we'd like it if you wouldn't
speculate until we can check on it."

He did know how the story had originated. Everyone in
Chinle had talked about little else following the appearance
there of J. C. Berchtol. Tonalea was sufficiently wise, too, to
the operations of the media to realize that no matter what he
said they would continue to speculate. However, making the
point kept the department in the clear and could be used as a
defense if the conservative Tribal Council asked questions.

While waiting further radio reports, he worked over the speech he would give, on behalf of the Tribal Council, to students leaving the reservation for various colleges. "Don't let the white man's prejudices prejudice you. Many of them don't like us but most do."

He struck that out. Too negative. He continued to the next paragraph. "Learn all you can from the white man but don't become one. Remember you're a Navajo and be proud of it but not too proud. We're a Navajo nation, and we're a part of the United States, and we're proud of that, too. We can live with the Anglos and the Anglos can live with us because we are now blood brothers. History has made us blood brothers. We have no choice but I think that this is the way we all want it, the Anglos and the Navajos."

Not bad. He would let that stand. "Learn all you can and come back and live with us and help us. There are many thousands who need you. They still die in the blizzards in wintertime. They still go hungry. They still have no work, and when a man has no work, he no longer is a man."

That was the heart of the talk. If he could persuade them that their people needed the skills and talents they would learn in the Anglo universities, then he would have contributed something to The Dineh.

"Don't forget the Blessing Way. Don't forget that in beauty we walk . . ."

He started to cross that out. He shouldn't inject religion. After mulling a moment, he decided to keep it. To hell with the Supreme Court.

Glancing at his watch, he found it was almost eleven. He called his home. "Looks like all night, Edith," he told his wife. "Go to bed and get some sleep and I'll call you around six or seven."

"You're not going down into that canyon?"

"How'd Kojak make out?"

She laughed. "You'll never know if you don't answer my question."

"Do you know what an FBI agent told me the other day? He won't let his wife ask questions. Internal security. An FBI agent can stay out as late as he wants and go anywhere he wants—and it's classified information."

"Don't try that on me or I'll classify you."

Smiling, he hung up, got into his rain gear, told Miss Burnsides he would be at the landing field, and, bowing his head, plunged into the storm.

He drove slowly, turned left on Highway 264, and across from the Tribal Arts Building took a narrow dirt road for several hundred yards. A sheet of water covered it, but like an old dog on an old trail he kept on it. It led him to a dirt runway on which sat a Bell Jet Ranger 206 helicopter. Back of it loomed a dark mesa with jagged teeth.

On his right was a Quonset-type structure. Inside a cubicle office, a single light burned weakly. A chopper pilot whom Tonalea had alerted, dozed with his feet up on a desk. Tonalea pushed them off and the pilot popped up like a jack-in-the-box, ready to fight bears.

"Can't go down," he mumbled, "can't see anything in this storm."

"Did I ask you to? I want you to warm it up—see if it runs."

"No need to—"

"We're taking off when this storms breaks and I don't want to find it won't fly."

"Major, it'll fly."

"I want to hear a little noise out of it. Now, this minute."

Tonalea had flown helicopters in Vietnam. He knew their eccentricities.

Still grumbling, the pilot headed into the raw night with Tonalea toward the great bird chained fast to moorings. On the side was an insignia in blue and white: THE GREAT SEAL OF THE NAVAJO TRIBE.

In Chinle, Captain Yazzie heard the roar of the Rio de Chelly in the background when Officer Ramona Davis came on the air with her next report. "We've run into high waters and have had to abandon the trail and take to higher ground. It's rocky and uneven up here and we're taking a chance on breaking an axle or upsetting. Please advise whether we should continue by vehicle or transfer to the horses."

He drummed the table. "Hold it for a minute, Davis."

He considered the options. He had none. The Rio de Chelly was the enemy and no man could outwit a canyon river at flood crest.

"Continue, Davis, but watch the river. Don't assume it will stay on its course." She knew this, and so did every officer and ranger with the party. But they needed to be reminded. No one in the canyon this night could be reminded too often.

"I'd suggest you send one car ahead to reconnoiter. Keep me posted."

He was gambling and he was frightened. A breakdown was a minor worry. The river was the peril. Canyon and desert rivers were notorious for leaving their channels and turning into raging monsters, caroming at will over new territories, sweeping everything before them, slashing deep, new beds. Only last year, the river had struck out at an ammo carrier, picked it up like a toy, and smashed it against the canyon wall. By a stroke of luck, the driver escaped.

An officer looked in. "A Mr. Delaney to see you. Says he's a close friend of the pilot."

Yazzie nodded and straightened. Entering, Bill hesitated about offering a hand. Yazzie stared coldly. He had a habit of casing a man, then remembering to be cordial.

"Captain, I'm a very close friend of Miss Wilcox."

"She's your fiancée."

Bill was taken by surprise.

Yazzie asked, "Is our information wrong?"

"I've got to get to her," Bill continued hurriedly. "I know you've got a rescue team in the canyon but is there some other way in? Maybe from up above, the other direction?"

"Mr. Delaney, we're doing everything that can be done.

Why don't you take a room here in Chinle tonight and we'll keep you posted."

"I've got to get to her. If there's no other way, I'll join up with your party."

"Absolutely not. We've got officers and rangers who know the canyon, and still they're risking their necks."

"I'll take my chances."

"No, you won't. Absolutely not."

Bill bristled. "You Indians don't have jurisdiction in the canyon. It's a United States national monument."

Yazzie said coldly, "We have an agreement with the park service and the Tribal Rangers to head this mission."

Bill could scarcely control his anger. "I'll see the park service about this."

"You'll get the same answer but if by chance you should get through their barricade, I will give strict orders to my officers to turn you back."

Turning on his heel, Bill said, "You do that, damn you!"

He took long steps, bumped into a couple of officers, and hit the outside door hard. Once in his car, he gunned it and roared down Highway 7 toward Canyon de Chelly.

The waters covered the canyon floor, spreading up to the walls, and the officers and rangers grew apprehensive. Working their way to the left of the main artery, where the rampaging torrent heaved and foamed and thundered, they followed an old track along the wall. Here the water flowed at a stiff clip a foot or more high and was rising. Adding to their concern was the womblike darkness which the headlights illuminated about as much as a flickering match in a cavern.

Constantly they had to keep in mind the rickety old horse carriers they pulled. The carriers were not balanced as well as the jeeps, and the fear lurked that one might upset. The horses neighed occasionally but were remarkably quiet considering the night. Bred to the country, they knew it. Like their humans, they had worked it in storms before. The carriers held twelve, one for each of the seven officers, four park rangers, and the paramedic.

In the lead vehicle were Sergeant Art Tachee, who was behind the wheel, the two U.S. park rangers, and a Tribal park man. Inching his way, Tachee would nose a boulder, back up, and circumvent it. The beaten-up old jeep slipped and slid, but the footing was gravel and fairly firm.

"Enough water for you, Art?" asked one of the U.S. rangers.

"You bum!" Tachee exploded.

"You don't need to tap the Colorado with all of this."

"You coyotes, you!" Grinning, Tachee gripped the wheel tighter. Depending upon whom one met, he was either a crusader or a rabble rouser in his pitch for more water for his country. With water, much of the desert would bloom, and the Navajo's economic woes of a century would be eased. Seven states and Mexico had divided the precious Colorado River and left none for The People. In Washington, the government discussed the matter, and discussed it, and a time or two Congress had voted for projects, but the end result was little.

Tachee said, "I'm going to get a cat and dig a ditch and let the Colorado spill out all over the reservation. All right?"

"You'll get arrested."

"Not by the Tribal Police. Not an officer around would bring me in. Do you know why? Because your Supreme Court —*your* court—it was about 1908, if I remember my history— ruled that Indian tribes had first claim to water on their reservation or running by it."

Lake Powell fronted some one hundred miles of Navajo reservation. To the horror of ecologists and many of The People, Washington had created the lake by building Glen Canyon dam across the Colorado River. Now water covered some of the most spectacular scenery in the world. And still The Dineh had little water or power.

"Forget it, Sergeant," said the other ranger. "A hundred thousand Navvies up against the big cities? We'll get another

Supreme Court ruling. We Anglos are good at that. But I'm with you. I'll help you dig some irrigation ditches."

The veering canyon wall forced Tachee out into deeper water. He stopped and blinked his red brake lights to signal the vehicles following. "We'll pack out of here."

Sloshing through heavy water in high cowpuncher boots, Officer Davis came abreast. "We're ditching the vehicles," Tachee said. "All right?"

"Sergeant," she answered quietly but firmly, "we have orders to go as far as we can as long as we're not taking too much risk."

"There's quicksand ahead."

"I know where it is. I grew up in this canyon. Let me take the lead."

She remembered the hogan with the bough-covered shadow house, open on one side for hot nights, and with a rock firepit outdoors. Remembered the apple, peach, and pear trees, the sheep she and her younger brother had herded along with a ragtag dog she dearly loved. Remembered the wrens, swallows, piñon jays, and house finches. Remembered her mother sitting at a loom weaving rugs from designs recorded only in memory.

The hogan, if it were still there, would be about a mile ahead. There would be no problem in moving that far. She had known other floods in other years.

Tachee said, "I'm not risking the lives of these people—and I'm in charge. The captain was—"

"It wasn't my idea," she assured him. "Believe me, I want to work with you, not against you."

He swung out of the jeep and heading back, yelled, "Okay, unload the horses."

She raised her voice to his level. "Hold it everybody!" To him, she said, "You will not issue orders without consulting me."

"Get some sense into that head of yours, woman."

"Don't call me woman!"

"The captain wanted to put me down—and used you."

"We can make another mile."

"You're making me look bad."

"You're helping! We'll see what the others have to say."

She went from jeep to jeep, and the consensus was that they should continue. Every mile helped. Packing in on a night such as this would be slow, laborious, and fraught with danger.

Tachee outmaneuvered her and took the lead again. She prayed that he knew where the quicksand was.

As she drove, her thoughts were with Larry. It was a good night for thinking. Strangely, there was peace in the beat of the rain, the slosh, grind, and groan of the jeeps, an occasional wheeze or neigh from the horses, the distant, muted churning of the river, the brush of cars against shrubs, the sleepy quiet of her fellow officers, the glow of a cigarette.

She was near a decision.

She was thankful for the darkness. No one could see the tears.

Bill kept his foot pressed firmly on the accelerator. Eighty miles an hour. No one was going to stop him. He would be with Sandy within the hour.

She'd be alive. Nothing could still that radiant, happy, at times recklessly wild spirit.

They had come this way. How long ago? A month? Dust devils were whirling like dervishes. Great white clouds skimmed across the turquoise sky.

Down they went, plunging without care or a thought over the trail to White House ruin, she in tight jeans and a thin shirt, and he in Levi's and a white tank stretched taut over his broad shoulders. He was puffing and she, laughing. She was a ballet dancer and he an awkward tackle.

"You've got to be part mountain goat," he said. And she, "I love men who flatter me."

On the canyon floor, they surprised a dog who backed off

in fright. She talked to him in Navajo, setting his tail to wagging. "Most of them speak Navajo," she said.

She called out to a cliff with holes that looked like wren's nests, and it threw back her low, warm voice. She dared him to race her the last hundred yards to the ruin, and won.

Eighty miles an hour, and the car skidded, and barely held around a sharp turn. Past a boarding school, Garcia's Trading Post on the left, low hills, much open country, Park Service headquarters, on across the new bridge, past Justin's Thunderbird and the public campgrounds.

The wooden barricade up ahead. Cars with revolving red lights. Men in heavy raincoats waving spotlights.

He never slowed. The crashing of splintering wood, a slight veering of the car, quickly corrected.

Eighty miles an hour. He'd make it—if he could only see where he was going, if this damn rain would only let up.

13.

Long after the last rock had tumbled, Sandy sat doubled up on the floor of the dank, cold cave. By forcing her legs against her body, she subdued the stabbing pain inside her. Her arm still hurt, but the first agony had disappeared. Her breathing was raspy and loud and distorted in her hearing. More than anything she wanted to sleep but feared she might not awaken. Death was still close by. Death had passed her over to lay its hand on Mr. B., and the why of it was beyond human explanation.

Back of her there was a quick scurrying of a small animal. Closer, she sensed rather than heard a wriggling, snakelike movement through the sand that lay an inch or two deep. She picked up the club which was an assurance rather than a necessity. Animals and reptiles seldom attacked unless set upon or trapped.

A mother. Skeet. Thinking of him steadied her. With Bill gone from her life, Skeet would be an emotional anchor to hold to these coming months. She would rear him as a Navajo. To do otherwise would be wrong. She would not scold or punish but, like most Navajo mothers, mold him by attention and love. He would gain confidence and know his worth to her and others. He would love her so deeply he would never hurt her by wrongdoing. Although she would have to prepare herself for a time when he might turn to the Holy People, she would hope that, regardless, he would live by the teachings of Christ. He would marry a girl of The People, and become a good and perhaps a great man, and lead the way toward accepting the best of the two worlds that history had destined The Dineh to live in.

By sheer will power, she summoned herself to her feet, and, taking painful steps, made it to the entrance. Outside an unbelievable transfiguration had taken place, such as happened in desert country. The rain had stopped, the stars were out, and a full moon hung close to earth. It seemed to dangle within the canyon proper, and cast a misty, diffused light. The sandstone walls wavered and so did odd forms deep within the canyon. It was an old Japanese print, done on a vast scale that the eyes reduced to a quaint miniature.

The passing of the storm resurrected hope. Despite the pain, she would make it to the rim. Slowly she trudged up-canyon with the river's roar as thunderous as ever. Even hours later, the mountain waters would still be rushing this way, to be absorbed eventually into the canyon soil itself and Chinle wash. Taking a deep breath, she was conscious of the good earth smell that followed a rain, a washed land pungent with spices.

Suddenly the rapacious, pitiless cries and barkings of coyotes tearing their victim apart stopped her progress. They were up ahead, to her right, very close. Oh, God, she thought, why all of this killing? At least they killed for food, man for much less. She resumed her slow, painful walk. They would pay no heed to her. They would be fighting among themselves over the leftovers.

She was well past them when she again sensed rather than

heard a noise out of context. It was no more than pebbles disturbed and a brushing against wet branches. Thinking it an animal, she plodded ahead, then once more went rigid. The noise was unmistakable, that of human beings, two or more persons.

She hurried, calling, "Hello, there."

A boy's voice called back, "Hello!"

Rounding a huge boulder, she drew herself up short. She was dead center in a blinding spot cast by four flashlights. Even so, she made out the teen-agers she had seen when Mr. B. was buying jewelry, and later in the Porsche at the Chinle airstrip. With them was a Navajo boy. She was so overjoyed she would have collapsed if there had been any place to do so. "Hello," she said, babbling, "my plane crashed. Back there. I'm so happy to see . . . how in heaven's name . . . ?"

The older Anglo swept her into his arms briefly. "Thank God. Sit down, sis. Over here." With his flashlight, he indicated a large, flat stone.

She thought he had said *sis*. Her brain, though, was badly fogged. She had misunderstood. "Don't you remember me? I saw you at the—"

He shut her off. "We heard about it over the radio. An awful shock. Sis here"—he indicated the girl—"went to pieces. The trader tried to stop us when we got supplies but nothing could, knowing you were down here. This is a friend, Jigger. I don't think you've met. And Charlie, our guide. I hate to ask, but what about the gentleman who was with you?"

She struggled to assimilate it all. Jigger appeared very pleasant. "Are you all right, miss?" he asked, seemingly concerned. Charlie hung back a step. His lips formed silent words she could not make out in the faint light.

She said, "I hunted and hunted for him. It was raining so hard. And finally I found his body. I think he died instantly. I don't think he ever knew what happened. I buried him. I didn't think I could do it but I did. I had to—because of the animals."

Charlie interrupted. "He is your brother?" He indicated Vince. "Also, the lady—she your sister?"

Vince said quickly, "You got a short memory, kid." He let Charlie see his hand moving toward the .38.

"What's he talking about?" Sandy asked. Vaguely, she sensed an undercurrent at odds with the appearance and seemingly normal talk of the teen-agers.

"Little joke between us," Vince said. "Didja bury the money and the jewels with him?"

"I thought I heard you call me *sis*."

Vince held up a hand. "Hold it, all of you." He cocked his head listening. In the distance, a strange noise grew ever sharper. At first it was unrecognizable, then it took form as that of a helicopter.

Vince shouted, "All of you, flat on your bellies. Over here." He indicated with the flashlight a growth of shrubs. "Get those flashlights out." To Sandy, he said, "I'll tell you what it's about later."

She stood her ground. "Somebody's looking for me."

His tone was a threat. "Come on, face down. Quick. You, too, Charlie." To Jigger, he ordered, "Get the damn fool's flashlight out before they see us."

She hesitated, torn. The roar of the rotor blades filled the canyon. The craft itself was in full view, illuminated by its own searchlight that played a spot from wall to wall.

Vince continued to yell. She stood confused, terrified.

For the first time, Penny spoke. "Please, ma'am, do what he says. Please." Her voice had a personal urgency, a pleading. *Something horrible will happen if you don't and I don't want it to happen.*

The next Sandy knew, she was conscious of a fist plowing into soft flesh. Turning, she saw Charlie, doubled up, sinking slowly to the ground.

Before Charlie landed, Vince knocked her legs out from under her, caught her, and laid her gently on the ground. "I'm sorry to do this, ma'am."

Terrified, she found herself alongside this girl they called Penny who whispered, "Don't fight him—ever. Please."

The thrashing of the blades was deafening. The canyon walls magnified the raucous roar a hundred times. Vince crawled alongside. "I've got a gun on you, ma'am."

The helicopter moved slowly, a giant, noisy bird almost stilled in flight. Its wide swath of light patiently swept the canyon floor.

From his post beside the pilot, Tonalea scanned the country below. He searched for anything out of the norm—foliage sheared off that might indicate the plane had fallen into a copse of cottonwood or other trees, the river current rushing around an obstacle, fresh footprints in soft sand, and the slightest movement. For years he had worked rugged terrain and his sight had been trained by a thousand cases.

"Can you set it down a little more?" Tonalea asked.

The pilot shook his head. "We're getting more turbulence than I had expected."

They could hear the increasing whine of the wind.

Shortly after entering the canyon, Tonalea had observed an old prospector and a mule. Looking up, the prospector had raised a hand in greeting, and Tonalea recognized him as Shonto. Tonalea had never met him but had seen a recent picture and interview in *The Navajo Times,* a well-edited weekly owned and published in English by the Tribal Council. Tonalea thought: Now what is that old character doing down there at this time of night? Then he dismissed Shonto from mind. In one way or another, these old prospectors were eccentrics.

They were well into Hidden Canyon when Tonalea spotted the wreckage. One glance told him there was little chance anyone had survived. Its cabin, tilted crazily, had one side sheared off. It was missing its nose and part of its tail. Although accustomed to death, he had never become inured to it. It was a shock, a sadness that persisted long after he had completed a case. There was, of course, an outside chance that one or both were alive. They could be pinned down by the wreckage or tossed free of it but unable to move because of injuries.

For minutes, the pilot kept the copter hovering over the site. There was no chance of putting down. Aside from air turbulence, the canyon was narrow, with sheer walls rising on each side and the river spread out over half of the floor. Enormous boulders, looking like play blocks a child had dropped, covered the remainder.

Tonalea called Chinle and when Captain Yazzi answered, said, "We're over the crash scene and there is no sign of survivors or bodies. The plane is badly smashed up. One side is completely missing. We'll be landing at Chinle shortly and will wait until morning to fly further sorties if we need to . . ."

The pilot was moving the copter down the canyon when Tonalea asked him to retrace the course. No, he had not imagined it. There below, half hidden by scraggly growth, was a prayer cairn, a little pyramid of rocks. The leaves of a twig, weighted down by a stone, suggested that someone had recently passed this way.

Now that they had completed their mission, the pilot speeded up. They passed over the rescue party which was unloading the horses. A short distance later, Tonalea saw a lone man on foot and wondered what he was doing in the canyon. After another half mile, they came to a car deserted on a rise well above the flood waters. Tonalea conjectured that the car belonged to the man and he had driven as far as he dared.

Strange.

Bill Delaney found the going rougher than he had anticipated. He should have stopped at home for his boots. With effort, he lifted his waterlogged shoes. He slid, stumbled, and, a time or two, fell. The slick rock, the pot holes, and hidden step-offs were traps. He had had no experience in canyon country, and the tennis he played occasionally had not developed the needed stamina.

He caught up with the rescue team when it was about to

move off. The horses had been unloaded and saddled. There were sorrels, paints, buckskins, and grays. They nipped at each other playfully and nickered low.

Both Sergeant Tachee and Officer Davis walked to meet him.

"Mr. Delaney?" Ramona Davis asked. It was more of a statement than a question.

He nodded.

"You're not supposed to be down here. I must ask you to leave the canyon at once."

"You're an officer?"

"Yes, sir." Her tone defied him to resist. She had a strength of purpose and speech that surprised him. She was a striking-looking woman. Not beautiful but earthy, a product of a rugged land.

Casually, he twisted his jacket to squeeze the water out. "Let me have a horse. I can handle one. Back in New England—"

She cut him off. "This is not New England. I have strict orders—"

Suddenly he was angry. "Don't you have any feelings? Any feelings at all?"

She forced back the lump in her throat. *No survivors found* pounded in her hearing. Gently, she said, "We might never see you or the horse again. There's quicksand up ahead."

"Don't tell me what to do. You don't have jurisdiction down here."

"But we do. I speak for the United States Park Service, the Tribal Rangers and the Tribal Police. I think you must know, too—since you've been on the reservation some time—that the Park Service has a strict rule. No one in the canyon unless he has a permit or a guide, except for the trail to White House ruin."

"I've got a friend down here. She may be dead—but if she's alive, I got to help her."

Tachee spoke up. "We've got to get going. Let's arrest him and be done with it. All right?"

She ignored him. "Look, Mr. Delaney, you may get in our way unintentionally, and keep us from getting to your friend as quickly as we should—and, too, we feel a responsibility for you. You could get caught in a flash flood before you knew what was happening."

"Hell," Tachee said, "let him go if he wants to kill himself. One more white, we won't miss. All right?"

"Please, Sergeant . . ." Davis began.

"Okay, you handle the stubborn bastard. Remember what I said so you can report it to the captain."

"You tell him," Davis retorted. "I'm no informant." She turned back to Bill. "I'll have to arrest you if you resist me."

He stood a moment staring at the river, then shrugged, and walked away, back in the direction he had come.

She said to a nearby officer, "Follow him for a short distance and make sure he goes back."

She watched until darkness enveloped both. He was a handsome guy, and direct in his approach, which she liked. Her heart went out to him.

"Come on, come on!" Tachee yelled from atop a brown horse pawing and neighing, anxious to be off.

"Coming," she said. She lingered, though, thinking of Larry. If something happened to her, such as to this Anglo girl, he would never dare show his love. It would have to be as though he had never known her. It would hurt, and hurt deeply.

Larry. It was inevitable that they would be seen together by someone who knew them. It happened in Farmington, New Mexico, a small agricultural town a few miles off the reservation.

Larry had to go there on business. As usual, he would pick her up on the highway a mile or more north of Chinle. She liked to hike and traffic was usually light.

Already at nine in the morning the pavement was hot, the heat partly held over from the day before. In places the asphalt was soft and sucked at her soles. The highway itself stretched endlessly, and the land, too, was without boundary.

And then, like her old dog, Mac, who knew her car a half-mile away, she recognized Larry's. Some distance behind her, he slowed down to let another driver pass. When there was no traffic in either direction, he swooped down alongside her. He slammed on the brakes and she could hear the tires digging into the heat-softened asphalt.

She pressed her lips hard against his and held until both gasped for breath. He pulled her to him in a bear hug, and she hurt where his big hand held her. It was a good hurt.

A huge truck rose up out of the pavement and she slouched down. She wore dark glasses, which she disliked, and a pancake Stetson that she could tilt over her face, partially hiding her features. In that moment she detested herself. She had never been furtive, not even as a child when playmates fibbed to their parents about little sins.

For miles they talked about their week. They commiserated over small rebuffs and savored little triumphs. Their love, she thought, was all the more intense concealed and protected as it was by stealth. Conspiracy itself was a bond sealed with epoxy.

In Farmington, he let her out near a motel. She would look over the town's shops and then rest and read in the motel's patio. Again there was the sudden stop, the surreptitious checking of faces about them, and hurried departures. All week she was a police officer, and then weekends, a skulking fugitive with criminal instincts for flight and deceit.

That day Larry assisted Peter MacDonald, chief of the Tribal Council, who had led the Navajos to a midway development that few peoples of the soil anywhere had achieved in such a short time. If he had headed one of the small African or Asian countries, he would have been considered an outstanding statesman. As it was, he was hidden away in a remote nation within a nation.

This day he appealed to the people of Farmington, as well as other off-reservation towns, to lay aside their prejudices and grant the Navajos the same consideration they gave their fellow Anglos. He asked for "faith and good will, to establish a beginning toward a better understanding and a better relationship." He asked for help with housing, a culture center ("if this town can spend $40,000 for a dog pound . . ."), health care, an alcoholic treatment center, recreational facilities, a school code "that will treat our youngsters equally and fairly," and employment of Navajos on the basis of skills and talents, the same as the Anglos.

He wanted, too, the prohibition of the sale of alcohol "in areas of high alcohol abuse." Each year the Farmington police took in many hundreds for twelve-hour "protective custody" under the Federal Detoxification Act. Indians accounted for 86 per cent. Liquor was the Navajo's greatest weakness, as it was the Anglo's. The difference was that the Anglo's friends took him home, and got him out of sight, while the Navajo often lived far away and landed in the police roundup.

Shortly after five that afternoon, Larry picked her up. He was late and the wait had been interminable. An old school friend had stopped to chat and ask what she was doing in Farmington. She was investigating, she said, an off-reservation angle of a criminal case. It was a plausible story, and yet she had answered stiffly, as if on the witness stand.

They had dinner in a small restaurant several miles out of town. It was not patronized by Navajos. The hostess met Navajo couples with a gracious smile and was very sorry but the restaurant was booked for the night.

Larry knew the Anglo owner and was welcomed. Often Larry argued with him about his policy. "Your people don't phone ahead for a reservation," the owner complained.

"Oh hell," Larry said, "that's an excuse and we both know

it. I can understand why you wouldn't want drunken bums in
here but when a decent-looking couple comes in . . ."

The Civil Rights movement had been slow in infiltrating
the off-reservation towns. Ramona Davis had explained once,
"We're not a docile people but we don't beg for rights we
should have. We've got pride and dignity, and when we get
rebuffed, we move on. But we don't hate the Anglo for it. Perhaps it's our faith. We know there's evil and good in everyone
and all people. Even the Holy People."

That night they had roast duck, candlelight, soft music, a
touch of hands, and eyes only for the other. When they left,
they walked beyond reality in that somewhere land of dreams
and fantasy. Tonight was theirs, never to end.

But it did end minutes later, with a shock.

Coming out of a bar two doors away was her uncle. He
weaved slightly and was bleary eyed. Turning sharply, she
headed in the opposite direction.

All the way home she was tortured and silent. Her uncle
might have seen them, and again, might not.

"I can't go on like this, Larry," she said.

"I know."

14.

Long after the copter had passed, Vince kept them
pinioned to the ground. Now that the beating of the rotor
blades had faded, the thunder of water in the wash was loud
again.

Mud oozed under and around Sandy's body. Unconsciously, she clutched gobs of it in a fist tightened by nerves
running scared. The shock of being sent sprawling was matched
by the realization the three teen-agers were after the cash and
jewelry. She doubted if she could absorb more punishment. She
was near the breaking point. If she could only double up to
strangle the searing pain in her abdomen.

The flight of the chopper gave her hope. Definitely, the authorities were looking for the plane. They would send a rescue team up the canyon from Chinle. She must play for time.

Vince said, "Okay, on your feet."

Slowly, she rubbed the mud from her hands on her Levi's, then instinctively finger brushed her hair, as if it mattered how she looked.

Vince said brusquely, "Here's a flashlight. Keep it pointed down. Don't raise it up if you want to go on breathing . . . Come on, come on, move your butt. We haven't much time."

Penny whispered, "He means for you to take us to the plane, ma'am."

"I'm hurt—bad." Sandy indicated her abdomen. "I can't make it back to the plane."

Vince nodded to Jigger. "Examine her and see if she's hurt." To Sandy, he said, "Unzip your pants."

Charlie emerged at that point from his own shock. "Mister, can I have my money? Also, I will go home—"

"Don't go," Sandy exclaimed without thinking.

"You hear that?" Vince said. "She wants you to stick around. She likes young boys."

Sandy backed away as Jigger approached. To Penny, she said, "Really, I'm in an awful lot of pain."

Vince took a deep, horselike breath. "Get away, Jigger. Can't you see she doesn't trust you. I'll check her out."

"Please," Sandy said quickly, "I'll try."

"Okay. Keep the flash down. Come on, Charlie. Single file. You first, Wilcox, then Charlie, then me and Jigger."

"Why do I always have to be last?" Penny complained.

"Logistics."

"What?"

"You're guarding our rear. A vital job."

"You mean I get shot."

"Wouldn't you die for me?"

Penny fell into line. "I don't like kidding around like this. Like something might happen. You'll take care of me, Vince?"

"Sure."

"Me, too," Jigger put in.

"Yes, you, too, Jigger," Penny said happily.

Playing for time, Sandy proceeded more cautiously than necessary, and took the longest way possible. She led them over slick, treacherous whorls of rock, in the hope one might fall, and once, along the edge of a precipice when they could have taken another route.

Vince suspected. "What'd we climb up here for when we could've stayed down there?"

"Safer."

"You've got something in mind, Wilcox, and you'd better get it out before I get it out for you."

Her anger surfaced. "You want to get us all killed?"

She sat down. Her body was drenched with nervous sweat. "Go ahead. You take over since you know so much about it."

He stared belligerently. He was uncertain of his ground. He had had no experience in this kind of country. "Okay, okay, have it your way. You're in charge." He turned to Jigger. "She'd make a great cab driver. Never take the shortest route."

Jigger laughed uneasily.

Penny said, "I know you hurt, ma'am, but he gets awful mad when he's crossed and I don't want to see anything happen to you."

The girl seemed genuinely concerned. Yet Sandy wondered if it could be a routine. She swayed a little getting to her feet. After steadying herself, she struck off.

A half hour later, they arrived at the cabin of the plane. The sight in the faint moonlight with the flashlights playing about sharpened memories only a few hours old. The crash, the wandering about, the finding and burying of Mr. B.

"Take a look around," Vince told Jigger. "Penny, keep an eye on our guests. Yell if you need me."

Sandy dropped to the soggy ground and buried her head in her arms. She had to get herself mentally adjusted. Long ago she remembered her father telling her, "If you've got a problem, don't moan over it or panic or worry, just sit down and figure out what you can do, all the possibilities, and then decide on one and do it."

"Are you all right, miss?" Charlie stood over her, his eyes troubled. A short distance away, Penny watched and listened. Behind her, Vince was exploring the plane. He kept them within sight.

Far away, she heard the boy called Jigger moving noisily through underbrush. Most likely, if his search were methodical, he would come upon Mr. B.'s grave. However, she doubted if he would recognize it. It was flat with the rest of the ground, and the rocks she had placed over it to hold the earth intact would have no meaning to an untrained eye.

"I'll be all right," she told Charlie, and mustered a reassuring smile. He was such a likable youngster.

"They are bad people. Most bad. Also, I think they are wolves. I took the medicine. Do you want some medicine?"

"Thank you, no."

"I wish I had a sister like you."

She was surprised and touched. "I'll be your sister."

Jigger returned to report he had found pieces of the plane but nothing else. "Too dark to do a good job. If we could wait until daylight . . ."

"And miss the bank deal?" Vince turned to Sandy. "What's that over there?" He pointed to the ruins of the pueblo she had seen while wandering about shortly after the crash.

"A cliff house."

"Looks in ruins."

"Has been for about seven hundred years."

"Nobody there at all?"

"A few ghosts."

"Come on, Jigger. I've found us a command post. Okay, Wilcox, you first."

Approaching the two-story pueblo, a condominium of its time, which was somewhere between A.D. 1100 and 1300, she experienced a strange, tingling sensation. She was walking out of the present into the past. Somewhere in the deep shadows people waited. The Anasazis, the ancient ones. Waited to sell highly polished pottery with intricate design. Waited to offer them food and water.

The enormous walls were of stone and some had fallen. The front ones stood only two or three feet high, but the rear ones had withstood time. There were holes near the top where poles supporting the roof had been anchored. The roof itself was long gone.

Looming over the apartments was a tower, perhaps used for defense, perhaps for religious ceremonies. Over all of the pueblo stretched an immense overhang of sandstone, an awning of rock. It looked as if it had been chiseled.

None of the ancient ones emerged from the shadows. Long ago, perhaps during the great drought of 1276 to 1299, they had abandoned their homes, and no one knew for certain where they went.

Picking her way over the rubble, she entered the first room. One wall was streaked with black where fires had smoked. There was a feeling the owners had run out for a pack of cigarettes and would soon return. The floor was dirt and not too wet. It had been windswept clean. A surprised lizard darted across it.

"What a dump," Vince said, though pleased. They stood on a slight rise and looked out over the plane wreckage, and beyond that, to the wash, and on to the opposite canyon wall. Yet they were hidden from the view of a helicopter unless it flew dangerously low.

To Sandy and Charlie, Vince said, "You two stay here. I don't want you wandering around getting lost. I'll take the flashlight."

He handed Penny the Saturday Night Special. "Use it if they try anything. Make it a clean shot. Don't wound them. Jigger and me don't like seeing people suffer, do we, Jigger?"

"Right."

"How long we got, Charlie, before the rescue guys get here?"

Charlie shifted uneasily. He had run through his mind some movie scenes in which John Wayne and Clint Eastwood and others had performed miraculous deeds against overwhelming odds, and he had decided to emulate them. Still, he had not figured out a course of action, and he was nervous. "Don't know. Might take long time."

"One hour, two hours? Come on, we're paying you fifty bucks."

"Maybe three hours. Also, maybe four."

"That should do it. Okay, Wilcox, what'd you do with the money?"

She took a deep breath. She had anticipated the question, but nevertheless hearing it produced a certain shock effect. It wasn't her money and she had no interest in it. But she would be damned if she would let a threatening punk hoodlum shove her around.

She said slowly, "I wasn't thinking about money. You don't think about money when you walk out of a crash alive. You thank God you're here, and I started looking for Mr. B., and I must've hunted an hour before I found him."

Vince stared until she shifted her gaze. "Wilcox, you're a liar. Isn't that right, Jigger? You saw how she couldn't look me in the eye."

"I saw."

Vince continued quietly, "Now, Wilcox, the old geezer had a fortune in all that Navvy crap. I'll make you a deal. You keep the jewelry, I take the money. That's fair, isn't it?"

"Why give it to me?"

"You live up here and can peddle it. I don't. I wouldn't know what to do with it. I don't know of a fence who'd handle the junk. Good deal for you, good for me."

She tossed her hair defiantly.

"I told you . . ." she began. He reacted violently. He slapped her so hard her neck snapped. She staggered backward, stepped on a rock, and lost her balance. She went down hard and lay sprawled on the dirt floor, breathing with effort. As pain jetted through her body, she let out a low, animal-like cry.

"Don't stand there, Jigger. Help the lady up."

Penny moved before Jigger did and took her by the hand. "Can you make it?"

With a struggle, Sandy got to her feet. Tears ran down her cheeks. She brushed them aside, squared her shoulders and pushed out her jaw. "Go ahead, knock me down again. Show your friends what a man you are."

Vince stared, amused. Dammit, what a fighter. He enjoyed women with fire. He could have fun with this one. This time they had picked up a live one.

Penny whispered, "Please tell him. I don't want to see you hurt."

Charlie stepped between her and Vince. "I'm a professional fighter. Also, I win all my school fights."

Vince crumpled Charlie up with a blow to the midriff. "Also, I win all mine." He stood over Charlie as if he might continue to pummel him, then relaxed. "I'm disappointed in you. Here we're paying you fifty bucks and you don't show any gratitude."

He turned to Sandy. "Okay, Wilcox, I'll take you at your word. But if I find out you lied to me, I'll break your arms and legs and leave you for the vultures. But first I'll rape you."

"He means it," Penny put in. "Please tell him."

Sandy stood motionless, in agony. She had bluffed and won. But only for the time being.

"Where'd you bury the old man?" Vince asked.

She whispered, "You're not going to dig him up?"

He nodded. "Why not?"

"I swear before God—"

"What d'ya care? What's he to you?"

"It was horrible burying him—and it'd be more horrible—"

"You show me where. Come on, Jigger, I may need you if she makes a run for it." He said to Penny, "Keep a few feet away from Charlie so he can't grab the gun—and let him have it if he tries anything."

Sandy started to follow Vince, then abruptly halted. Charlie, too, had heard the faint, alien sound. It had to be man-made. And the very fact they could hear it at all above the river's roar would indicate that more than one person was approaching. Her heart sped up and the night's weariness and pain dropped away.

Vince held up a hand. "Sh-h-h . . ." He squatted and motioned for the others to do likewise. Deliberately, she hesitated. If she could buy a little time, only a few seconds, then the party thrashing through the brush might see her. Jigger stepped over, and she cringed, expecting a blow. "Excuse me," he said and gently pushed her down. He was a paradox she could not fathom.

When Vince pulled his .38, Jigger followed suit. However, the Saturday Night Special languished in Penny's hand like a popsicle. With each minute, the sound grew more distinct. Definitely, there was more than one person. Vince skirted off to one side to crouch behind a wall about three feet high.

A low whistling came over. Charlie buried his head. Whistling in the dark meant that a ghost was about. Knowing this, Sandy crawled on her hands and knees and put an arm about him.

In the full moonlight, a form took shape over toward the wash and headed toward them. It was a thin form, and behind, another, that was a pack animal, a mule or mustang. By the time they reached the wreckage, Shonto and the mule were well outlined.

While Shonto poked about the plane's cabin, Vince disappeared. A few minutes later, Sandy watched as Vince, gun in hand, slipped up behind the old man. He put the weapon to Shonto's head and slowly Shonto raised his hands. Vince frisked him, there was talk, and then they headed toward the ruins.

With great deliberation, Shonto led the mule in. His

rheumy old eyes switched quickly from one to the next, taking stock of them and the situation. He walked as if on stubs.

"Put the mule over there." Vince pointed out a corner.

Shonto had to push to persuade Sam to move. "I hate to do this to you, boy, but I got no choice. Don't you fret none." Once he had Sam in a corner, he buckled a hobble on him, then gave him an affectionate pat. Silently he berated himself. If he had hurried, he could have had this claim worked by now. It had never occurred to him that anyone else would be down here prospecting. Especially kids. Kids with guns. He had never trusted youngsters with guns. They often panicked.

Jigger asked, "Who's he?"

"Old prospector."

"This time of night?"

"What you say your name was?" Vince asked Shonto.

"They call me Shonto."

"Got any other name?"

"None I care to remember."

"Hell of a name. Where d'you live?"

"Here and there, most everywhere. Wherever the good Lord leads me and Sam."

"Sam?"

"My friend over there. We've been friends for nigh on to . . ."

Sandy liked the quiet, sensible way he talked. His deep, blue eyes—sad, understanding, intelligent—hinted that he could handle almost any situation. Now there were three of them to match wits with the three teen-agers. She doubted if in a crisis she could count on Charlie. He was too impulsive and outspoken. But Shonto struck her as a cool, calculating, though slow-minded collaborator. He was up in years, arthritic, and none too stable on his feet, but those seeming drawbacks might prove assets. Vince would consider him little threat, the same as he obviously did Charlie.

She was the one Vince watched. He needed her; he had to have her; he would not kill her, she didn't think, until he had exhausted every possibility of wringing from her the whereabouts of the half-million dollars. Still, he was unpredictable, he might kill on impulse, in a burst of anger. He had a quick, penetrating mind, but exactly how much control it exerted over him was yet to be determined.

For the last half hour, she had debated whether she should turn over the money and the jewelry. They were not her responsibility. Too, why risk death for a half-million dollars the authorities probably would recover eventually? The thought kept recurring, however, that she risked death also if she surrended the money. Once he had it, would he not kill her and Charlie to quiet them? If he let them go, they would be witnesses against him in case he should be apprehended. Most telling of all in her final decision, though, was the feeling that Vince would enjoy murdering her. Jigger would watch, completely hypnotized by the daring of "the great man." Penny would be disturbed, but not overly so. She adored her two boy friends, and whatever wrongs they committed she put quickly out of mind.

"How come you're down here tonight?" Vince asked Shonto.

"Well, the good Lord—"

Vince exploded. "Don't talk to me about the Lord! Any time anybody starts talking about the Lord, watch it, man, here comes a con job. I'll ask you once more, and you'd better answer me. What're you doing down here?"

Shonto ran a hand through his thin hair. "Couldn't sleep. I've got arthritis bad and I reckoned me and Sam better get to Chinle and see one of them doctor fellows."

Vince shook his head in disbelief but spoke quietly. "You heard it on the radio and you're down here to pick up a half-million bucks. Why, you old scoundrel. You ought to be ashamed of yourself. At your age, lying, stealing, dragging a poor jackass out in the rain, calling on the Lord . . ."

Jigger interrupted. "Beautiful! Criminy, Vince, but that's beautiful."

Vince continued, "Get over there with the other stooges. Meet Wilcox. She's the pilot. And Charlie, our guide."

"Glad to meet you folks," Shonto said. His gaze stayed with Sandy, taking a reckoning, sizing up what kind of a partner he had.

"Well, don't be too damn glad. You three are prisoners of war under the Geneva convention which says we can execute you for certain crimes."

Charlie spoke up. "No, mister, you got it wrong. We studied about it in school—"

"You did, huh? Guess you didn't read the paragraph that says we can plug you in the back if you try to escape. Come on, Wilcox, let's dig up the old guy. Jigger, you better stay here since we've got another prisoner."

He looked Sandy up and down. "After we do the digging I might find a nice soft spot of sand where Wilcox and me could get to know each other."

Penny took Vince aside and they talked very low. Charlie sauntered over to look at the mule. "My father had a horse," he told Shonto, "but we had to sell him after my father died. We couldn't feed him."

He pretended to listen while Shonto recalled where he and Sam had met. Charlie, though, was taking the lay of the land. At the other end of the room, Sandy sat on the dirt floor. Jigger was looking out toward the wash. Vince and Penny were a few feet beyond Jigger who partially blocked them out. In the wall behind Charlie was a small, deep, three-by-four opening, a primitive window. Beyond the window was thick brush. He studied the window and the brush, measuring his chances. He could be through the window before anyone reacted. The brush was the danger area. If they opened fire, he could hide but he would be trapped.

Penny said, "I'm your girl. You don't have to do—to do anything to her."

"Like what?" Vince teased.

"Promise me, Vince, you won't. I'd feel awful."

She held him in a tight embrace. His left hand patted her, reaching as far down her backside as it could. She felt his right hand forcing its way between them, along her stomach. She grew excited with anticipation. It stopped and she realized it had pulled the weapon from his belt.

She backed up screaming. "No, Vince! No!"

The explosion of the .38, fired inches from her head, deafened her.

In the window, Charlie dropped without a cry.

15.

Until he came upon the rock slide, Officer Frank Ramah had found the trail not too hazardous. A former football defensive end, track star, and basketball guard, he easily jumped the narrow chasm between ledges and snaked along the cat-sized trail where one slip of a knee would plunge one into eternity.

In the low-wattage light cast by the moon, he studied the slide. His flashlight helped little. Its beam barely reached down to the precipice. As near as Ramah could tell, the plunge went right to the brink. The question was: Was there solid footing a few feet this side of the drop into the canyon? Possibly. The boot tracks of four persons—one set possibly those of a young female—indicated they had gone down the slide. Still, they might have started a small avalanche which had changed the course. For all he knew, they might have plunged over the precipice.

He was about to report to Chinle that he was returning when he noted the lone scrub tree at the foot of the slide. It slanted out over the canyon. Would it hold him if, finding no firm footing, he grabbed it? The root system for scrub trees varied greatly. The roots might have drilled deeply to locate precious moisture, in which case the tree would hold him. However, the roots might be surface ones shooting out only inches below the soil.

He knew he had the strength to pull himself back up if he went over the brink and seized hold of the scrub tree. He remembered Captain Yazzie's warning about gung-ho tactics. But this move, he assured himself, was more like a calculated risk.

He relaced one boot that was too loose, zippered his jacket up to his neck, and flexed his arm and leg muscles. Taking a deep breath, he walked into the slide. Immediately the downward pull caught him and he moved faster than he had anticipated. He lost his sitting balance and floundered badly. He experienced a moment of outright terror before he straightened himself out. Like driving a car on an icy road, the trick was not to make sudden moves. He dug his boots in as far as he could and slowed his descent. With the storm gone, he saw the canyon depths coming up rapidly. He was on a roller coaster with no ups. His heart pounded and his breath came hard, but he had played too many football and basketball games to panic.

He felt a rock gash an elbow, and saw the moon tilt over backward. His own thrashing was thunderously loud in his ears. He resisted a compulsion to use his hands to brake himself.

And then the foot of the slide came up fast. He tried standing up, and struggled desperately to locate solid footing. He was going over, and below him was a thousand-foot drop. His body would strike a dozen jagged edges and be tossed about like a dummy.

He guessed at the distance and the timing. Right on the split second, he reached for the tree. He got hold of a branch that gave a little, then snapped. But before it broke, the branch stopped his wild fall. Twisting around in space, he got a hand on the trunk, and then his other hand anchored him tightly.

With a heave of his body, he brought himself up on a ledge that the avalanche had covered with a foot of rocks and smaller aggregate. A surge of relief swept him as he found his footing firm.

Once on the canyon floor, he stood a moment collecting himself. His trousers were ripped and muddy, his shoes caked, and his hands and arms badly scratched. Moreover he was winded.

Playing his flashlight about on the ground, he discovered numerous fresh prints. He examined them and then, waiting until his breathing was normal, took out the two-way radio he carried inside his jacket. He listened to assure himself he was alone. It was difficult to tell, since the furious pounding of water down the wash, only fifty or sixty yards away, obliterated most other sound.

"Captain, Officer Ramah," he said when he reached Chinle. The static crackled loudly and he had trouble hearing.

"Where are you, Frank?" Yazzie asked.

"At the foot of the trail."

"What shape's it in?"

"It's suicide. Pieces are missing and you jump and don't know where you're jumping. There's a rock slide, too, that goes over a precipice. There's been a recent avalanche. A small one but it's made the trail impassable."

"If it's impassable, how'd you make it?"

"Lucky, I guess."

"I know—you were a damn fool. I told you—"

"Yes, sir. I was into it before I realized . . ." He hurried on. "I wasn't the only one. A party of four preceded me."

"You mean . . . ?" Yazzie exclaimed.

"Yes, sir. Three males, one young, probably a boy. One female. All slender judging from the impression their boots and shoes left. The prints are fresh, made since the rain stopped. And down here I found one male and a pack animal. All the prints point down the canyon . . ."

In Chinle Major Tonalea sat across the desk from Captain Yazzie. Tonalea had had the pilot put down on the Chinle landing strip and instructed him to refuel and ready the craft for another flight.

He said to Yazzie, "That would be an old prospector named Shonto and his mule."

Yazzie relayed the information into the radio. "Hold on, Frank. The major wants to speak with you."

While Tonalea took over the radio, Yazzie went to the door and called in Officer Ybarra, who only a few weeks before had completed his training at the Navajo Tribal Academy. "Officer Ramah reports that a party of four went down the trail ahead of him," Yazzie said. "Three males and one female. Ring up the Big Rock Trading Post. No, better still, drive out there. Get the trader up and find out if they got outfitted there. Then scout around in that area and see if you can find anybody who saw them and might know who they are."

While Yazzie was talking with Officer Ybarra, Tonalea asked Ramah again about the trail. "You're positive it's impassable?"

"Absolutely—until there's some work done on it."

"I see. Call us as soon as you reach the crash scene. In the meantime, we will try to identify the party of three males and one female."

Lost in thought, Tonalea leaned back. It was strange that a girl or a woman would have gone down into the canyon over a treacherous trail. And just as strange that her companions would have made a trip on a night such as this. They would have to be strongly motivated.

"Odd, isn't it," Yazzie said slowly, "five people heading for the plane. A half-million dollars, they say, besides the jewelry."

Tonalea rose. "I've had the same thought. A few months ago I wouldn't have had it."

That was before two major crimes had been committed barely off the reservation. Raiders had cleaned out the vault of one trading post of a million dollars in jewelry and stolen a small fortune from another.

Tonalea continued, "We should advise Ramah to approach with caution. He should scout the layout before he moves in. Of course, these five could be curiosity seekers. A crash holds a morbid fascination for some people."

The static still crackled badly when Officer Davis came over.

"Davis in," she said. "Davis here."

Davis here. How often these last four years had she said that? But Davis was not here to the men who wanted to date her—the police officers, the Navajo park rangers, the young government workers. What was the matter with Davis? they asked. She never went out with a man. Why had she fenced herself in?

What did she do during her days off? The weekends? Where did she go? They didn't set out with premeditation to create a mystery woman, but they had. In time, someone would unriddle the mystery woman, and she would stand stripped.

In time.

Now and then a horse would neigh, but for the most part the mounts stood quietly in moonlight with a swift current running against their legs. They and their riders were a ghostly group, a strange apparition, in a canyon where all life had fled except for them.

"What does it look like?" Yazzie asked Davis.

"Not good, sir. We're in water well up the shanks of the horses. But if we can make it another quarter mile, there's a crossing I think we can ford safely."

Tachee said into his mike, "Captain, Sergeant Tachee. I think you should know that we're in a bad way and may have a casualty or two if we keep going . . . Davis wants to ford the river. She'll get us all killed . . ."

One of the U.S. park rangers prodded his horse near, and Tachee added with a grin, "We could send the U.S. park rangers ahead. If we lost one or two of them, nobody would notice . . . Captain, I do not hate the white people. You got me all wrong. I just think their God made one horrible mistake . . . Okay, here's Davis."

Davis listened, then said, "There's a rock bed we could cross over. It would be slick and we would have to move slowly. If we can get to it . . . very well, Captain."

She put the radio back into a saddle pouch. "What'd he say?" Tachee asked.

"We ford the river."

"Davis, you're a catastrophe."

"Thank you, Sergeant."

Looking back, she saw the riders waiting for a signal. It was all so real—the night, the storm, the river running wild—and yet it was unreal, a dream done in dim shadows, even the dream a fantasy. She was tired, so tired.

An officer came shouting, sloshing through water which was up over his knees. "My horse! Some guy stole it!"

"Stole it?" Tachee found that hard to believe. "Nobody's around except us. How could anyone steal it? What were you doing off it?"

"I had to get off, sir."

"Oh . . ."

Davis asked, "Couldn't you hold onto the reins?"

"I did, and someone yanked them out of my hands, and before I could get going . . . I didn't see anyone, no one at all as the horse took off. He must've been on the blind side, riding low like they do in the movies. He put the spurs to the horse and I barely saw him at a distance when he swung up into the saddle."

Letting the horse take the bit, Bill Delaney sat the saddle well. This one was not bad for a Navajo mare. They all were a scrawny lot and looked mangy but weren't. Back in New England, they had meat on their bones, and held their heads high, and had a certain distinction about them that became the land of Puritans, Paul Revere, Concord, and the Kennedys.

He hummed "La Paloma," the Mexican song the mariachi band had played for Sandy and him that night in Gallup. He could see her sitting across the table from him, smiling, laughing, filled with the joy of living, and later, he was to know, the joy of being with him. It wasn't much of a restaurant, actually, a little on the shabby side. Never before, though, had there been a restaurant that floated through the clouds.

Well, that was all over, washed out. He had never known anyone as stubborn, unreasoning, illogical as Sandy. Lucy sided with him on everything. She didn't have to, and sometimes he wished she wasn't so agreeable. She would be a terrific asset to his career. When he brought important personages home she would have everything exactly right from the flowers to the silverware, and herself, and her conversation.

He wanted to prod the horse but restrained himself. That Navajo woman officer had said that he did not know this country. She was right. But he didn't need to. He had a mount that knew it.

He wondered if they still hanged horse thieves.

16.

Sandy stood paralyzed, staring at Charlie slumped in the window. There are some events the mind rejects. Since they are too horrible to contemplate, they hold no reality. Only after a time does the mind begin to assimilate the stark facts, and even then there is a long delay before the reasoning admits that a tragedy has occurred.

No one moved. It was a tableau frozen by death. Shonto stood immobile by his faithful mule. Jigger had half turned at the explosion of the shot. Penny had her mouth open, but shock had strangled the last scream. Vince held the weapon ready for another squeeze of the trigger should that be necessary.

Sandy broke the tableau. She was beside Charlie. Lifting his head, she examined him with the hope of one who knows time has run out but clings in desperation to the thought that it simply could not have.

Within seconds, she knew, and turned toward Vince. She was half sobbing. "You killed him! Killed him!"

"Strictly business," Vince broke the .38 chamber to replace the bullet.

Crying, she walked toward him, forgetting the pain searing her. "He was only a kid. A little kid."

"Girl," Shonto said kindly, fearing for her.

"I don't know how anybody . . . anybody . . . He didn't do anything to you. He didn't hurt you."

Shonto wrapped his big arms about her and pulled her back.

"He did his best . . . and you killed him." Her voice rose. "You killed him!"

Shonto buried her face in his chest. "There, there, girl." He felt her quiver like a bird held in one's hand.

Bill. She wanted Bill.

"Didja have to?" Penny asked, stunned. She was not accusing, only wanting him to say he had had no choice.

Vince was his old self. "You don't understand these things, sweetheart. Shonto, hustle your ass over there and take the kid and put him down under those bushes. The ones down there. Get him out of sight. We'll give him a full military burial later. We always pay proper respect to the dead, don't we, Jigger?"

Jigger stared at his feet.

"Jigger?" Vince demanded.

"Yes, of course," he said weakly. "Right."

"You'd better be a little quicker on the uptake if you want to stick around. Now where was we before the little creep tried to pull a fast one? Oh yeah, come on, Wilcox. You're going to show me where you buried the old man."

She straightened, brushed the tears away, and steeled herself. He could torture her before she would tell him. "I don't know! It was raining pitchforks."

She could sense that she had reinforced his conviction that she had buried the money and jewelry with Mr. B. His look hardened. "I was right all the time."

"What d'ya know," Jigger said. "What d'ya know."

"Jigger, go take another look around the wreckage while I'm refreshing Wilcox's memory and scout around under the bushes out there."

"Sure." Jigger left on the run, eager to be of service.

"Now, Wilcox, you wandered around looking for the old guy and then what?"

She hesitated, thinking. She wanted to clam up. She wanted to tell him off, let her hatred and anger explode.

Shonto said, "Go on, girl, tell him. Won't do no harm."

He was as calm inwardly as he sounded. No one bounced around for seventy-nine years without mashing the inner springs down a little. He was composed but nevertheless concerned for this tall, thin girl. From the first nod, he saw her as his own daughter. He and the girl had to play along with this mad killer—or get shot. Even if the stupid kid dug up the half million, that did not mean he got to keep it. The night was young and, Shonto figured, given time, he could outwit him. He had a feeling he and Sam were going to strike it rich tonight.

She stifled her emotions. "He was stretched out full length on the ground under a cottonwood not too far from the arroyo. It was sandy there and I dug a grave—"

"Hold it. What was he using to carry it all in when you left Chinle?"

Charlie. He was still crumpled up where he had fallen. She wished they could lay him out on a dry spot and cover him. She saw Skeet. What if it had happened to Skeet? Oh, God, take care of Skeet.

"I asked—"

"I heard you. The money was in a traveling bag and the jewelry in an attaché case."

"Where'd he have them on the plane?"

"The case at his feet. The bag he was holding."

"So when he fell out of the plane, they dropped out, too, and they were near the body."

"The plane disintegrated. He didn't just fall out. The bags could be miles away—and you know it. Or they could still be in what's left of the cabin. I didn't look."

"I did."

She shrugged.

"What didya use to bury him with?"

"A metal strip—it was like a shovel—from the wreckage."

"You don't look strong enough to handle a big man."

"I got a blanket from the cabin, and wrapped him in it, and rolled him in."

"Now let me get this. You returned to the plane, got the blanket, and then didn't have any trouble in finding your way back. But now you say you don't know where you buried him. Wilcox, I only took so much from the Indian kid and I'm only going to take so much from you."

He turned to Shonto. "What didja say your name was?"

"Shonto."

"Yeah, Shonto." He returned to Sandy. "You know him?"

She shook her head.

"Never seen him before?" Again, she indicated in the negative. "You wouldn't mind then if I blasted him?"

Her nervous system reeled. She struggled not to show it. "You mean—?"

"That's what I said. You either tell me where the old geezer is or we'll bury Shonto with Charlie."

Shonto raised his voice. "What did you say your name was?"

"None of your damn business."

"Don't matter none," Shonto continued. "I'm seventy-nine, son, and I go to sleep hungry most nights, and my arthritis is killing me, and you'd be doing me a big favor if you'd end it now."

"No!" Sandy screamed. "No!"

Shonto patted Sam. "All I ask, girl, is that you take good care of Sam and give him a good home. He's like me, getting along in years and won't have many more."

Vince was amused. "You must've been a great poker player in your day. But I'm calling your bluff." He eased the .38 out but didn't raise it. "Wilcox, you want to sit in on this hand?"

She started to leave the ruins. "Come on, as you're always saying."

He caught her by the wrist, held it tightly. "You stay with me. I haven't any handcuffs but this will do." He tightened his grip until she could have screamed but she refused to give him that satisfaction.

Jigger materialized and took Vince aside. Vince said to Shonto, "Hurry up and get that kid out of here. Penny, go with him and see that he comes back. Remember, sweetheart, if you have trouble with him, make it a good, clean shot right through the heart. And Shonto, your mule will be dead five minutes after she kills you. You may not care anything about your own carcass but don't forget your old buddy."

While Vince and Jigger talked in whispers, Shonto pulled the body out of the window by slow degrees. He groaned and puffed. The pain in his joints was subdued by the necessity and urgency of the moment. If he had been younger, he would have cried. A mere boy. No need to kill him. The hood could have stopped him with a shot fired into the air.

Moving slowly for fear she would arouse Vince, Sandy reached Shonto. Sobbing quietly, she helped him. Heading for the bushes, Shonto staggered. With each step, he seemed about to collapse.

Sandy was following him when Penny said sharply, "You stay here."

Penny trailed a few feet behind Shonto. She pointed the way with a flashlight. In the other hand, she held the Saturday Night Special, her finger about the trigger. Sandy knew that

Penny would not hesitate to pull it. Under Vince's spell, she was a lethal weapon.

Shonto tried lowering Charlie to the ground, but his back would not bend. By a series of maneuvers, he managed to sit down while still holding the boy. He stretched him out, and taking off his jacket, put it under Charlie's head and over his face.

The fast-moving glint of something reflected by the moonlight diverted Sandy. She watched surreptitiously as Jigger slipped Vince a piece of turquoise and silver and a hundred-dollar bill. She trembled in the knowledge that Jigger probably had found them near the spot where she had come across the bag and case. Vince nodded and pocketed them.

When Shonto returned to the rubble, there were tears in his eyes. "Don't try nothing, girl, until we're ready," he whispered to Sandy. "I got some notions."

"Shut up!" Vince yelled. "If you got anything to say, say it out loud."

"I was saying we ought to say a few words over the boy—"

"Sure, when the time comes. I've got to take off now. Wilcox, don't forget where you put the old man. I don't want to have to shoot grandpa. Penny, how about getting us some coffee and sandwiches? I'll be back soon."

Then he yelled, "Down everybody. Flat on your bellies."

Before they knew it, the chopper was over the crash scene, its searchlight crisscrossing the canyon floor and walls. Shonto could not make it to a lying position fast enough, and Vince cracked him behind his knees. Shonto collapsed in a heap. Sandy rolled on her side and doubled up.

For minutes, the copter hovered over the wreckage. Its giant spot reached back repeatedly and probed. It lighted the ancient pueblo like day. But they were crowded up against the front wall, about six feet high at this point, and the beam shot over them.

"I sure as hell could bring it down with a couple of shots,"

Vince said to Jigger. "But it wouldn't be a smart move. Nobody knows we're down here or what we're doing. We're pulling a big heist and no one knows it."

"Fantastic," Jigger said. "I don't know how you do it, Vince."

17.

Before the Big Rock Trading Post, Officer Ybarra parked his car alongside the orange Porsche with the California license plates. He took down the number, QDD-223, and checked the doors and trunk. They were locked.

Repeatedly he pounded on the big, much scarred front door of the post and called out. He knew the trader lived in the back with his wife and two children. After several minutes, a light came on inside, and at the door, before opening it, a sleepy voice asked who it was.

"Officer Ybarra. Navajo police."

Another minute passed while the trader unbolted the enormous door. It swung open with a groan that might be expected from rusty hinges a half-century old. The trader with his hair askew and eyes straining to see was in a faded, frayed robe that had not many more washings to go.

Ybarra said, "I'm sorry to get you up."

"Thought you was some drunk. We get 'em sometimes this time of night. Come up from Gallup."

"That car over there, the Porsche, do you know who it belongs to?"

"Yes, I do. Some teen-agers from Los Angeles. They stopped here before starting down the trail. Why? Anything wrong? I took an American Express credit card for better than two hundred dollars from the older one."

"Just a routine check. We got a report they were in Hidden Canyon and couldn't figure why they'd go down in the storm."

"I can tell you. The older boy's sister was flying the plane that crashed. I felt terribly sorry for him. I suppose she was killed?"

"We don't know yet. About how old were they?"

"The older one, eighteen or nineteen, and the other boy, maybe a little younger. As for the girl, hard to tell. Didn't look much over fifteen."

"And the other one?"

"Just the three. Oh, and the Navajo boy, Charlie Begay. They hired him to guide them. I warned them they were crazy to try it and likely would get their necks broken."

"How about names?"

"No—except for the older boy. Come on in. He signed the credit slip."

For Ybarra, the trading post had the same old familiar smell. He had been in and out of them since he could walk. It was a distinctive odor, a combination of mustiness resulting from too little fresh air, sheepskins, wool that had been recently sheared, carded, and woven into rugs, bags of grain, and assorted items that had disappeared a generation ago from most communities.

Finding the slip, the trader read the name. "Rudolph Circassian." He looked up. "Name's different 'cause he's her half brother. Nice bunch of kids. Polite. I knew from their looks I could trust 'em."

In Chinle, Captain Yazzie hung up the phone and repeated Officer Ybarra's report to Major Tonalea. Two salient points stood out: one, the older boy was the pilot's half brother, and two, his name was Rudolph Circassian.

"I'm relieved to know they have a legitimate reason for being in the canyon," Tonalea said. "I don't understand why they didn't check with us first but a bunch of kids . . ."

Yazzie rubbed the scruff of his neck. He was dog weary. "Probably thought we'd stop them, which we would have."

Tonalea stood at Yazzie's desk looking down at aerial photographs taken over the crash scene. He pointed out heavily circled objects. "There's the prayer cairn I mentioned. It looks recent. Here are all kinds of tracks—which we can sort out later—and over here in the cliff dwelling is Shonto's mule. There's only one thing missing."

"What's that?"

"Five people. We hung over the scene for several minutes, and I never saw one single person. Five people down there and I didn't see one. Usually somebody would've run into the clear and waved to me, and told me by sign language that there was no survivor or there was one or both."

Yazzie sucked in his breath. "They forgot to hide the mule —if they were hiding from you. Still, the boy did go down, presumably to determine what happened to his sister."

"Presumably."

"Yes, presumably. You know, what you suggest would indicate a collaboration and I don't see how the kids and the old prospector could be in this together. He's hardly the type . . ."

"But what's he doing down there? Why is he roaming around in a storm at night?"

Yazzie yawned. "Excuse me. I was up at five. Let's say the prospector heard about the money on the radio. He arrives at the crash scene and the kids are there. So he pulls a gun on them . . ."

"At his age? He's lived around here most of his life. Never been in any trouble."

Yazzie nodded. "I think I'd better get a check started on the license plates, and ask Kayenta and Page if they know of a Rudolph Circassian, presumably Sandra Wilcox's half brother."

Officer Ramah sat on a wet rock under a dripping cotton-wood. He was drenched and miserable. Yazzie's voice came over clearly. ". . . half brother of Miss Sandra Wilcox, the pilot. We do not know this for a fact and Major Tonalea believes you should approach the crash scene with caution. We want you to determine exactly what the five persons are doing before you make your presence known."

"Six," said Ramah. "I just picked up a sixth track, that of a woman. She's wearing cowpuncher boots."

"Six!" exclaimed Yazzie. "Where'd the prints start? You mean the prints just started out of nowhere?"

"That's about it. I may have missed them before or they were rained out. The prospector is moving by himself but the other five are moving over mostly rock ledges where they leave few prints."

The rescue party came to the crossing over the Rio de Chelly. The canyon and the river had turned and the moonlight slanted down on the raging torrent at the most propitious angle. Officer Davis raised a hand in signal to halt, and she and Tachee sat their horses side by side. Each estimated the force of the water and whether a horse could stand up to it. From here the river appeared to be about a hundred feet across. Of this footage, sixty in dead center would be the most hazardous. A little the other side of midway the torrent split when it smashed against a boulder. It shot up a geyser that fell heavily over the course they would take.

"I don't like it," Tachee said, raising his voice above the thunder. "You sure there's a rock footing?"

She pushed her soaked hair back under the rain hood. "I played here as a child."

Her childhood. She could still see her mother sitting at the loom in the shadow house working on the nine-by-twelve rug. She had sheared the sheep, carded and spun the wool, and dyed and balled it. When the rug was finished, she had cleaned it in sand, as had her mother before her, and her grandmother.

Every day for two and a half years, she had labored from dawn to sundown in hot sun, snow or rain. Only when a friend or neighbor was very ill or dying had she taken time off. She and Ramona were alone. Ramona had only a misty remembrance of her father who had died when she was five.

The rug was to pay for Ramona's first year at college. A

trader had contracted to buy it for three thousand dollars. He had sold it for eight thousand dollars. The difference, however, did not represent all profit. He had staked them with food and other necessities. All through the years, too, her mother's and father's clans had assisted them. ("If you are wealthy," the saying went, "then you are not helping your people.")

Her mother, who had never learned English, had amazing perception. To cope with a changing world, her daughter must have an education. Her mother had sacrificed and had been happy in doing it. All she asked of Ramona was that she follow the Blessing Way.

Twice a year Romona visited her mother, who now lived near Mexican Hat in Utah where she had been born and where she wanted to die. To please her mother, Ramona would fix her hair into a silyelth, the traditional knot tied with white wool. Her cradleboard hung in the hogan, and the squirrel's tail that would have protected her in case of a fall was still tied to it. Always the old bond was renewed as they sat on a sheepskin on the hard-packed earth floor, talking. In living over the old days, they gave expression to their love.

"The day goes into the night, and the night into day, and the birds sing and are quiet and sing again," her mother said. "I live in you, and when I go, as I must before many seasons pass, I will still live in you. It comforts me to know that. You are all I ever wanted in a daughter."

"I have forded here many times," she told Tachee.

"You better be damn sure it's the same spot."

From the rear, someone yelled, "Let's go!"

She put the spur to her mount and the horse moved into deep, turbulent water.

"Damn fool woman!" Tachee muttered.

The horse started to rear. She calmed him by talking and holding a tight, firm rein. He took one step, then another. The water moved with a powerful thrust around his legs, tugging, shoving, and whirling angrily. Like a mad dog, the river foamed about them. One step, then another. Each time the horse explored the next and advanced only after careful testing.

More ominous than the pounding of the water was the deep-throated roar, an organ with the bass stops pulled out. Noise alone, she thought, could be more devastating to the nerves than danger itself. Man was not so far from the Neolithic age but that thunder told him the gods were angry and would wreak some horrible vengeance.

She had no fear; she knew what she was doing. Her confidence imparted confidence to her mount. Long ago she had learned that animals, as well as people, needed to be reassured in meeting unknown or strange situations. Hysteria or even moderate fear could be transmitted.

The water rose until it was running almost to the underbelly. She bent low to pat him and talked quietly. A time or two he stopped to survey the situation and she waited patiently. He was a fine, intelligent animal. She could strangle people who said horses had low IQs. At no time did he lose his head. Nothing would ever spook him.

Tachee followed a few feet behind. At the far side, they rode up on a sand bar. She threw the flashlight ahead, and on the ground, firmly imprinted, were the fresh tracks of a horse. In the same instant, Tachee spotted them.

"You take over here," he said angrily. "I'm going after that horse thief."

"Sergeant," she called, and he stopped. She said quietly, "He's in an emotional state, and when you apprehend him, will you keep that in mind?"

Suddenly he grinned. "I'm not going to kill the *bi la gáa naa*—but just the same you'd better get a stretcher ready. All right?"

He's in an emotional state. Not as much so as she had been—and was. At times, especially in the predawn hours, her mind went whirling out of control, and she lay in a stupor of fear. In daylight, though—and once she had her coffee—she controlled herself by the stern, personal discipline her mother had taught her. No matter how turbulent the night, she was cool, appraising, impersonal, and once in action, her tired, rebellious brain functioned sharply.

Apparently her uncle had not seen her with Larry. Recently, when she talked with him, he was the same as ever. But there would be other nights and other chance meetings.

The problem defied solution. They would ruin either her mother's and his parents' lives by the shame they would bring down on them, or their own.

In recent nights, though, her thoughts had dug up a third choice, one too terrible to contemplate.

18.

Frank Ramah switched off his flashlight. He would proceed as best he could to avoid tipping off anyone at the crash scene. Even though, the moonlight seemed brighter, he slowed his gait to avoid a fall.

He was happy he had descended the trail without suffering more than a wrenched ankle. Every assignment was important now. Shortly he would be up for promotion. Six months ago he might have made sergeant except that he had fired at a shadowy figure in the dusk that he thought was a fleeing criminal. The "fugitive" turned out to be a frightened sixteen-year-old. Fortunately he had not hit the boy. He was severely reprimanded, and later, Major Tonalea, on an inspection trip, had counseled him. Tonalea said he was too impulsive. The department wanted officers with initiative and guts but only if their actions were tempered by thinking and judgment.

Ramah had a special reason for wanting the promotion. For the past year he had dated a very mod receptionist at Window Rock's Navajo motel. They had gone bowling and dancing, and to the movies in Gallup. Both thought much alike. They had no compunction about giving up the old traditions.

They were proud they were Navajos but didn't think that meant they had to live in the past. They wanted to be part of the Anglo scene and enjoy the luxuries the Anglos had. He had set himself a goal: if he made sergeant, he would ask her to marry him.

He had covered only a short distance when he caught the first flash of a spotlight up ahead. It was bearing his way and bobbing like a buoy in a rough sea. The column of light would shoot up in the air, go suddenly to the right, veer left, then disappear. Seconds might pass before he saw it again.

Stepping into thick brush, he bent low and waited. A minute later, as a figure passed, holding the spotlight, Ramah emerged. "Hold it there," he called. "I'm a police officer. Navajo Tribal Police."

The figure stopped, turned, and threw the light in his eyes, but only for a second. "Oh, thank God, you're here, sir," Vince said in anguish. "My sister . . . she was flying the plane . . . she's badly hurt. Do you have a first-aid kit with you?"

Ramah thought he looked like a good youngster who was distraught and desperate. "No, but I can get our helicopter to drop anything we need."

Vince started back the way he had come. Ramah stopped him. "Just hold it a minute. One or two questions."

"Please, she's suffering so, sir. Can't you ask the questions after we get to her?"

Ramah hesitated. He had a compulsion to hurry to the aid of a woman who might be dying. He was coerced, however, into adopting a firm tactic by Major Tonalea's warning that he should approach the setup with caution. "What's your name?"

"Vince Roberts."

"The others in your party?"

"Jigger Hardin and Penny Thompson."

"Anyone else with you?"

"We picked up a Navajo boy for a guide. Please, sir . . ."

"Rudolph Circassian. Who's he?"

"My sister's dying and you . . . that's my real name. I'm an actor and use Vince Roberts as my professional name."

"What're you doing over here from California?"

"Why, visiting my sister, of course."

"The girl with you, what's she to you?"

"Jigger's sister. I'm sorry, mister, but I'm not going to stand around and—"

"Where were you going when I stopped you?"

"Back up the trail to get a doctor. I don't know what all of this is about, asking me all these questions."

"I'll call the copter over."

"Please, sir, take a look at her first. I don't know what she needs. I suppose you've had a course in first aid?"

"Yes." Still Ramah hesitated. He was satisfied with the answers. He could not allow a woman to die. "Lead the way."

Half running, Vince took to high ground. He slowed only when he encountered rough underfooting. Occasionally he turned to assure himself Ramah followed.

When they were a few feet from the ruins, Ramah stopped to reconnoiter. The people inside the enclosure were little more than shadows. The old prospector sat on the floor by his mule, his head on his chest, as if dozing. Penny and Jigger stepped out to greet Ramah. The woman pilot was stretched out on the floor, doubled up on her side.

"My sister's over there," Vince said, and stepped aside. When Ramah passed him, Vince tripped him. He went sprawling, and before he could recover his balance, Vince grabbed Ramah's gun from the holster and was standing over him.

Shonto awakened, blinked his eyes, and struggled to rise but couldn't make it. Despite the pain she suffered, Sandy came to her feet and backed up against the wall.

"Get up," Vince ordered. "Check him out, Jigger. Penny, where's the coffee?"

She hurried into a back room where she had water boiling on a Sterno burner for the instant coffee. Reappearing, she brought not only the coffee but sandwiches, which she handed to Vince and Jigger. She tore hers apart and offered half to Sandy.

"Thank you," Sandy said, touched but puzzled. Penny smiled in return.

Jigger ran his hands lightly but thoroughly over Ramah. "Nothing," he told Vince.

Ramah was shocked and crushed. He had been given a fairly routine assignment, and then had been advised to proceed with caution. And he had. How could he possibly have foreseen this kind of a trap? But the captain accepted no excuses.

Sandy said, "I'm Sandy Wilcox. I was flying the plane. And this is Shonto, a prospector. These others—"

"Shut up!" Vince ordered. "I'll tell you when you can talk."

"I'll talk any time I want to, and you're not going to kill me because you think I know something you want."

She had decided to change tactics. There were people who trampled you if they could, but respected you if you showed mettle. They hated weakness and admired guts.

He was amused. He stared at her torn shirt, still wet and plastered to her body. She tugged it loose.

He smiled insolently. "Gag her," he ordered.

Jigger approached only so far. He knew she planned to resist and he had no stomach for slapping a woman around. Vince had turned back to Ramah. Shrugging, Jigger returned the kerchief to a hip pocket.

Together with the others, she watched Vince. He was threatening but quiet, deadly but without histrionics, confident but not swaggering. He had a brilliant mind, and could go far, perhaps as a lawyer, but she was certain he had never considered the future. Like most criminals, he lived for the present. He had killed without remorse. He was not alone, only one of thousands who destroyed human life without reason. They were the assassins, the terrorists, the stranglers, the compulsive murderers. They were the nothings who roamed the streets in the guise of normal individuals, out to kill the somethings, the John F. Kennedys and Martin Luther Kings. Most of their victims, however, like Charlie, were unknowns except to family, friends, and their community.

How frightening it is, she thought, *that I walk the streets with these wanton killers. I meet them, I talk with them. If one could only "see" into the mind, if we could X-ray thoughts the way we do bones.*

Who would be next: Shonto, the Navajo officer, or herself? If it were she, she wondered what would happen to Skeet. Bill would probably take him. They liked each other. A week ago, when she had been away on a charter flight, they had driven up into Monument Valley to visit the sites where John Ford created his classic of the Old West, *Stagecoach.*

Vince said to Ramah, "You do as I say, copper, and no one'll get hurt. But if you don't, what's one more dead Indian? We've already got one out in the bushes who got smart with me. You understand that?"

Ramah nodded. He was ashamed and angry. The first shock over, he searched his thoughts frantically for a way to reverse the situation.

"Who else is coming down the trail?"

Ramah shook his head, said nothing.

"You know you're dead if anybody shows up on that trail. I can't stand a liar. Can I, Jigger?"

"Right."

"How many in the rescue party?"

"I don't know."

"You sure as hell do." Vince turned to Jigger. "Remember that game we used to play? We'd kidnap some snotty little kid, stand him up against a door, and see how close we could throw darts and still miss him? We don't have darts but knives will do."

"Three," Ramah said.

"You're lying."

"Why send more? With me, there would be four."

Vince concealed his elation. He and Jigger could easily handle three. It would be like shooting ducks in a gallery. Still, you couldn't trust these pigs.

"Okay," Vince said. "Now here's what I want you to do. Get out that walkie-talkie job and get Chinle. Tell them you found a couple of bodies. No survivors. They don't need to hurry. Okay, get with it."

Ramah unzipped the radio set. Vince continued, "One more thing, you speak English. No Navajo. You say one word in Navvy and you're a dead Indian."

Ramah stared defiantly. "We talk only English on the air but we say very few words to save time. Like a telegram."

"Okay but no Navvy."

Ramah reached Captain Yazzie. "Officer Ramah here. At scene wreck. Bad scene. Much wreck. Find two bodies. No survivors. No need rescue party hurry. No one here except Ramah. You tell me: I stay? . . . Okay, I stay. How soon party arrive? Two hours? Okay, two hours. Good-by."

He turned to Vince. "They told me to stay. What do I do now?"

"Turn it off and shut up." Vince put an arm about Penny and squeezed her. "Not the best night you've ever had, is it, sweetheart?"

He turned toward Jigger. "He may be lying. We'd better figure on one hour though they say two. So we got to hack it. We can wait until we see them coming to set up an ambush since they don't know we're down here . . ."

His words ran out. He stared at the mule. "The mule!"

"What about him?" Jigger asked.

"I forgot about the damn mule. He's in plain sight. They could've seen him when they came over the last time. Shonto! Get your jackass out of here. There's a room back of this one. Get him in there. Through that door there. Penny, keep an eye on him. Hey, Wilcox, get over here. We're going to dig up the old guy—unless you've got a better idea where the money is."

She felt her fingernails bite her hands. "I'm not going."

He turned abruptly about. His eyes tightened. "I want to tell you something. I've been too easy on you. I'm going to get the money within the next sixty minutes one way or another, and I don't care which it is."

"Go ahead. Kill me."

He struck her face with his open palm and she reeled backward. "I'm not going to kill you—but you'll wish I had."

19.

Major Tonalea was furious. "What does he mean, talking pidgin English, a university graduate?"

Yazzie was dumfounded. "Kidding around, I suppose."

"Joking? At the scene of a tragedy? Two dead?"

Yazzie rubbed his neck cords. "It's not like Frank. I've seen him come in from an accident all choked up. He's impulsive but not insensitive."

Tonalea paced about the room. "Never happened before?"

"You know . . ." Yazzie began.

"Yeah, I was thinking the same thing. He was trying to tell us something."

Yazzie picked it up. "Someone was standing by him—with a gun poked into his side, and—"

"—and the gun would go off if he didn't report what he had been told to."

"That's it," said Yazzie.

They fell silent, thinking through Ramah's conversation in light of this speculation. Tonalea asked, "What about the report itself? No survivors?"

"Maybe so, maybe not. The party—we'll call him X— wanted Frank to report that to us since X knew we would take our time if both were dead. And the motive, money. They need time to locate it. It won't be easy with wreckage scattered about."

Simultaneously, they glanced at the wall clock. It was

seven to two. They realized they might unknowingly be in a race against time. X had only a short while to find the half-million dollars before the rescue party arrived and doubtlessly knew it. Tonalea and Yazzie had only so much time to work leads and develop facts that might identify and pin down X.

"We'd better talk Navajo over the air," Tonalea said. "They may be listening in."

They tried repeatedly to reach Ramah. They had expected no answer and there was none. The frightening possibility existed that X might have executed him.

Already officers had requested the California Department of Motor Vehicles at Sacramento to determine the holder of license number QDD-223. By telephone they asked the Los Angeles police to check their indices for the name of Rudolph Circassian. They requested the American Express in Phoenix, Arizona, to give them the home address of Rudolph Circassian and data regarding recent credit card charges that might reveal his travels.

Yazzie put in a call to Charles Murphy, the resident FBI agent in Flagstaff. The FBI had jurisdiction in the investigation of fourteen major crimes when committed on the reservation. "I'm sorry to get you up, Murph," he said, "but we may have something breaking that would interest the FBI. We're not sure . . ."

He gave Murphy a concise rundown. Murphy advised he would leave at once for Chinle.

Next Yazzie telephoned the Apache County sheriff's office at St. Johns, Arizona. The sheriff had jurisdiction, too, over certain crimes. Yazzie knew the deputy on the graveyard shift. They had served together in the Marines. Yazzie would forever remember the day the war had ended. Everyone was celebrating. They would be going home soon. Everyone, that is, except Chee Yazzie. He was near tears. As a Code Talker, he had been somebody. He had commanded respect, worked hard, and drawn good pay. Now he would be returning to a bleak, arid reservation, and probably destined to run sheep the rest of his life. He would be locked into a form of peonage with a trading post, and hungry in the wintertime. His wife and children would scarcely have sufficient clothes. He would be encountering unfriendly Anglos who would dismiss him as one more lazy Indian. That it had turned out differently was a stroke of luck. For many it had not. For some it had ended in suicide; for others, in the anesthesia of liquor, drugs, or sex.

As soon as Tonalea left for the airstrip, Yazzie contacted Officer Ramona Davis to advise her of developments. She estimated her party would reach the scene within the hour. She reported that Sergeant Tachee had taken off after Bill Delaney in an effort to apprehend him and recover the horse.

Yazzie was astounded. "Why didn't you stop him or send someone else?" His tone was highly critical.

She bristled. "Captain, I only share command with the sergeant. I'm not over him."

Yazzie calmed himself. "I know. I just hope he keeps his head. How'd he act when he took off?"

"Like a bear with a sore paw, to quote my mother."

Yazzie groaned, and signed off, and groaned some more.

Bill let the horse set her own gait. He didn't prod her. If he had, she might have bucked. He wanted to pull leather, to ride hell-bent, but restrained his compulsion.

His legs were scratched, cut, and bleeding. They had been raked by cactus thorns and jagged sandstone outcroppings.

He wished he knew the horse's name. He had never gone into any home without asking the name of the dog or cat. It was a silly habit, but he liked to call animals as well as people by their names. In doing so, he had the feeling he knew them, that there was an affinity.

Carefully, his mount picked her way over slippery ledges, soft sandbars, and finally loose sand into which she sank inches. She was beat and blowing a bit. When they returned, she would need a good currying. She was caked with mud splattered by her hoofs.

The night was eerie. One moment the moonlight lay a mystical gossamer mantle over the scene. Up ahead, shadowy forms stood tall and threatening and mysterious. Then huge clouds, sailing across the sky like so many ships, would pass before the moon, and the curtain would drop. At those times he was wrapped in a black world.

From time to time, he would rein in his mount and listen intently. He must not be caught unawares. He had no idea what the Tribal Police would do if they hunted him down, and had no intention of finding out.

By the minute he was growing more exhilarated. He estimated there was not too much ground to cover before he reached Sandy. He would take her into his arms, not as the sweetheart she had been, but as a dear and old friend.

He wondered if the crashed Cessna was the same plane that she had flown, with him beside her, that sun-blinding Sunday over Lake Powell. They had been gloriously happy. This was the land she loved, and her affection for it showed in pointing out the landmarks. He doubted if he could ever love a country that intensely. A city person never developed the intimacy one had for a land where one walked outdoor paths and trails, and smelled pines, and listened to waterfalls. There were no sunsets in a city worthy of comment, no good, warm smell of the earth after a hard rain, no feeling for cattle or sheep, no laughter over the antics of raccoons or other wild life that timidly spied on the human folly.

Below them had spread a fantastic tapestry, beginning with Eisenhower Dam, better known as Glen Canyon, that had taken seven years to build. With a teen-ager's excitement, she pointed out the steel arch bridge, the highest in the world, rising as tall as a seventy-story building above the Colorado, a tempestuous, temperamental, gruff, old river. But most of all, she talked about Lake Powell, the man-made body of water the dam had formed, 186 miles long with 1,900 miles of shoreline.

Along more than 100 miles of that shoreline the Navajo reservation stretched.

"Before the dam was built, the scenery upriver was fantastic," she said. "Great gorges and sheer walls and mesas. Just staggering. Now look at it. Covered with water. Gone forever. Future generations will never see it. And all because cities like Phoenix and Los Angeles want power at any cost. They don't care how they get it, how many people they hurt, the lives they destroy.

"And look, over there's Rainbow Bridge. It's really an arch rather than a bridge." She flew low over the lake for a better perspective, and suddenly he saw it, a great, slender monolith of red sandstone rising over three hundred feet into the intense blue sky. It straddled a wide, dry creek which aeons ago had gnawed its way through the soft rock to form the graceful arch.

"Take a good look at it. It won't be there much longer. They're backing up the water and the lake's getting bigger all the time. It's sacred to the Navajo people. The bridge is, I mean."

Later she was to show him a copy of an affidavit filed by several medicine men before the U. S. Supreme Court when they had asked to be admitted in a particular case as "friends of the court." It read: "The bridge is our means of communication with our gods and is our altar and the foundation on which our religion is based . . . Rainbow Bridge is like a mother for our people. It stands like a temple or church to the Anglo Christians. We do not destroy the white man's sacred articles and shrines, nor do we destroy their religion. Therefore this water should not be allowed by the white man to rise and cover our holy shrine of prayer."

She had become quite heated. "Can you imagine what would happen if we buried a Christian or Jewish holy place under water? The trouble is that the Navajos can't make enough noise. The blacks and Chicanos can get a hearing because of their numbers but who cares about 140,000 people out

of two hundred and some million? We talk about how we take
care of our minorities, equal rights and all of that, but we
ignore our very small minorities."

He was amused by her earnestness. He went along with
her, agreeing with a casual "yes." At that point of their relationship, he thought of her as being refreshing and with a fey
quality he found most charming. He loved the fire in her quick-
moving eyes and the tight set of her upswept lips. He thought
her a reincarnated leprechaun.

But leprechauns, he believed, should not poke their noses
into matters they knew little about. The dam, he wanted to
point out, produced sufficient electricity to light up several big
cities. Americans had to scrape up all the energy they could. It
was the lifeblood of the country. So what did it matter if a few
burial grounds, sacred places, ruins of the Ancient Ones, and a
little scenery were buried under the lake's waters? It was, of
course, too bad. He regretted it. But in our kind of society, he
thought, these matters had to be studied in full perspective.

His keen ears caught the faint click of metal on rock, the
strike of a horse's shoe. He strained his hearing, hoping to
bring in corroborative sounds. He could have imagined it.
When one expected to hear a specific noise, one usually could.

Playing it safe, he reined in his mount and firmly pulled
her against her wishes into a dark recess under an enormous
cottonwood. For a few exciting moments, he thought she intended to take the bit and continue the course she had set. She
was restless and apprehensive, fearing danger in this black hole.
Gently, he stroked her and she calmed. If he had dared, he
would have talked to her. Whether a horse, cat, or dog, they
understood him. He was inordinately proud when Sandy re-
marked once that he spoke a universal language.

He listened intently. He remembered telling Sandy he
thought nature had missed a bet by failing to devise an antenna
that would rise up out of the ears. He recalled her full-throated
laughter. His little jokes never failed to amuse her. Lucy never

had laughed much. She was serious-minded, anxious to cope with problems near and distant. Any problem. She was not selective.

Without an antenna, he was conscious of little noises under the big one stirred by the onrush of water. The dripping from the cottonwood . . . the spattering of drops around him . . . the call of a bird . . . the distant bark of a coyote . . . the rustle in nearby bushes.

He heard then a lone horse picking its way. A foot at a time, the horse struck rock, a water-filled pot hole, a sand trap, and hard-packed earth. Clicks and splatters and crunches and the normal fall of hoofs.

His own horse heard. Up went the ears, the head cocked, and the nostrils distended for fuller breathing. One restless stamp of a foot or a slight neigh would betray them.

Then the sergeant—he couldn't recall his last name, if in fact he had ever heard it—took shape, first as a murky shadow and when he stopped not more than twenty feet distant, as a well-defined silhouette. His horse let out a low neigh. The animal had picked up the scent of Bill's mount. Anxiously, Bill rubbed his own horse's neck. Any second he feared she would answer.

Turning slowly in the saddle, the sergeant surveyed a ninety-degree arc with a spotlight that threw a wide, bright beam. Every few seconds, Bill checked him, then averted his eyes. He had read that if a person concentrated on another, the latter would eventually sense that he was under scrutiny.

Bill was tense, ready to react instantly should the sergeant spot him. He planned to dig in the spurs and outrun the sergeant's animal. He realized that this might prove a dangerous course. His horse might slip or stumble, and throw him.

Poking here and there with the beam, the sergeant shot it under the big, old cottonwood. Bill set his muscles to propel him into action on the count of three. They never had to, though. The shaft of light faded before reaching him.

Finally, the sergeant threw one foot over the saddle and

dropped to earth. Bending low, he studied the tracks. Bill had no qualms. Before entering the cottonwoods, he had walked his horse down a gully filled with runoff.

After a few minutes of concentration, the sergeant stepped to the saddle. He sat a little while, perhaps baffled, then rode on.

Bill smiled to himself. He had no desert experience, but even a New Englander knew he had to lose his mount's tracks if he was a fugitive.

20.

When the copter came over the next time, they were flat on their bellies with their arms around their heads. At gunpoint, Vince had ordered them into this position. Their bodies were crowded together on the south side, where the partly fallen wall was high enough to prevent a searching spotlight from locating them.

The performance was a repeat one. Again, the chopper hovered above the crash scene. This time, however, the pilot dropped the craft dangerously low.

On one side of Sandy lay Vince. She could hear his labored, nervous breathing, and was conscious his eyes covered them. If anyone attempted to attract the attention of the officers in the copter, that person would die the same instant he made his move.

Vince's hip crowded hers. She felt his warmth, the steady, deliberate pressure, and the flexing and playing against her of a thigh muscle. She tried pulling away but had only inches.

Close to her on the other side stretched the Navajo officer with the quick eyes of a hunter. He frightened her. If he saw a chance, or could create one, he would move swiftly. If he failed to calculate the chance correctly, he might get them all shot.

During these quiet minutes, the pain surged back into her abdomen, a succession of sharp, searing stabs. When she was confronting Vince, however, the pain receded. If she had to, she could react physically with all swiftness.

She wondered if Bill had heard about the crash. She doubted if he had. Oddly, he seldom listened to radio news. He preferred the daily newspaper. If he had heard, would he come for her? In a flash, she answered herself. He would. If she were dying ten thousand miles away, he would come. They had parted friends, and friends they would always be.

Again, as so often in the last few days, she canvassed the avenues possible for a reconciliation. She toyed with the idea of compromise. She was a strong exponent of it. She believed in employers and workers, or any groups at odds, sitting down to discuss their differences. But how could you compromise your beliefs? She could not live with herself and neither could Bill. She would not respect him if he did, which he never would, and she admired him for his constancy. She disliked persons who vacillated.

On her right, there was a slight, slithering movement that ran the length of her body. Her flesh literally crawled. A big-eared head passed close to hers and she was conscious of faint, whispery breathing. It was abnormal, stilled by will power. A man's sweaty smell was in her nostrils. He crept only an inch at a time. Soon a muscular shoulder was opposite her face. And then came his slender torso. It had to wriggle to propel itself. It was an understatement of a wriggle, so slight that she alone was conscious of it.

Officer Frank Ramah was setting in motion a deed of der-ring-do. She had no idea what his plan was. However, she had pegged him right. He was the marshal of the Old West, walking down Main Street with guns blazing. As of this moment, the odds were all against him. He couldn't know, as she did, that Vince had him under surveillance.

Buried under her side, her right hand snaked forth, moving as deliberately as Ramah. Only her arm shifted. The rest of her was as immobile as if she were asleep. Once freed, her hand climbed over his leg below the knee and tightened like a vise about the leg. She had a strong hand, developed by throwing sheep to the ground for shearing, playing tennis, changing tires, and bowling. Her mother, who had complained about jar lids being turned too tightly, said she had a strangler's hands.

Surprised, Ramah stopped and was very still. He had intended to get into a position whereby, when the copter left and Vince rose, he could tackle him and seize his gun as he fell. He had thought it out carefully and the plan appeared feasible. The risk, he figured, would be minimal. Some risk had to be taken, since otherwise Vince in the end would gun them all down. Ironically, the timing of the killing would be set by the rescue party. When it appeared, Vince probably would execute two of them before fleeing and take one along as a hostage. He and his accomplices would be unable to move fast if he held the three as prisoners. Eventually he would kill the hostage.

She tightened her hold, and Ramah felt the long, sharp fingernails. They were the talons of a mountain cat he had caught when a boy. He forced himself to remain quiet. It was evident she had stopped him because she knew of a danger he did not.

He knew now he could work with her. He needed a partner who had brains and guts, and he had found one. Shonto was too old to be effective.

The trouble was: they had such little time.

Vince, too, had little time. Once the whirlybird had clattered away, he told Sandy, Shonto, and Ramah to line up against the far wall.

"Vince, don't—please . . ." Penny began.

Ramah broke in. "As a police officer, I've got to warn you—"

"Shut up!" Vince threw the flashlight beam head on into their faces. "You're prisoners of war, and if you talk, we'll keep you alive. It's that simple. Okay, we'll take the broad first."

He aimed the .38 at Shonto, in a dead line with his heart.

She had sworn she would take a hard stand. No matter how much he slapped her around . . . now, however, with the weapon set dead on Shonto . . . the burst of gunfire that could come any second . . .

"I said I'd show you where I buried him." She had difficulty talking. The night's events had drained her strength and left her thick-tongued. Physical discomfort burgeoned, too, the pain of her injury, tortured muscles, clothes clinging cold and wet to her body.

"You didn't say anything of the kind. You said you didn't think you knew where it was. Isn't that what she said, Jigger?"

"Right."

"I can't be sure. How can I?"

Vince took another sighting on Shonto. "Either you tell me exactly where or we bump off Grandpa."

Shonto rubbed a hairy hand across his rheumy eyes and squinted, to see better. "How much didja say is in the bag?" He edged closer to Sandy. "Don't you worry your pretty head, girl. We'll work this out."

He rubbed his gnarled fingers together. He could feel the gold. No one could understand his emotions unless he had dreamed for a half century of a strike, and slowly, as the eyesight failed and the step got more uncertain, realized it was not to be. And now old hopes long dead stirred anew. For a half century he had wanted the strike for his daughter, his and Maggie's. Only now he knew she was no longer his daughter, if ever she had been. Too many years had run their course. Intuitively, he sensed he craved it for a reason hollow to many men: a strike would fulfill a wild, compulsive longing. It would give meaning to his life. It would remove him from the failure list, the winos of Main Street, the grubbers of the desert.

"What you got in mind, Grandpa?" Vince asked.

"I heared a half million, which strikes me as plenty for us'uns all if we divvy it up."

"That'd be theft," Ramah said. "You can't do it. You'd go up for grand larceny."

"You hear that, Grandpa," Vince said. "You'd be a criminal. Jigger, give me thirty seconds."

Jigger held his wrist watch close to his eyes to follow the second hand.

Vince continued, "Wilcox, you've got thirty seconds before we send Grandpa to the mortuary."

"I said I'd find the grave, didn't I? What more do you want me to say?"

Vince drove a fist into her stomach. She doubled up and fell against the wall. Gasping, she held her arms tightly about her midriff to press out the hurt. Nothing could shut out the shock that exploded in her mind.

Ramah advanced on Vince. "I got a fist here says you can't do that to a lady."

"Get back, copper!" Vince yelled, and fired a shot aimed a little to the right of Ramah. Ramah stopped, paralyzed, then began moving again.

"Hold it!" Sandy said, and then shouted, "Not now! Not now!"

She got through to him. He backed up to the wall.

Shonto said quietly, "How much in it for me if I stake out the money?"

Sandy noted the craftiness in his watery old eyes, the avarice. He would find the prayer cairn, would know it had been recently put up, and would figure it marked the spot where she had buried the money.

Shonto continued, "Me and Sam've been workin' this country for years. We know signs and tracks and things a man new to this desert don't rightly know to look for. I can tell right off when somebody's been monkeyin' 'round buryin' people and things."

"How much you want?"

"Fifty-fifty."

"Twenty-five."

Shonto nodded. "Don't have much choice, I reckon."

"You don't—and you know it. You're a lot smarter than some other people around here."

Sandy straightened and it hurt. "It's come to me—something triggered it, I don't know what—exactly where I buried Mr. B. I'll show you the grave and you don't have to split with me."

"You remembered? Just like that?" Vince snapped his fingers.

"Do *you* remember everything right off?" she retorted. She would brazen her way through. She had to stop Shonto.

"You've known all along, Wilcox. You lied to me—and if there's anything I hate worse than liars I can't think of it. If you didn't lie to me—and are now . . . Maybe you're taking me out to kill time. You'll say, Funny, I can't seem to find it. Then I'd have to waste some ammunition and I don't like to waste ammunition. So I'm saving a bullet and your pretty body which I can use later. Jigger, take Grandpa wherever he wants to go, but watch the old devil."

"Shonto," she said softly, "it's a ripoff. Once he gets the money he'll kill us all. You, too. You don't think he'd let you get your hands on any of that money?"

Shonto looked the other way.

Vince would have hit her a knockout blow but Penny stepped in front of him. "Vince!" she cried. "Vince!"

He shoved Penny aside. "I don't want any more mouth out of you."

He turned to Shonto. "I give my word, I keep it. Ask Jigger."

"Right, he does."

"So you get your share, Grandpa, when you find it and then you scoot out of here free."

"And get a shot in the back," Sandy said.

Vince stood trembling. She had tapped a hairline crack into his cold façade. It could be shattered, she thought.

"She doesn't want you to get any of the money, Grandpa,"

he said calmly, though the erratic movement of his lips and
eyes betrayed his anger. "Wants it all for herself. Let's see, a
quarter of a half million comes to more than a hundred thousand. Not bad."

Shonto avoided her eyes, which spoke of betrayal, and
ambled off. His rocking walk was slow and painful. His eyes,
though, were sharp, and any desert rat worth his salt could
decipher recent diggings at a glance, even after a rain.

Jigger hung behind to get last-minute instructions from
Vince, then hurried to catch up with Shonto. Jigger took him
by the arm as if to help him along. Once Jigger looked back
and raised a hand. Had Vince given him orders to assassinate
Shonto on the spot if Shonto uncovered the half million?

Frightened, Sandy watched the dancing, disembodied
beams from their flashlights dwindle until they were only stars
hanging barely above the earth's surface. High up over the
roaring wash a full moon hung. Any other night she would
have felt close to nature, close to God. To relieve the tension,
she breathed deeply and her spirits rose. She would need to
bolster them if she were to survive this long, black night.

Slowly terror seeped through her. The moving pinpoints of
light were set on a course bound for the prayer cairn.

Squatting on the ground, Vince idly poured pebbles and
dirt through his fingers. "Get the radio back on," he ordered
Ramah. "They're going to think something's wrong."

Sniffling, he asked Penny for a tissue. She turned her back
on him, pouting over the shove he had given her. "Cheer up,"
he said. "You'll have enough money tomorrow to buy all the
clothes in Beverly Hills."

"I don't want clothes."

"Slob."

"I want you."

"You've got me, sweetheart. Only when I'm on a deal, you
deal yourself out. Understand?"

Sandy listened with mounting interest. Penny was not as

hardened as Sandy had thought. If Sandy could get her by herself and have a talk . . . it was a long shot.

Penny handed Vince a tissue. "I love you, Vince."

He boxed her on the bottom. "Love me tomorrow."

His stare zeroed in on Frank Ramah. Vince never underestimated an enemy. Ramah was dangerous. He had the eyes of a killer, the killer instinct. And he feared nothing, as proven by the fact he had challenged Vince to fight it out. The damn fool. That was the trouble with guys like Ramah. They failed to recognize superiority. One had to prove it, and Vince was getting weary of flattening every challenger who chanced along in his bailiwick in Los Angeles.

He wished he were back there. When he had the half million, minus fifty thousand dollars apiece he would give Penny and Jigger, he would like to return. Wisely, though, he planned to head for San Antonio. In L.A. there was the case pending against him of the little kid he had knocked off. Too, he was not about to put up any longer with his mother. He had taken a shot at her a couple of months ago and missed. He pretended it was an accident and she believed him. Maybe. She said she did, but possibly she was playing the fox and would be laying for him one night with a shotgun.

Now he said to Ramah, "Figure it out this way, copper. You cause me trouble and you get your guts shot out. You sit there like a good boy scout and you get to play detective again tomorrow."

Ramah was the stereotype of the stoical Indian. Not by an eyelash did he register thought or feeling.

Vince shrugged. "Have it your way." He accepted a cigarette Penny offered and took a slow puff.

He turned to Sandy and his gaze moved leisurely over her. "You remind me of a broad I raped once. She got a kick out of it. Said it was different."

He waited for a reaction but she refused to give him the satisfaction of one.

He continued, "I trapped you, Wilcox. You can't play

games with me. I'm too damn good. Way ahead of you. You're
a smart broad but you think you're smarter than you are."

He rubbed the cigarette in the dirt. "At first you couldn't
remember where you buried the old man, but when I sent
Grandpa out, you remembered fast enough. You figured
Grandpa was going to find the money—and it wouldn't be in
the grave because all of a sudden you were ready to show me
the grave.

"So now you'd better remember fast what you did with the
money, just in case Grandpa's eyesight isn't so good. You come
clean with me, and I'll let you go, and like I said, you get to
keep the jewelry. But if you don't, Wilcox . . ."

The radio came alive. "Yazzie calling Officer Ramah.
Yazzie calling Ramah. Come in, Ramah . . ."

"Oh, what the hell," Vince said, exasperated. "Who's this
guy, Yazzie?"

"Police captain," Ramah answered. "Heads the Chinle
district."

"Okay, answer him. See what he wants. But don't try any
tricks. And don't talk Navvy."

As Ramah picked up the radio, Vince shoved the .38 into
his side. "Ramah here . . . Sorry, been busy. Explain later . . .
All A-okay here, no change . . . Repeat, two dead. Pilot
Sandra Y. Wilcox, Y as in yak . . . No, y-A-k, not O. Also,
man about sixty. Identity unknown . . . You have ident? Two
sons, one daughter in military . . . Please, hold it, Captain.
Much static. See what can do."

He turned to Vince. "The captain wants to know if I've
seen an old prospector. They have a mule on an aerial photograph."

Vince nodded. "What was that about two sons, one daughter?"

"He's survived by them. The old man she buried."

"Who the hell cares?"

Ramah shrugged. "I'm only repeating what he said." He
put his finger on the "talk" button. "Correct, Captain. One old

prospector, mule . . . No, no boy with him . . . How long before rescue?"

Vince grabbed the radio to listen. Yazzie said, "We project under an hour if we don't get more rain."

Vince returned the radio. When Ramah finished, Vince turned on him, furious. "You damn, lying geek, telling me two hours. But I had you figured, copper, to the minute. I divided it by half. I'm ahead of all of you stupid, scheming, little geeks."

Penny said, "You're something awful smart, Vince."

Sandy went rigid. The flashlight beams were little more than fireflies. They hypnotized her. She followed them as if her life depended upon them, which it well might. They appeared to do a choreographed dance, sweeping to the ground, soaring high. For several minutes, they had flown about in a very small circumference.

Shonto had found the money.

21.

Although many people thought the Navajo nation was a remote place, lost somewhere in the Great American Desert, it was as close by communications to other parts of the country as any town or county. The California authorities responded quickly to the leads set forth by the Tribal Police at Window Rock.

The Department of Motor Vehicles at Sacramento reported that license plate QDD-223 had been issued to Rudolph Circassian, forty-nine, blue eyes, five feet ten, hair brown, and address: 1401 Mountain Avenue, Sherman Oaks. Since each California driver's license carried a photograph in color of the party holding it, the department would send a print to the Tribal Police if they should so wish.

From the Los Angeles police department's communication center came a phone call stating that a check of the indices for the name, Rudolph Circassian, had disclosed that one Vincent Roberts, aka Vince Roberts, and Ronald Hardin, aka Jigger

Hardin, were wanted for the mugging of Circassian, a stock-broker, and the theft of his orange 1975 Porsche. Roberts and Hardin were also wanted for the slaying of Louis Mercado, age six.

The FBI, the Los Angeles authorities advised, wanted Roberts and Hardin for unlawful flight to avoid prosecution for murder. Roberts was described as highly dangerous. The report said they were accompanied by Georgiana Thompson, aka Penny Thompson, age fifteen. A check of juvenile authorities revealed no criminal record.

The above information was forwarded by Window Rock to Chinle, where Major Tonalea, Captain Yazzie, and three other officers had set up a command post about a long, much-scarred table. Before them were spread the photographs that Tonalea had shot on his last sortie into Hidden Canyon. He had used high-speed Kodak film that utilized the light from the copter's searchlight.

The pictures revealed myriad tracks which the officers studied. From the footprints they knew that two females, a young male, and three adult males had been—and might still be—near the scene of the crash. One photo showed clearly two feet sticking out from under a bush. Obviously they belonged to a body in a prone position. The party could be either dead or in hiding. The officers conjectured that he was most likely dead since anyone in hiding would have concealed himself more carefully. The size of the feet was indeterminate. They were in cowpuncher boots, a fact that eliminated J. C. Berchtol, the New York jewelry buyer, since the police had established that he wore ordinary oxfords.

As in a previous photograph, the prayer cairn stood out in bas relief to a desert-trained eye, although the average Anglo would not have noted it.

Yazzie ran a rough hand through his thick black hair. He was puzzled. "Nobody's lived or farmed in Hidden Canyon for at least fifteen years, and I don't know why anyone would go down there. Even if someone did, why would they stop in that particular place to set up prayer rocks?"

A secretary brought in hot coffee and Tonalea took his black. He indicated on the map the prayer cairn. "Look at the twig. It's impossible to judge how fresh it is but it was placed there recently or the leaves would have fallen off."

A second secretary brought in typed copies of the taped radio conversation with Officer Ramah. "A few words were blurred," she said. "I left them blank."

Yazzie thanked her and quickly scanned a copy. "We have the pidgin English again which would indicate he is still talking under duress."

Yazzie read: "All A-okay here, no change . . . Repeat, two dead. Pilot Sandra Y. Wilcox. Y as in yak . . ."

Yazzie looked up. "We have already established that her middle name is Rose. So when Ramah says it is Yak, he is setting the word up obviously as code for something."

He returned to the transcript: "He says, 'No, y-A-k, not O.' Since I made no comment on the yak but he pretends I did, he must be telling us something. Yak. What does that mean?"

Tonalea took a deep breath. The coffee had rallied his weary spirits. "He makes a point in spelling it without an O. So the O had to be considered in juxtaposition with the yak, some way or other."

"That occurred to me, too," said Yazzie, "but it is too simple. He ran a risk in using a code—if you can call it that—so simple. Yak spelled backward—which is what my thirteen-year-old boy does all the time when he doesn't want me to know what goes on—is kay. Put an O in front and you've got Okay. Sandra Okay Wilcox. I think he's telling us that she's alive. And to back that up we have the tracks of a woman we haven't been able to identify."

"Could be," said Tonalea.

Yazzie continued, "Ramah says, 'Also, man about sixty. Identity unknown.'"

He looked up. "I did not comment on that, as the transcript shows, and yet he pretends that I did, and says, 'You have ident?' and then he fakes some more, repeating what I am supposed to have said, 'Two sons, one daughter in military.' In other words, two boys and one girl armed, which is what we already know but he has no way of knowing that we know."

Yazzie gulped down a long swig of coffee. "Now we get on to the prospector. 'No, no boy with him.' Again, I had said nothing about a boy but he pretends I did."

For the next few minutes, they discussed every possible interpretation. Tonalea summed up the consensus: "He's telling us that the fourteen-year-old boy is dead—and the feet sticking out from under the shrubbery here in the photograph would tend to corroborate that premise."

They sat quietly with their thoughts. Who would wantonly murder a fourteen-year-old boy? And for what reason? Only too well they knew that a killer did not need a reason. Tonalea pointed to the Los Angeles police report: wanted for the slaying of a six-year-old boy.

Finally the situation had crystallized. Originally they had believed the three teen-agers had descended into the canyon out of curiosity. Then they had been misled into thinking one was a brother of the pilot. Now it was evident they intended to steal the half million and the jewelry, and at least one would murder on the whim of the moment or to gratify an overwhelming ego.

All who sat about the table were seasoned police officers accustomed to grappling with the criminal mind as well as the criminal body. Over the years they had established a high percentage record in apprehending killers, rapists, and others who employed violence as a weapon. At times the cases had been solved by brilliant detective work. Usually, however, the cases had been cracked simply because criminals were a stupid lot who, given time, trapped themselves.

Now, though, they confronted one who had a decided advantage: he would shoot to kill without provocation, and in so doing, create terror. In such an ugly, highly dangerous atmosphere, even Officer Ramah might hesitate to strike. He might hesitate because he had not only his own life to consider but two others, Sandra Wilcox and the old prospector, Shonto.

Each officer experienced a certain degree of apprehension. For the next hour they would work with fear tempering and shaping their strategy. A little fear would work in their favor. It could highlight dangers an officer might not consider otherwise, and prompt him to evaluate whether the risks involved in a plan were too great to merit putting it into operation.

Yazzie pulled the radio up. "Come in, Officer Davis. Come in, Officer Davis."

Come in, Officer Davis.

Larry had called her Officer Davis back in the days when they joked and laughed. Before fear of exposure turned them solemn and furtive. Now they hid their laughter as they did themselves.

Only a week ago they had last met. Yet it seemed so long ago.

It was a storybook day, the air warm and laden with scent, the birds noisy with seeming joy. Taking different trails, they had climbed by horseback up Lukai peak, beyond Three Turkey ruin, a cliff house, and come together on a slab of slick, smooth rock that overlooked the immediate world. In the distance were mountains old and tired, the wrinkles furrowed deep, the shadows heavy. On the highway far below, cars plowed through the waters of a mirage.

They went into each other's arms and clung out of love and desperation. They kissed tenderly, then hungrily. Afterward, they sat on a boulder facing each other, their hands touching, feeling, finding love by contact. Then the glow disappeared from her ruddy, strong-boned face. She stood up and walked about.

"I didn't sleep last night," she said, avoiding his eyes. "I cried half the night. There's no use talking about it. We've talked and talked."

"I got a letter from an old friend yesterday," he said slowly. "He can get me a job in Washington."

"Washington." Her thoughts dug dreamily into the past. "When I was a little girl, I wanted to go to Washington, and walk into the White House, and tell the President that my people needed him."

She smiled. "Childhood. It was so easy and simple to solve problems then. I don't know why we have to grow up."

She returned to reality. "Sure, Washington's far away—but sometime someone would see us, and it'd get back here."

She stood on a sandstone ledge and stared down at a drop of several hundred feet. She felt the pebbles under her boots, and with a toe, rolled one back and forth. It spun off, hit a jagged outcropping, and bounced out into space.

"Ramona." He was frightened.

She turned to face him. "I was awake most of the night. I said that, didn't I? I'm like an old woman. I don't remember what I said."

"We're tired. Too tired."

She rushed on. "You've got everything going for you, and can be anything you want to. I'm not going to ruin you. I'm not going to kill Mama, either, or disgrace your parents and maybe shorten their lives."

She swallowed hard. "We've got a responsibility, too, to our clans and to The Dineh. We're Navajos, Larry. Not two crazy Anglos who shack up and don't care whom they hurt."

He tried to take her into his arms but she backed away. He said gently, "We're not going to hurt anyone, Ramona. We haven't yet—and we won't. In two years, nobody's ever seen us together."

"My uncle may have." He had never mentioned that evening in Farmington but she thought he might be protecting her. During her childhood, they had been very close.

"Sometime . . ." she said.

"We'll deny it. We'll say they're mistaken and people will believe us."

"Deceit, hiding, lying. What kind of a love do we have?" In shock, she put her hand to her mouth. "I didn't mean that. I love you so much—too much. Yes, Larry, too much."

"We'll go on just the way we have been."

"Even if we went on," she whispered, "what do we do? We can't have a home or children or friends."

"We'll have each other," he answered softly, "and that's all I want. You're all I live for."

She looked away. "You'll need a wife to help you in your career. A wife you can show off and be proud of. The time will come when you'll wish . . . you'll wish . . ."

He seized her and, kissing her, said, "Don't talk nonsense."

Gently, she ran her hands over his face, then turned. "I've got to get back. I'm on duty in an hour."

"Winslow, Saturday?"

She put a foot in the stirrup and swung up. She was crying. She never looked back.

"Yazzie here. We have a couple of developments. We have reason to believe that the pilot, Sandra Wilcox, is alive and being held hostage by one or more of the teen-agers. Also, we are certain that Officer Ramah and a prospector named Shonto are being held. We want you to push as hard as possible, but after you've gone up Hidden Canyon by roughly a half mile, call a halt and get in touch with me. At that time we will give you final instructions. The older teen-ager, name of Vincent Roberts, is a fugitive and extremely dangerous. He killed a six-year-old boy in Los Angeles and may have killed the fourteen-year-old they picked up as a guide."

"What about Sergeant Tachee?" she asked. "He's up ahead looking for the Anglo."

"Tachee, are you on?" Yazzie asked.

"Yes, Captain."

"Return to the rescue party. We'll forget the Anglo until we wind this up."

Davis said, "He may drift into the crash scene and become a hostage himself."

"I don't know what we can do about it. We asked him to stay out of the canyon, and you did, too. We're not responsible."

When Yazzie signed off, he sat a moment in thought. He had promised: "At that time we will give you final instructions."

What instructions? They had none yet to offer.

They had forty-five minutes, more or less, to come up with them.

22.

Vince moved about, restless and apprehensive. He took out a pack of cigarettes, found it empty, wadded it up, and threw it beyond the rubble. For several minutes, they had been unable to locate the swinging beams of the flashlights. Sandy was thinking—and it was evident Vince was, too—had Shonto done away with Jigger, seized the money and fled on foot?

Sam, quiet all this time, brayed loudly. He sounded like a siren gone wrong. The canyon picked up his protest and boomeranged it along the walls back to them.

"I hear voices," Sandy said.

Vince swung about. "Voices?"

"The voices of the dead. The voices of the chindi. They're all about us. They're coming for us."

"Think you're damn funny, don't you?" He turned to Penny. "I'm going out there. You hold your Saturday-nighter on them, and if they move a foot, let 'em have it. Don't talk, just fire. Wound the broad. I don't want her dead. But kill the Navvy. Okay?"

She nodded. She was proud Vince trusted her with a re-

sponsible assignment. At the same time she was terrified. She
had never fired a gun.

He turned to Sandy. "I'm expecting Grandpa to deliver,
but you'd better be ready when I get back if he doesn't."

He looked at Penny. "You heard that, Penny. I warned
her."

"I heard," Penny said, aiming the weapon in the general
direction of Sandy and Ramah. Her index finger wormed its
way about the trigger. She held the gun steady, yet Sandy wondered if a minor surprise, such as an animal moving about in
the bushes, might not activate the finger.

I warned her. Vince had said that about Charlie after he
shot him. *I warned him.* As if that justified a killing. He had
warned the party, and the party had disobeyed. In his mind,
that was sufficient reason to murder him.

Once he was gone, a silence they had not known since ar-
riving settled in. For the first time, Sandy felt the sadness of
this ancient ruin, the kind of nostalgic sadness that envelops
any deserted, moldering home in a forlorn place. For generations, people had lived here, and had their children, and gone
forth to hunt and grow things with primitive tools. And then
something catastrophic had happened, probably a drought that
brought thirst and hunger, and they had moved on. They had
left behind their hopes and dreams. One caught the essence of
wishes and longings by walking the same paths and climbing
the same steps.

A sadness centuries ago, and a sadness this night. When
the sun came up above the canyon walls, relatively late in the
morning, would they be here? Would Shonto or the Navajo
officer or she have survived?

Her thoughts went to Bill. He was organized, always punctual. She never was. Invariably he had to wait a half hour when
they had a date. She would stop to do the "immediate things"
("they'll just take a second") or drive an old person some-

where ("I couldn't run off and leave her"). He never scolded or complained.

A couple didn't have to be alike, did they? One could be punctual, the other late, if there was understanding and love. One could think one way, and the other, another, couldn't they?

And Skeet. The last she saw of him the morning she took off he was sitting on the ground with several little friends, playing a string game, usually a winter pastime. She remembered her mother had called it "cat's cradle." Skeet and the other boys would see how many figures and designs they could make by twisting a piece of string between the hands. They made up stories to go along with the designs.

Life is a string game. Life is the string, and we weave our own stories as we go along, and sometimes the string snaps.

God, if anything happens to me, take care of Skeet.

Ramah shuffled a foot, as if restless, and her eyes went to his. Without moving them, he signaled that this might be their chance. How he communicated, she would never know.

Penny stood by a wall that had disintegrated with the centuries until it was no more than three feet high. Sandy said, "I feel faint. I've got to sit down."

Now Penny had Sandy at one side and Ramah straight ahead. Penny said, "Don't try anything. I don't want to hurt you."

She had a softness they might exploit.

"You mean it, don't you?" Sandy said. "I mean, you really don't want to hurt anybody."

Penny smiled faintly.

Sandy continued, "You got any folks?"

Penny hesitated, thinking that over. "No."

"It's nice to have folks." Sandy edged a little closer. If she could get within range of cracking Penny's gun hand with a sharp blow . . .

"Maybe for some," Penny answered wistfully.

She's only a child, Sandy thought. What a tragedy that at her age, she should set her life in a direction that would lead inevitably to grief and ruin. *Maybe if I get out of this alive, and she does, too, I can do something for her. It may not be too late. She does seem to have good basic decencies.*

Two more inches gained.

Keep talking. Helps splinter her concentration.

"I had wonderful parents," Sandy went on. "Both gone now."

"I got Vince and Jigger. They're all the folks I want."

"You run around with them, and they kill people, and the police will say you're in on it."

Penny raised her voice in defiance. "I haven't done nothing."

"I know you haven't," Sandy said, gaining a few more inches, "and I don't want you to. Why don't we get together and rap some when this is over? We could go shopping together."

"Jigger took me once."

"That's a Saturday Night Special, isn't it?"

"Vince bought it for me. He's awful good to me."

"I got one at home but I don't know how to load it. Could you show me?"

Penny retreated. "Get back!" she shouted. "Don't come any closer. I don't want to hurt you, but I do what Vince tells me."

Penny backed into a corner. Sandy heard the little putt-putt of her excited breath. Her childlike face was glazed by desperation. Sandy sized up the distance. She would need more than a lunge to reach Penny's gun hand.

Sandy sagged and said softly, "You can go to prison doing what Vince tells you to do."

"I love him!" Penny shouted.

"I know you think you do, but maybe you're confusing love with sex, and pretty as you are, you can find some other boy who's good for you—who doesn't murder kids." She indicated the bush under which Charlie Begay's body lay. "He didn't even call out for him to stop, just shot him."

Penny stared at her. *Maybe I got through to her,* Sandy thought exultantly. *If I can create a doubt.*

"He had to," Penny said weakly. "You blame him for everything. You don't know him."

At the sound of pebbles rolling, Sandy turned. Vince, Jigger, and Shonto were coming in. As if rehearsed, their flashlights moved in unison.

"He didn't find it," Vince told Penny.

"Course'n if I had me a dog to smell around . . ." Shonto began and rambled off.

"Any trouble?" Vince asked.

Penny held the Saturday Night loosely.

"Well, was there?"

"No, no trouble."

"Something's bothering you?"

"Did you have to shoot Charlie?"

Vince swung on Sandy. "So that's what you've been up to?" He turned to Penny. "She's brainwashing you, sweetheart, like the Commies do."

He put an arm about her and squeezed her hard. "Soon as we finish up here, we'll have fun again. You and me and Jigger. Right, Jigger?"

"Sure will."

Sandy studied Penny. Despite her adoration of Vince and sexual tie with him, she was disturbed. Her gaze was set on distant focus. She could identify with Charlie. He had been only a year younger and had been nice to her. Sandy made a mental note: every time she had a chance, she would talk about Charlie. She would hammer on the truth, that he was killed in cold blood.

Sandy's mental appraisal went next to Jigger. He appeared an even better bet than the girl. Hero worship was such an ephemeral thing. It could be punctured by doubts alone.

Vince glowered at Shonto. "You know what I'm thinking? You're holding out on us. An old desert rat like you—"

"And lose my cut? Mister, many's the night me and Sam've gone to sleep hungry. You ever been hungry? Or had to live off the country? Time's been when Sam and me's lived for weeks off the yucca plant. I'd beg me a little goat's milk and squeeze the juice out of the roots, and mix'em up, and let'em set a spell, and I'd have cheese. Or I'd put the bananas in hot ashes, or make mush cereal—"

Vince yelled, "Grandpa!" Shonto quieted like a dog admonished. Vince looked around at them. "I don't want any running off at the mouth unless I ask you something. That goes for all of you."

He turned to Jigger. "Where'd you go?"

"All the way to the river from the plane."

Shonto said, "Give me a little time to get my legs back and I'll try again. They're hurtin' somethin' awful. Ain't much down there when you get to my age."

When Vince turned to Penny, Shonto attracted Sandy's eyes and smiled knowingly. Out of his peripheral vision, Vince caught the look.

Vince straightened, and anger rose in his tired eyes. "You old double-crossing scoundrel!"

"What did he do?" Jigger asked.

"He found it, sure as hell. You found it, didn't you, Grandpa, and you're holding out on us? Going to sneak back later and get it all. Cut us out without a dollar. Your friends who trusted you, made you a fair deal considering the spot you're in."

Shonto indicated Jigger. "He was with me all the time."

"He's right, Vince," Jigger said. "I never left him."

A little to the right of Vince, Frank Ramah squatted on the ground, unnoticed in the excitement. His hand moved slowly until he found a sizable clod. Then very deliberately he rose.

Vince chastised Jigger. "You're no desert rat, or boy scout, or Indian. You didn't see what he saw."

Penny spoke softly. "Don't hurt him, Vince. He's a nice old man."

"You again! Clear out! Go sob for this bastard some other place." To Shonto, he said, "Okay, you talk, you old creep." He pointed his .38 toward Sandy. "Or she gets it right here and now."

Sandy cut in. "You talk and we both get it. He's not killing us until he gets the money—and then he will."

Vince said, "Okay, Grandpa, which is it? Listen to her and she's dead—and you're next."

"God help me, son, I ain't got nothin' to tell you. I ain't holdin' out on you. I couldn't use all that money if I had it, an old man like me. What you givin' me will take care of my wants rest of my life."

Ramah had maneuvered until he had their backs to him. He threw the clod as a baseball pitcher would, straight into a large tamarisk some thirty feet directly in front of the ruin. In one unbelievably swift movement, Vince swung about, drew and fired into the bush. Ramah leaped on him, grabbed his gun arm, and the two fell to the ground. With a powerful lunge, Vince threw Ramah off. Both sprang to their feet the same second with Vince firing. Ramah weaved a moment uncertainly. Vince got off a second shot, then Ramah spun about and dropped with a thud to the dirt floor. He groaned and twisted. Standing over him, Vince would have fired into his brain but that instant, Sandy fell to her knees by Ramah's side, blocking the shot.

Ramah struggled to talk. In the dim light she could see blood oozing from his chest. "Throw the light on him, some-body." She looked up at Penny, who averted her eyes. "For God's sake, I've got to see what I'm doing."

Shonto reached for Jigger's flashlight, and Jigger offered no resistance. Shonto held the beam on Ramah. After tearing off his shirt and undershirt, Sandy found an ugly and heavily bleeding chest wound. She soaked up the blood with the undershirt and held it firmly to the wound. If she could stop the bleeding . . . if the wound was not too deep.

Holstering the .38, Vince turned away. "I've got to get in some target practice," he told Jigger. "I should've killed the creep on the first shot."

23.

Bill sat rigid and tense, holding a tight rein. Floundering in the soft sand, his horse threatened to panic. She tried to take the bit in her mouth, all the time working sideways, attempting to escape to more solid footing. She appeared to be struggling against suction, and the more she struggled, the more she slipped back.

Alarmed, Bill sought to soothe her by talking low and confidently. He remembered one of his Navajo foremen telling about an old pony getting spooked and running into quicksand. The Navajo had shouted the pony's name, and the animal had struggled to free himself but slowly disappeared from view.

Summoning all his strength, he pulled the horse to a halt. As the seconds ticked off, he tightened a grip on his nerves to still the trembling. There was no suction, no dropping, and he breathed a big sigh. Nevertheless, he turned his mount into an arroyo, a small gully cut by runoff water from higher ground. He would gamble that it had firm footing.

First, though, he listened. To his left was the thunder of water. Strange as it might seem, he knew that he could distinguish noises underneath that high level of sound. A horse's hoof on hard rock or a low neigh. Fearing he might overtake the sergeant, he had let the mount choose her own slow gait. There was the danger, of course, that at some point the sergeant might decide to quit the chase, retrace his steps, and they would meet.

The arroyo proved a good choice. Once out of the soft sand, the horse settled down and carefully picked her way around rocks and over tree roots that the storm had exposed. Soon they were on higher ground. As he rode, he scanned the country beneath and saw no movement. The lightning was errant and spectacular. At times, clouds chasing each other blocked the moonlight. The effect was that of a child playing with a light switch.

Never had he been so uncomfortable. His wet clothes clung to his hot, excited body. His cuts hurt, and one continued bleeding badly.

Unexpectedly the canyon narrowed and he was forced to lower ground. He was so close to the river that he could see the foam on the rushing torrent. Keeping as near as possible to the canyon wall, he passed a small overhang that protected a cave about the size of a double garage. He was barely past it when a voice called out, shocking him to the marrow, "All right, white man, that's as far as you go. I've got a .38 on you. I can riddle your back like a target board."

Bill had planned, if he met the sergeant, to make a run, but with Tachee only a few feet behind him, he had no doubt the sergeant could bring him down. And would.

Tachee emerged from the darkness. "I've got orders to bring you in. Put your hands behind your back."

Defiantly, Bill swung in the saddle to face him. "I told you back there, you don't have jurisdiction over a white man on government property."

Tachee patted his holster. "This is my jurisdiction—and it's all I need. It's all the white man has needed for more than a century. It's been his jurisdiction. All right, hands behind the back."

"I'm no criminal and you know it, Sergeant. I'm a guy who's got to get to his girl friend—if she's alive."

Tachee offered no comment. He wound a piece of rope tightly about Delaney's hands and tied a solid knot. "You're a horse thief, among other things."

"I borrowed a horse. You know I would've turned her back to you when I got to the accident."

Tachee snorted. "We're going back. You first. Come on, Chia."

So that was the horse's name. Bill wished he had known.

Talking the bridle, Tachee turned the horse about. Chia was anxious to follow orders. Retracing her steps could lead to food and a warm stall. She moved faster than before.

When Officer Ramona Davis sighted the two approaching, she held up a hand to stop her party of twelve. Quietly she said into the radio: "Sergeant Tachee has apprehended the subject and is bringing him in. I don't want to spare a man to return him to Chinle. May I place him in effect under house arrest and take him with us?"

Yazzie answered immediately. "Anything you say. Be firm, though, and explain that if he fails to follow orders we'll press every charge we can against him and make life hell for him."

Tachee rode up. "Here's the prisoner." He said it as if he had caught a desperado.

"Untie him," she instructed. "The captain's order." To Bill she said, "You're under arrest for interfering with peace officers in the performance of their duty. However, we're releasing you on your own recognizance provided you agree to follow all orders given you by the sergeant and myself. Agreed?"

"I'll have to think about that."

Davis wheeled her horse preparatory to riding away. "Tie him up, Sergeant, to the cottonwood over there. And I hope we remember where we left him."

Bill called out quickly, "Okay, okay."

She turned back. "I want to talk with you." With him following, she rode out of the hearing of the others.

She maneuvered her horse so that she faced him. "My superiors have established that Miss Wilcox is alive. We don't know what her condition is, but she did survive."

Bill sat shaking. "Oh, God," he said at last. "I knew she was all right. Nothing could've happened—but still—I didn't know."

"I understand," she said softly, then continued, again businesslike, "My superiors want to know what your relationship is with Miss Wilcox."

"We're friends."

"Engaged?"

"I don't see what that has to do—"

"Answer my question."

"Not any more. I don't know what happened. We got into an argument. She doesn't like strip mining and that's my business. I guess it sounds a little ridiculous—to split up over that . . ."

"No other reason?"

He shook his head.

"And you love each other?"

"I really don't see—"

"Answer the question, please."

"Yeah. We'll always love each other. It's just that . . ."

"You had an argument."

"I guess you could call it that although at the time . . ."

She sat motionless, looking past him. If only she and Larry had had nothing more than an argument to come between them . . .

Suddenly she was tired, so tired. If she could only lie down somewhere, and sleep. Sleep and never wake up.

There would be tears for her and love. They would say she had lived the corn-pollen way.

Wheeling her mount about, she rode off.

For a long moment, until the sergeant yelled at him, he sat submerged in the happy euphoria of knowing that Sandy was alive. His Sandy. Not alive in his prayers and hopes but really alive.

A strange conversation he had had with this officer they called only Davis. Strange questions that couldn't possibly concern the crash and the ultimate rescue. But they had to. Otherwise she would not have asked them. She was not the kind to inquire out of curiosity. An attractive woman but too abrupt and businesslike for his taste. Not much feeling there.

Like a tableau, Tonalea, Yazzie and the other officers sat in the same positions. Occasionally one would rise and walk about, seeking to ease the weariness from his bones, only to return and fall back into the same chair.

As well as exhaustion, the tension showed. It had been a long night. Now, though, the pieces had fallen into place to reveal a crime of terrifying proportions that was approaching a climax. Within thirty minutes, it could be resolved. So much depended, as did most cases, on the plans drafted, their execution, and even more important, on the breaks they got. The unforeseen could descend with tornado fury and speed to wreck the best plans and the most clever execution.

Outside, tires crunched on the soft, wet earth, a horn sounded, splitting the silence of the night, a baby cried as a mother passed by on a mysterious late-night mission, and on the main highway, big trucks rumbled at high speed. In an adjoining room, the murmur of officers came over as they handled the usual night business: an accident, a suspected burglary, a drunken fight.

Yazzie asked, "What about using Delaney as an intermediary to bargain for the hostages? The subjects would trust him since he wouldn't make a move that would harm the girl."

Tonalea considered the proposal. He considered everything. He didn't like it. "In the first place, you can't bargain with someone who's killed a six-year-old for target practice. He'll take whatever you give him and still do away with the hostages. And then, I wouldn't want to trust Mr. Delaney's judgment. He's inexperienced in criminal investigation and under too much emotional stress to think clearly. By that, I don't mean to deprecate him, but it's dangerous to use untrained people in a high-risk situation."

They rejected, too, the possibility of dropping officers by helicopter at the crash scene. They decided (1) Davis had a sufficient number under her command, and (2) a ground attack would take the subjects by surprise whereas dropping men by rope or ladder would alert them. Parachuting was out of the question. The department had no parachute unit, and even if it had had, the terrain was too rough for landings.

With the others' approval, Tonalea decided to fly another sortie, and perhaps several, over the accident scene. "We may surprise them in the open in some kind of operation we should know about. But even if we don't, we will bother them, and increase their tension, and may interfere with something they are planning. I don't see how it could hurt. They still don't know that we know."

On the possibility that the case might not be resolved before dawn, he dispatched three sharpshooters with high-powered rifles to a point on the canyon rim looking down into the cliff house across the way. He wanted them as a backup crew if a gun battle should ensue after daybreak.

After much discussion of details, the group agreed to a suggestion by Tonalea that officers should descend by ladder down the canyon wall directly over the cliff house. He marked a narrow ledge on the photograph where they could land that would be within a few feet of access to the cliff house's tower. The descent would have to be undertaken when the subjects were inside the ruins. Because of the overhang above them, they would be unable to see the maneuver.

Finally, the anticipated call came from Officer Davis. "We're in position, Captain," she said.

He gave her the instructions they had worked out. Davis, Tachee, and their party were to tie up their horses and proceed on foot. When they were within sight of the ruins, they were to crawl as near to the subjects and their hostages as they safely could without risking discovery.

They were to approach on a broad front that would extend well past the cliff house on each end, to block any attempted flight. An officer on the extreme right would serve as a decoy. He would emit a coyote bark but overdo it, so that the subjects would recognize it as a fake. Vincent Roberts might go himself to investigate or send one of the other teen-agers.

Prior to that, an expert shot, whom Davis would choose, would position himself as close to the ruins as possible, and on signal, pick off the subjects if they refused to surrender and opened fire. "From now on we will call this officer our number one man, for the sake of identification when we're talking about him."

Yazzie continued, "We will try to get word to the hostages, without the subjects knowing, to fall flat the second they see the number one man. I won't go into details of how we will do this but it should get them out of the line of fire. At the same time the number one man shows himself, one of the officers who has come down by ladder and is already in the back of the cliff house will emerge and either protect the hostages, if they need it, or join in the apprehension of the subjects.

"The other officers will remain in hiding on the ground and will be available to you if you need them. You will position yourself so that you can observe the action but will at all times remain in the background. In other words, you will handle the command post."

"What about Sergeant Tachee?" she asked.

"He could be the decoy if that meets with your approval."

"Captain, I'm not certain—"

"I'm giving the orders, Davis. Sergeant, are you on?"

"Yes, Captain."

"I've put Davis in charge."

"Yes, sir."

Yazzie could imagine what he was saying under his breath.

Yazzie continued, "Remember, the roar from the wash will cover your movements except possibly for a sharp noise such as a cough. Please warn the officers."

"Yes, sir," Davis answered.

"One more thing. If this plan fails and the subjects manage to seize and flee with one or more hostages, you will withdraw

immediately and await further instructions. You will not pursue
them. Is that understood?"

"Yes, Captain."

"That's all for the time being. Wait. I've had second
thoughts about Miss Wilcox's fiancé. Tie him up, Sergeant,
when you leave the horses."

24.

Shonto got an old, threadbare blanket from his saddlebag,
and after smoothing the ground, spread it in a corner of the
room. Half staggering, he and Sandy managed to carry Frank
Ramah and place him on the blanket. He was slipping in and
out of consciousness and still bleeding copiously.

"We've got to get help," Sandy told Vince. "He'll bleed to
death." Her own personal fright had been submerged by another.

"Sure, pick up a phone and call a doctor."

Taking a deep breath, she stilled her anger. "We could
get the copter to drop us what we need. Shonto could call
Chinle and tell them the officer fell—or something."

"Got a cigarette?" Vince asked Penny, who lit one, took
a puff, and handed it to him. "Come over here, Wilcox. I'm
not finished with you and Grandpa."

Sandy turned to Penny. "Talk to him, please. He's going
to die if we don't . . . For God's sake, you wouldn't let him
die. I know you wouldn't."

"She's conning you," Vince said, enjoying the smoke.

"She tried to con me while you were gone," Penny told
him.

Vince took another puff, then said, "Okay, you two. Get
over here."

Sandy stood defiantly. The terror that had partially paralyzed her had given way to angry resistance.

Grabbing her roughly by an arm, Vince pulled her to the
spot where she had stood before. Shonto hobbled after them.

Letting her go, Vince backed up a few feet to stare coldly.
"Strip her," he said to Jigger who hesitated. Vince repeated
sharply. "Strip her!"

Still Jigger made no move.

The old terror surged back through her. "You don't have
to, Jigger," she said quietly. "I'll do it. What're you doing
with this guy anyway, a good kid like you? Let me tell you
something. Get out now before he hangs a murder rap on you
and you spend the rest of your life in prison."

"Shut up!" Vince shouted. "I've had enough of your
mouth."

"Please don't do anything to her," Penny said.

"You, too!"

Sandy felt a shimmer of hope. He was beginning to crack.
The tension was telling.

Shonto said in his raspy old voice, "I've got my legs back.
What say you and me go out and have another look? Might
strike gold this time around."

"You're nothing but a damned old con man. Okay, Wilcox, hurry it up. Everything off."

Penny hung her arms around him. "I'm your girl. And
Jigger's. Aren't I enough girl for you? You told me last time—"

"You're jealous." He pried her arms loose and pushed her
aside.

"She's an old woman," Penny yelled.

"Would you rather I broke her arm?"

Penny was half sobbing. "I'm your girl."

Shonto broke in. "I got a feelin' I could walk right up to
that money."

"You damn could if you would because you know where it
is." To Sandy, he said, "Okay, Wilcox, what d'ya want. Some
fun with me, or your arm broken, or tell me where you hid the
haul?"

Tears were in Penny's eyes. "Don't I always give you all
the fun you want? You and Jigger?"

"I don't think you ought to hurt Penny's feelings," Jigger said.

Vince swung about. "You're nothing but a damn weakling. You gave up your flashlight to save the bastard and now you won't strip the broad."

To Penny, Sandy said, "Don't worry. He's not going to attack me. He just says that to terrorize me—to break me down. With him, rape's an amusement, and he's got too much on his mind right now."

Startled, no one spoke, then Vince said, "What a cool, tough-minded bitch!"

"Thanks."

"Go on, play it cool or scared, makes no diff. I got maybe fifteen minutes to get the money."

"You're not going to kill me or rape me. Okay—as you're forever saying—so now what?"

He would torture her. He had no other recourse. But she would play for time. Perhaps the copter might come over again, perhaps the rescue party might arrive. Another few minutes, and another . . .

Shonto was thinking along the same line. "I got a feelin'," he began.

"To hell with your feeling," Vince stormed. "Tell me where you saw what you saw and we'll quit playing games. Tell me now!"

"I don't rightly know from here, but if Jigger and me went back over the same country . . ."

Ramah moaned. Sandy pleaded, "I don't care what you do to me, I've got to look after him."

She started to Ramah. Vince shot out a hand and seized her lacerated right arm. She cringed in agony. "You're stalling. You and Grandpa. You think the cavalry will ride in to save you?"

He twisted her arm slightly and the torn muscles screamed. "Okay, Grandpa, first her arms, then her legs."

Shonto's voice hinted of panic. "God, son, don't do that to an old man. This ticker of mine ain't so good."

Pain exploded deep inside her. "Don't tell him anything! He'll shoot you in the back!"

Slowly Vince twisted her arm and she doubled up. "Remember, Jigger, that kid that got smart with us—and I twisted his arm slowly and his eyes almost popped out before it snapped. Didn't sound much more than a twig breaking."

Her eyes automatically squeezed themselves shut, as if suffering was an object that could be blotted out. She bit her lips until they bled and swallowed the scream that fought to get out.

Shonto went into a nervous coughing spell. Between hacking, he said, "It's a pile of rocks she put up so she'd know . . ."

Vince barely loosened his hold. "Where?"

Shonto breathed as if each heartbeat would be his last. "Over that way." He indicated to his right. "A couple hundred yards . . . easy to see . . . a small pile of rocks . . ."

Vince thrust her away. As she fell, she struck the ground hard. She sat stunned, a spasm wracking her abdomen.

Vince was exultant. "Okay, you old buzzard, it'd better be like you say or it's all over for you. You know that, don't you?"

Shonto struggled to help Sandy up. "I can manage," she said, rising on her own.

"I'm sorry, girl, but I'm an old man and I couldn't stand by while he broke your arm. Time was when maybe I could've. I don't rightly know whether I ever could—but an old man can't."

She patted his cheek. "You did what you had to. In the end, we all do. We don't have much choice sometimes."

"The rest of you stay here," Vince ordered. "Penny, you take care of Wilcox if she tries anything. Jigger's weak when it comes to a broad."

"I wish I wasn't," Jigger said.

"You can't help it. Some of us got it, some haven't."

He squeezed Penny and patted her fanny. "Just you wait till we get this wound up."

He slapped Shonto on the back. He felt good. He was still the overman. These were nothing but inferiors. He had outthought them, including the cool broad. "Let's move the carcass, Grandpa, and if you're leading me on, me and Jigger will bury you alive. We wouldn't waste a bullet on you. Right, Jigger?"

"Sure wouldn't, Vince."

Before they left, Shonto said to Sandy, "If I don't get back, girl, take care of old Sam for me. Find him a home. And I got me a daughter somewhere I'd hoped to see afore I died but . . . I got her name and an old address in the saddlebag. She might want to know . . ."

25.

Tied to cottonwoods, the horses pawed nervously. They shook their heads, setting their manes to flapping. Their occasional neighs were low. Seemingly, they knew they were a part of a secret maneuver about to unfold.

Stroking her mount's mane, Ramona Davis studied an endless succession of dark, piggy-faced clouds scudding across the velvet sky. When one blacked out the moon, she counted slowly. Sixteen seconds. Three were hooked together in elephant style. Forty-eight seconds. Almost a minute of near total darkness. Since they changed constantly in size and rapidity of movement, a man on the run would be unable to determine how long he would have before the moonlight set him up again as a target. Still, it was a factor to consider in darting from boulder to boulder or bush to bush in approaching the ruin.

She was keyed up. She had her first important assignment: three subjects to apprehend and three lives to save. She was both frightened and confident. It would be nip and tuck

whether she could bring the stratagem off without the loss of
life.

She could if she executed a certain daring plan that was
shaping up sharply in her mind. As the details fell into place,
she grew more and more obsessed.

Her thoughts were blasted out of mind by the echoing,
canyon-magnified roar of the helicopter. Within minutes, it
hovered over them, and Captain Yazzie dropped a packing box
by rope. A cloud passed off the moon's face, and he waved and
shouted but they could not hear. Then the chopper soared like
a lumbering dinosaur up the canyon toward the crash scene.

Working quickly, they unpacked the weapons: .357 mag-
nums, twelve-gauge shotguns, rifles, tear gas, and Mace canis-
ters, flares, battery-operated spotlights, and restraining devices.
Except for the .38 Smith & Wessons they always carried, the
officers had left Chinle unequipped for a venture that might
require considerable firepower. They had thought they were on
a mission of mercy.

Other items in the airdrop included aerial photographs of
the area they would be infiltrating. The photos pinpointed
shrubs, trees, and boulders. Some of the latter were high as a
man and wide as a truck.

They gathered silently about her and Sergeant Tachee for
a final briefing. Previously they had agreed that only the police
officers would take part in the attack. The park rangers, both
U.S. and tribal, would stay with the horses. The paramedic
would accompany the officers but remain well in the background, subject to call by radio if needed. Ramona Davis
wanted no amateurs endangering the lives of her men or herself. The success of the mission called for judgment based on
experience, and split-second timing gained from working other
cases of extreme violence. It called, moreover, for good marks-
manship and desert tracking.

Including herself, there would be eight. They formed a
circle about her with flashlights in hand, pointed downward.
They were a tense lot and their attentiveness to what she said

reflected it. She diagramed in the sand and on the photographs exactly where each man would post himself and what his assignments, step by step, would be. They discussed every conceivable eventuality, how to handle it, how to block it. But they knew that the mind could not foresee every possible development, and that was where the danger lay. The unexpected was as much their enemy as the subjects.

Tachee would signal the start of the operation with a coyote bark. He was pleased with the assignment. He anticipated that Vincent Roberts would leave the cliff house to investigate, and that he—Tachee—would ambush him.

After consulting Tachee, Davis chose her number one man. He was twenty-three, the best sharpshooter in the department, and had a reputation for making gut decisions under fire. He acted and reacted quickly. He had agility of both mind and body.

Working with him, they drew up a time schedule. Time was all-important. He must be upon the subjects before they realized they were under attack. The showdown would be his speed matched against the speed of eyes spotting him, searching out the why, and interpreting, and, in the last seconds, against the speed of a trigger finger.

She herself would stay at the command post to the rear of the maneuver. She had chosen a knoll that overlooked the scene. It was covered with scrub growth that would fairly well conceal her yet was low enough to permit her to watch.

Throughout the briefing, Bill Delaney had sat nearby on a large rock, his feet drawn up under him. As he listened, he grew increasingly apprehensive. He foresaw the possibilities: Sandy used as a shield, Sandy shot by a teen-ager reacting in panic to the surprise assault, or Sandy gunned down in cross fire.

When Davis was finished, he called to her. "I've got something to say."

"Say it," she answered.

"Somebody's going to get killed. You can't get to the hostages fast enough. Why don't you let me go up there and do some talking and offer to ransom them?"

"You'd do that? Take a chance on getting killed yourself?"

He nodded. *She saw Larry standing there, heard Larry, and she was the girl he would do this for.*

She shook her head. "I can't let you. But thanks."

Tachee came up. "The captain said for me to tie you up to a tree." He took a pair of handcuffs out. "I guess these will do the job."

"Forget it," she said.

"The captain said—"

"I'll take the responsibility, Sergeant."

"You're disobeying orders."

"Yes, Sergeant, I am." She turned to Delaney. "I want you to get this straight. Don't follow us or get in our way. If you do, you may jeopardize the girl as well as the others. And don't forget you're under arrest and you're to report to the sergeant when we wind this up."

Delaney nodded.

Larry. Where are you, Larry? Why weren't you an Anglo, Larry?

"You agree?" she asked brusquely.

"I agree."

"Hell," Tachee said, "they've broken every promise they've made. Why should this one be different?"

She held up a hand. "Let's move," she called out.

26.

Sitting Navajo fashion beside Frank Ramah, Sandy took his pulse. It was weak. She had stopped the bleeding but he had lost consciousness. For several minutes, he had not moved.

She turned toward Penny and Jigger who lolled against the

back wall. Jigger was kissing and fondling Penny who, nevertheless, held the gun tightly and never took her eyes from
Sandy.

"He's dying," Sandy said. "We've got to get an airdrop in
here. Let me use the radio. I'll tell Chinle anything you want
me to."

They exchanged hasty, frightened glances.

Penny shouted, "Vince said no." She shouted to bolster
her courage.

Rising quickly, Sandy started for the radio. Penny yelled,
"I'm pulling the trigger! I'm going to kill you!"

Sandy sat back down. "Oh, God, what gets into kids like
you?"

Jigger said, "We do what Vince tells us to do."

Sandy thought: the tragedy was that there hadn't been
someone good in their lives they could have admired and been
devoted to. We're all so busy; we never think what we could
mean to a younger person.

*Nearby a meadowlark began singing, too filled with happi-
ness to wait for dawn. Floating across the sky was a family of
clouds, small ones running, followed by parents hurrying to
catch up. In the turmoil of the river, she imagined she heard
strains from Finlandia. Closer she heard the whine of the rising
wind through the ruins.*

*Life went on. For some. A man dying and she sitting
quietly doing nothing. People would say it was a shame, he was
so young, he had died before his time. But what was a person's
time? No matter what one's age, death loitered in the offing.
Yet not until a friend was ill or dying did we see ourselves and
others as they were, and our treatment of them, and the days as
we should live them. Death was life's great clarifier.*

*Bill and Skeet and she. The glorious days that lay ahead if
she could only shape them as she saw them in this hour of
dying and terror. Nothing mattered except their love, and their
love of others, and their love of God.*

If I live out this night, God, keep me close to this night. So

that I will live in love and above the pettiness and trivia that
destroy life. So that I will walk the Blessing Way.

"You all right?" Jigger asked.

She nodded.

"You hate us, don't you?" Penny asked belligerently.

She thought that over. "No, I think I could love you two
kids. I think I could love you for what you could be."

Vince was talkative. If he didn't keep Shonto's mind oc-
cupid, the old buzzard might figure out a trick to pull. Like
walking him into a patch of quicksand. He wouldn't put it past
Grandpa to commit suicide. What did he have to live for? All
gnarled up with arthritis, hungry half the time, and no one to
care for him. That would be a neat stunt. Walk them both into
quicksand. He would save the broad, and an old man might
feel noble about that.

"Have you ever found any gold, Grandpa?"

"Been near it many times. Bedded down many a night on
the big uranium find up at Four Corners. I guess the good Lord
didn't intend it. Be ridin' 'round today in one of them fine cars
and have servants and everythin'. It wasn't in the cards. You
got to have the cards turnin' up right."

"You got something there. I keep telling Jigger it's all luck.
Look at us now. If I hadn't been listening to the radio, we'd
missed out on this. What if I'd been asleep or reading the
paper?"

Shonto stopped and turned.

"What's the matter with you?" Vince asked.

"You won't do nothin' to the girl 'cause she didn't tell
you?"

"Forget it. Once I get my hands on the money . . ."

Shonto rubbed his beard, thinking. He liked the girl. She
had fire. He'd like to be sure she'd be all right. No way, though.

"You back out now . . ." Vince was threatening.

"Just restin'." He got the legs moving again.

Before Vince was aware of it, they were treading soft sand.

In panic, Vince stopped. "Grandpa, you go on. I'm going to take my time."

"We're only a mite away. By that wild olive up there."

"I'll be there in a minute." Vince watched him hobble along. With the greatest effort, he lifted and put down his feet. He weaved in the sand like a drunk. Any minute Vince feared he would begin sinking, but at last he arrived at the olive.

Vince followed, careful to keep his feet in the old prospector's tracks. Obviously puzzled, Shonto waited. He pointed out the rocks. "We got to get somethin' to dig with."

Scouting around, he found the strip of metal Sandy had used. As usual, he had difficulty getting down on his hands and knees. He had not expected Vince to offer to dig, and Vince didn't. Shonto realized only too well his position. He was a prisoner who followed orders abjectly and implicitly.

He dug slowly, purposely stalling. "Hurry it up!" Vince ordered. He pulled his .38. "You want your share or a bullet?"

Shonto stopped and looked up. "I got arthritis bad, son."

Dropping to the ground, Vince seized the metal digger and pushed Shonto away. Like a demon possessed, Vince dug into the earth. The soil was wet and soft, mud on the surface. He tossed the digger aside and began clawing with his hands. He went faster.

He stopped and froze. He heard in the distance the muted racket of the copter.

He dug wildly, at the same time shouting, "Get over under that tree. Hurry it up."

Taking his time, Shonto lumbered bearlike toward the tree.

Vince's fingers clawed at something hard that resisted. With both hands, he scooped out around it, and brought up the attaché case. Opening it, he discovered the Navajo jewelry. Angry, he threw it aside and resumed excavating.

The clatter of the rotor blades grew louder.

Once again he used the metal shovel. He struck an object that gave but was not dirt. Once more, he dug carefully around it and this time let out a happy obscenity as he unearthed the moneybag.

The first peripheral rays of the copter's searchlight were lighting up the area when he ran, doubled up, bag in hand, for the protection of the tree. Shonto was sitting under it. Vince pushed him down. "Flat. Get flat on your belly."

He stretched out himself, then opened the bag. A handful of bills fell out and a few floated away. He let out another cry while his hand plunged deeper into the bag, feeling the money. More bills spilled out. He smelled them and tasted them and stuck some inside his shirt.

Overhead the copter halted and stood as if anchored in space. Its searchlight illuminated the night almost like day.

A voice came over the loudspeaker, a deep-throated voice electronically blown up to a volume that would ride over the roar of the water still spilling down Hidden Canyon. Someone talking in Navajo. At once Vince knew—without knowing how he knew—they were giving instructions to the Navvy police- . man. They had to be. No one else understood Navajo—unless it was Shonto. The Navvy officer didn't matter. He was beyond hearing.

Vince stared at Shonto to determine if he were listening. He had his eyes closed. It was difficult to tell. "What's he saying?" Vince asked.

Without opening his eyes, Shonto shook his head. "Never learned the gibberish. No reason to."

He might be faking, the old buzzard. Not that it mattered. Somehow the police knew that something was taking place. He and Jigger and Penny had to clear out fast. They could do that. They had the money. A cool, half-million dollars. They could thank Vincent Augustus Roberts for it. He was probably one of the greatest overmen who ever lived.

In the helicopter, Yazzie sat where Tonalea had on the previous sorties. Yazzie had asked to fly this one. Once again, as in the Pacific theater in World War II, he was the code talker.

As the chopper hovered deep in the canyon, there surged back memories of steaming islands and hot jungles where the humidity sapped a man's strength and his morale. Island by island, he had gone with General Douglas MacArthur and the Allied forces. From Guadalcanal to Leyte he had talked with fellow Navajos working behind enemy lines and with Navajos aboard the great ships preparing for the Battle of the Coral Sea. To the bewilderment of the Japanese, who could make nothing out of the "code," he had talked straight Navajo and Navajo backward. It had never dawned on the Japanese that the "code" was a language.

Tonight, as in those early years of the 1940s, he remembered Talking God and the sacred prayer stick Talking God had given the Hero Twins to guide them. May the prayer stick guide them all this night. May Talking God be with them.

Tonight the "enemy" would be Vincent Roberts, the other boy, and the one girl. They spoke no Navajo. He had had the Los Angeles police check that out. It was probably ridiculous to consider that they might, but Yazzie never assumed anything. At the same time, he had had his Chinle officers inquire about Miss Wilcox and Shonto. They learned that she spoke fluent Navajo and the old prospector, a smattering.

Before the broadcast, he surveyed the scene below. He spotted the freshly excavated hole where the prayer cairn had been. He correctly surmised what had been buried and dug up there. He spotted, too, the attaché case tossed nearby.

He pushed the button that put him on the loudspeaker. His voice, magnified electronically, startled him. He talked in Navajo which could not be translated literally into English. The gist of it, however, was, "This is Captain Yazzie of the Tribal Police. We will be moving in very soon to rescue you. On the first shot, fall flat. Do not attempt to apprehend the subjects. I repeat, do not try to apprehend the subjects. You will be given future instructions in Navajo on the scene. If it becomes necessary for you to flee, Officer Ramah will take charge. Except for Officer Ramah, do not give any indication you understand

Navajo. Do not take any action that would upset the subjects. That is all. I will repeat . . ."

He broke off. He thought he had heard a muffled ping. On the underbelly. There it was again. This time more like a sharp crack.

"Take it up!" he shouted to the pilot. "We're under fire!"

Vince stood out in the open, took careful aim, bided his time, and squeezed the trigger. That second the copter lurched upward and forward, and he missed. He swore to himself. If he had had a rifle, he could have felled the big bird. Easy.

Picking up the moneybag, he yelled, "Come on, Grandpa. Let's go."

Shonto had difficulty getting up. Vince seized a hand and yanked.

I ought to bump off the old buzzard right here and now instead of waiting. He's stalling, killing time.

He shoved the revolver into Shonto's ribs. "I'm getting awful nervous."

27.

Crouching, they made their way along the river. Davis was in the lead, followed by Tachee and the other five officers and the paramedic. Although they could not yet see the ruins—and hence, the subjects and hostages could not see them—they moved silently through a heavy growth of trees and shrubs. There was the possibility someone could be out scouting.

Davis held up a hand to signal a stop. They could hear Captain Yazzie talking from the helicopter but could not make out the words. They watched as the chopper appeared to jump, and rose faster than normal.

Then Yazzie came over the radio, "We have been fired upon. The gunman is out in the open below us, but I cannot distinguish his features. Apparently our aircraft is okay. The rescue party should proceed with extreme caution. We'll keep

above the range of hand guns and will report movements
below, if any."

The officers gathered around Davis. They were apprehensive. They could be ambushed.

Davis said, "Let's hold it right here until we get another
report. No talking, no smoking, and no moving about."

On the canyon rim above the cliff house, in a high, howl-
ing wind, four officers worked quietly. From a four-ton truck,
which they backed up and parked dangerously close to the
precipice, they wrestled with an enormous three-hundred-foot
roll of nylon-cord ladder.

The men pushed the "wheel" off the truck, down a ramp,
and rolled it up against a boulder. They unwound the sixteen-
inch-wide ladder, which was light in weight and looked like an
ordinary rope one. The top had a couple of metal hooks which
they fastened to the truck's bumper. Each man tested the hooks
to assure himself they were secured. They had already checked
out the bumper.

Slowly they dropped the ladder down the canyon wall.
They worked only when the moon was clear of clouds. In the
moonlight, far below, they could see the narrow ledge that was
their target. They looked beyond the ledge into eternity. They
experienced a twinge of fear, a sudden, involuntary sucking in
of their guts, but they did not panic. This was their business—a
job where a slip of the foot or a crumbling or splitting off of
sandstone could plunge them to their death.

A couple of times the ladder caught on rocky points and
they had to swing it clear. In doing so, they tangled once with a
prickly pear cactus growing out of the wall and another time
knocked off a cliff swallow's nest.

By the time they finished, they were sweating. For a few
minutes they sat on their haunches. One moved back from view
of the canyon to light a cigarette. The pungent odor of
sagebrush after a rain saturated the air.

Only two would go down, Nathaniel Smith and Carlos

Aguilar. They already had their packs strapped on. They carried pitons, nuts, stoppers, braided perlon cord, small picks, and other mountain-climbing equipment. The other two officers were reserves who would remain on the rim unless summoned.

On the ladder they would be protected from sight of the subjects by the great stone overhang that covered the cliff house—as long as the subjects remained within the ruins. If one decided to explore, and looked up, he might see them. Even with only moonlight to go by, a good marksman could pick them off. They knew, though, they would not be ordered to descend until the officers in the helicopter reported no movement in the area.

Now Aguilar said into the radio, "Aguilar here. We're in position and ready."

"Proceed as instructed," was the cryptic answer.

They had not expected to move so soon.

A few minutes before, Captain Yazzie had advised Chinle and Davis that Shonto and the party who had fired on the copter had returned to the ruins.

Still talking in Navajo, Yazzie said, "All seems clear, Davis. Proceed as fast as possible. Since the subjects apparently have the money, there is no further reason for them to keep all three hostages alive."

Davis said, "We're splitting up with each officer leaving for his assigned post. We should be in position within fifteen or twenty minutes."

Yazzie roared, "Davis, we haven't that much time. Make it ten. It's got to be ten. Don't you realize—"

"Ten then."

Ten minutes. The hostages could all be dead in less time than that. What the thunder was the matter with Davis?

He took a deep breath, shook his head. He was being unreasonable. Regardless of how much Davis and the others hurried, they never could cover the terrain in ten minutes. Logistics were logistics and no amount of pressure could alter the physical setup.

The pressure, of course, could be for naught. The principal subject could have shot his prisoners immediately on his return to the cliff house. Probably not all three. He would save one to guarantee his flight out of the canyon. Probably Miss Wilcox. Ramah would pose too much of a threat and Shonto moved too slowly.

"We've got ten minutes to be in place," Davis said. "Captain's orders."

"The crazy fool," Tachee said. "I've got to crawl halfway there on my belly."

"That's going to take some doing," somebody commented.

She was in no mood for levity. "Ten minutes. We can do it."

She gave final, brief, curt instructions. No coughing, no blowing of noses. Keep the radio so low you have to hold it to your ear. Keep your back to the ruins when you talk into the radio. Crawl, once in sight of the cliff house. Take care about dislodging stones and pebbles.

"The operation starts as soon as the sergeant's in position," she concluded. Tachee had the longest distance to cover.

"Let's go," she said.

Two minutes gone. Eight to go.

Crouching, she struck off alone. For the next hundred yards, she stayed under the giant old cottonwoods. Once she stopped to listen and heard only the thunder of rushing water. In addition to the roar, the rain-soaked land blanketed their movements. There were no dry twigs to snap, no hard-packed earth to record the passing of feet.

Away from the others, she found herself trembling and on the verge of tears. Back there she had been a police officer. Now she was a woman reacting to emotional stress.

The cottonwoods ended and she fell prone. After the darkness, under their thick, interlaced branches, the moonlight seemed extremely bright. Reconnoitering, she lay quiet. Raising up on her hands, she saw the cliff house as through a gauze. It was a shadow play with shadow actors.

Wriggling fast, she reached the thicket that would serve as a command post. It was exactly as she remembered from the aerial photograph. The stunted growth permitted her to stand without being seen. By pulling branches apart, she had a good view of the cliff house. She was approximately one hundred feet away and about seventy feet behind the number one man. When Tachee reached his post, he would be on a parallel with the number one man and some two hundred feet to his right. Two officers were posted near Tachee to assist him if one or more of the suspects investigated the coyote call. Two others were on her left to protect that flank in case the suspects fled in that direction.

Holding the radio to her ear, she heard only slight static with an occasional crackle. No messages would be exchanged, barring an emergency, until Tachee advised he was in position.

She was tense, again thinking clearly. Her body was taut, ready to react on command. Once more, she was the police officer.

Then her muscles tightened. At the ruins, a woman—that would be Miss Wilcox—and a stooped man—the old prospector—stood against a wall. On the other side of the room, facing them, was a man with a gun.

A cloud crossed the face of the moon, and they faded from view.

She fought back an overwhelming compulsion to order an attack. Her reasoning, though, told her that a trigger finger was far quicker than officers storming the site. Her emotions cried out that any second she would hear gunshot.

Six minutes gone. Four to go.

28.

When Captain Yazzie broadcast the instructions in Navajo, a surge of relief swept Sandy. Now rescue would be a matter of perhaps another half hour. He had said soon, hadn't he, or had she imagined it? It was growing increasingly difficult to sort out the facts from the bits and pieces her imagination tossed into the hopper.

Perhaps it was Yazzie's voice, or the sound of his native tongue that stirred Frank Ramah briefly back to consciousness. Gasping, he struggled to convey something in Navajo. She pretended she did not understand. She could not do otherwise. Behind her, Jigger and Penny watched closely.

"You know Navvy?" Jigger asked.

She shook her head. "He's delirious. Doesn't know what he's saying."

That was partly true. He wanted his parents given a message, and a girl friend in Window Rock, but his thinking was too muddled to be intelligible. Sandy leaned close and asked him to repeat but he slipped back into unconsciousness.

Does he know he's dying? Sandy wondered. How horrible it would be to know . . . at the very moment.

Then came the shots, and her mind exploded. Vince had killed Shonto. There could be no other explanation. Any minute Vince would be heading back, to murder her.

She continued bathing Ramah's forehead. She must not permit herself to disintegrate. She would stand up to Vince and play for time. She didn't think he would kill her quickly. He would torture her with threats. He wanted to watch her squirm and beg for her life. At some point, however, she would have no recourse left but to try to escape. Then as he had with Charlie, he would shoot her down. He might miss; she might be too quick.

"How's he doing?" Jigger asked, indicating Ramah.

"What do you care?"

He turned away but not before she caught the hurt in his eyes. What a horrible thing for her to say.

Then there was a sudden floundering through brush. Pulling Shonto along, Vince hurried toward them. He yelled, "We got it! We hit the jackpot!"

Vince dumped the bills on the ground. A slight breeze

scattered a few. Shouting, Penny and Jigger scooped them up by the handfuls. "What d'ya know!" Vince kept repeating. "A half-million bucks! What d'ya think, Jigger. Think we got a half million here?"

"Who cares? You did it, Vince. You did it!"

"I'm going to get me a nightie," Penny said. "A black nightie you can see through."

"Clothes," Jigger said. "All the clothes in the store. What you getting, Vince?"

"A Cadillac. One of them neat little new ones."

Vince stuffed Shonto's hands full of bills, stuffed them inside his shirt, and took off one of Shonto's shoes to cram bills into it. "There, Grandpa, I don't know how much you got. We'll settle up later. Okay?"

He turned on Sandy. "You bitch! See, I did pay off. Vince Roberts always keeps a promise."

"Right!" Jigger said.

"I'd put a bullet through you, Wilcox, if I hadn't promised Grandpa I wouldn't."

Shonto moved the bills to his pants pockets. His pockets hadn't bulged so much since he was a kid with frogs and the like in them. His old heart kicked and pounded. For sure he thought he was going to croak off. What a strike—and after grubbing all these years. It was more money than he had ever dreamed of.

Vince turned all business. "Flashlights out. Come on, come on, douse them. We got to get the hell out of here—and fast, man. Fast."

He grabbed the radio, pushed a couple of switches, and shook it. He kicked Ramah in the side. "Wake up, copper, and get this thing going."

"He's dying," Sandy shrieked.

Jigger found the right switch, and handed the radio back to Vince who yelled into it, "Listen, you pigs, get your damn chopper out of here if you don't want the broad shot. I'm knocking her off if anybody comes around. You hear me?"

Tonalea's cold voice came over. "I must warn you, Roberts, you cannot escape the canyon. The canyon will drown you, or pull you down into its quicksand, or kill you in a rockslide. You cannot escape the canyon."

He whispered to the pilot to take the copter out of sight. He wanted to remove the pressure that the craft might exert on the subjects. The very fact they were under surveillance from above, and could do nothing about it, might trigger a hasty, fatal decision.

As the chopper started back down the canyon, Tonalea continued talking over the loudspeaker. "You're a city man. You don't know what you're doing. Think about it, Roberts. You've got the money but what good will it do you if you die? And you're going to die."

Tonalea had decided, after considerable thought, on this unorthodox approach. He could have informed Roberts that he was surrounded. That, however, would have tipped him off, and while the ploy might have worked with another killer type, it never would have with Roberts. He was too much the superman to surrender. He considered himself impervious to gunfire. Tonalea could have pointed out, too, that if he murdered the hostages, he would himself die. Tonalea knew, though, that a scare technique would not faze Vince Roberts. So perhaps a thought planted that the forces of nature would eventually engulf him might at least disturb him—might cause him to choose a foolish escape plan.

Vince answered by throwing the radio as far as he could.

"How are we going to get out?" Jigger asked fearfully.

"Fast. We've got to make the Chinle landing field in a couple hours and nail the bank courier before he takes off."

"We got enough," Jigger said. "Do you think we ought to take the chance, Vince? Why take a chance—"

"Get over there against the wall you two," Vince ordered Sandy and Shonto. He said to Jigger, "Because no guys in all history ever pulled two big heists the same night."

"All I want is a nightie," Penny put in.

"Look," Vince said, pulling a gun on Sandy and Shonto, "you think this is an execution? It could be. It's all up to you."

"I told you he'd kill us," Sandy said, stalling.

"Shut up! I've had a stomach full of you. I ought to give it to you but I promised Grandpa . . . All right, I can go two ways. I can kill you both, and get out of here fast, and I'll have speed and mobility if I wasn't hauling you around.

"Or I take you along—and you, Grandpa, can show us how to get out—and Wilcox, we'll use you for protection if we run into the cops."

He paused to give them time to think. He had discovered that sometimes thinking could scare the hell out of a person.

He continued, "What about it, Grandpa? Will you get us out of here? You've got better than a hundred thousand at stake. If they catch us, they'll take it from you."

Shonto's eyes brightened. "Me and Sam knows a trail nobody uses except us. Only me and Sam knows where it's at."

"The mule stays. I'm not dragging any mule around."

"I don't know how to find the trail without Sam along leading the way. Besides which I don't make much time on these old legs of mine but ridin' Sam I reckon I'd keep up with you."

Jigger said, "I thought I heard something."

Vince listened. "They're probably out there but we've got a passport, huh, Wilcox? You want a bullet now or you coming along peacefully and do what I say?"

"Thanks for giving me so many options."

"I'm going to have to execute you yet."

"Never been any doubt about it, has there?"

"We'd better get moving," Jigger said.

"Okay, Grandpa, we'll take the mule, although I know you're stringing me along. But I like you, you old buzzard."

"Where's the jewelry?" Penny asked. "You said you'd get me—"

"You'll get it. A whole case of it. We'll pick it up on the

way out. See, Wilcox, what you missed by being a stubborn ass."

"Surely you're not going to leave the officer to die?"

"Why not?"

"Someone dying—and you ask—"

"He tried to kill me, didn't he? Okay, Grandpa, get the mule and we'll be on our way. Beats all. Escaping after a big heist with a jackass."

Suddenly the air was rent with the barking and whining of coyotes. They were close by.

"Coyotes," Jigger said.

"Yeah." Vince listened intently. "They're awfully near. What about it, Grandpa? Do coyotes come this close?"

"Could be—if they's after somethin'."

Vince swore under his breath. "Indians. They're putting us on. Go take a look around, Jigger."

Jigger started away. Vince called him back. "Forget it. They want to split us up. But we'll stay together—as a fighting unit."

Shonto left to fetch Sam, and Sandy dropped to Ramah's side. His heavy, agonizing breathing continued, but his pulse was stronger. She called to him but did not get through. She could do nothing except offer the comfort, if he should come to, of one person close by who cared.

In this moment, as never before, she longed for Bill. When she was with him, all the wearisome, daily cares dropped away. If she got out of this alive, she would borrow Rinni's car, drive to Kayenta, pound on his door, wake him up, ask for breakfast, and demand that he marry her.

That was a wild thought. Problems and difficulties were never solved in such buccaneer fashion. Or were they? Or might they be?

The coyote cries grew sharper and nearer. They frayed her nerves. She had the feeling she was about to fly apart, a sensation inherited from the fears of childhood. When very young, she had lost a dearly loved cat to a coyote pack. For weeks she had awakened nights crying. No grief could compare to that of childhood, she thought, no terror. Not even this night.

Skeet was her childhood all over again. So many things he said reminded her of little episodes she had lived at Far Mountain. She was thankful he was sleeping, and unless some thoughtless person had awakened him, didn't know about the crash.

Her thoughts hedgehopped. Shonto. Did he understand Navajo? He should. For years he had lived in Navajo country. Still, many Anglos taught school and worked as nurses, in trading posts, in clinics, and in other jobs without ever learning the language. Not too many years past, it had been an unwritten tongue. Now, though, there were books in Navajo, mostly for school use. She had bought several for Skeet. She wanted him to read his own language as well as speak it.

Anxiously, she wondered if Shonto had understood the instructions. Communication between them was impossible. Vince watched them like a vulture. He, too, wanted to know, and hoped to surprise them in an exchange of glances.

She wished she knew whether Shonto stood with Vince or with her. She had seen the ecstasy—and there was no other word for it—in his eyes when Vince gave him the money. If somehow Shonto got away with it, he would rationalize that this was the same as discovering uranium. He had made a strike.

Very likely, he did know of an old trail out of the canyon. The ancient ones had left many behind, overgrown with the centuries and no longer visible. To a desert rat who had walked the treacherous terrain, they were still usable. Once on the rim, Vince would kill him—and her. Shonto might think otherwise. The basic fact still remained, though, that if Vince should be caught, she and Shonto would be witnesses against him at his trial for the slaying of Charlie Begay.

Vince thought he had the operation all wrapped up. And maybe he had. Without a doubt, he had a strong lever in two hostages.

Bill Delaney was as restless as the neighing, stamping horses. He walked constantly and aimlessly. He never noticed the curious glances the rangers sent his way.

He berated himself for having given his promise to remain behind. He had offered it in good faith, though now in reviewing the circumstances, he concluded he had not committed himself voluntarily. The promise had been extracted by threats and intimidation, namely that otherwise he would be handcuffed and held prisoner. The woman officer had been stern, high-handed, brusque. Obviously, she never had been in love.

He had pledged his word, however, and was dutybound to honor it. But uppermost in his mind was the possibility that if he caught up with the officers, he might get in their way and jeopardize Sandy. His emotions cried out for him to participate in her rescue. His intelligence informed him he would be acting recklessly.

He found a boulder away from the others and sat down. He couldn't engage in idle conversation. He had to be by himself to wait out the minutes.

A high, pleading wind whipped along the canyon wall and set the ladder to swaying. Nathaniel Smith shifted his body in an attempt to steady it. He searched the wall, too, for toe and hand holds. He was young, sturdily built, and had the lungs of an opera singer.

Barely touching a foot to the wall, he braked the sway. In doing so, he suffered a cut and bruised ankle. He had not anticipated such bright moonlight. He was a target and the knowledge hurried his descent.

He heard a rock falling from above, covered his head with one hand, and crouched. The rock, big enough to knock him off his perch, missed him by a foot. Standing up, he took a deep breath. He was fearful that the subjects might have seen or heard the tumbling rock and would look upward. He had the queasy feeling he was standing out in space.

When he reached the ledge, he signaled for his companion officer to start down. The ledge was about three feet wide. The sandstone seemed stable. Even at the edge, it furnished solid footing.

He had to have a cigarette. He had to, even though someone below might see the glow. Reaching into his shirt pocket, he took out a pack, and threw it out into space. He groaned but it was the only way he could conquer the urge. He rummaged around in the same pocket and came up with a piece of hard candy.

Cautiously, he made his way along the ledge. Reaching the overhang, he sat down to puzzle how to get under it. He didn't dare use a flashlight. He waited minutes until his eyes brought into focus the topography of the wall below, and more minutes until a cloud slowly passed off the face of the moon. Elated, he saw what looked like niches cut into the rock. Very possibly, the Anasazis who had built the cliff house had cut a trail to the rim. He was careful not to dislodge pebbles, which would be telltale.

He took his first step, then the next. The third, though, was missing, worn off by the centuries. Keeping one foot solidly placed, he lowered the other. It came within inches of the fourth step. He held his position while debating what to do. He decided to gamble. As he dropped his body, his poised foot scrambled wildly but missed the niche. His hands clawed desperately at hard rock, and found a jagged piece protruding. He held onto it for seconds before it gave way. The time was sufficient, however, for him to get his other foot anchored.

After a few more steps, he edged himself under the overhang, and saw the tower of the cliff house. In the moonlight, it looked foreboding and eerie. From below, voices rose faintly. He could not decipher them.

His shirt and trousers soaked, Tachee wormed his way over the wet ground. Pulling himself along on his elbows, he held the revolver on the ready in his right hand. The going was

slow and difficult. Yazzie was right. He must reduce. He
blamed his pot belly on too much time spent at a desk. He
should get out into the field more.

After each move, he paused. From time to time, he let out
a coyote bark or whimpering. Soon one of the subjects would
have to come to investigate. Otherwise, Tachee would crawl so
close he could pick them off. "I'd sure like to get me some
Anglos," he had told Yazzie.

Yazzie had erupted—which had been Tachee's purpose in
making such a statement. Tachee prayed he would not have to
kill anyone ever, be the party Anglo, Navajo, or Chicano. The
same as with most Navajos who followed the Blessing Way, he
abhorred killing.

He raised up until he could see the ruins. He was nearer
than he had thought. One suspect, a teen-age kid, was looking
in his direction. Tachee dropped quickly, fearful he had been
seen.

29.

By now the night was warm and fragrant, and the moon
cast a soft shimmer over the land. Her land, her canyon, her
people. The turmoil that in recent months had been within
Ramona Davis was mysteriously gone. She knew not why but
in this moment when gunfire would soon break out she was in
harmony with the Holy People and herself.

Eight minutes gone. Two to go.

She could wait no longer. She took a deep breath, flounced
her hair back, and left the command post. Moving as fast as
a snake, she writhed over rough terrain dotted with thick,
scraggly, stunted growth. It clawed, scratched, and tore at her.
Her arms and legs were bleeding and her shirt ripped. Yet she
was oblivious to physical pain and discomfort, conscious only
of what lay ahead.

The number one man heard her coming. Crouching, he

was in a firing position. "Davis," she whispered, and he relaxed.

"I'm taking over here." She heard her words but it was another's voice. A few feet away she sat and watched herself.

She was amazed at how calm she was, that there was no quickening of the heartbeat. "You're to take charge of the command post."

Puzzled, he hesitated. "Captain's orders," she said, and he nodded and left.

Stretched flat, her head raised only inches, she took reconnaissance. Through a break in the desert growth, she had a raccoon's-eye view of the ruins. It was a stage, elevated slightly, with side walls serving for wings, and the rear wall, for a backdrop.

She easily identified the cast of characters. The three subjects stood out. The boys, huddled together talking, faced toward Tachee. The girl, with gun held loosely in hand, watched a woman—it had to be Sandra Wilcox—who, oddly, was kneeling.

Two were missing. The old prospector and Officer Frank Ramah. She was disturbed and fearful.

Very slowly, she crawled toward the ruins only thirty feet ahead. With every foot, she ran a hand over the ground ahead. She kept well away from shrubs. She wanted nothing moving that would betray her. Neither a shrub nor any living thing she might accidentally disturb.

The stage lay ahead, and she a character in this slow-moving, tortuous play. Within minutes, it would be over. Strange, all those hours wasted on trivia, and the living and dying that took place in minutes.

Leading his mule, Shonto stumbled out and almost fell. Sandy hurried to his side. "It's all right girl."

"Come on, get your jackass over here," Vince ordered. He clutched the moneybag under his left arm, which freed his right

for gun play. Occasionally, a twenty-, fifty-, or hundred-dollar
bill would escape and float to the ground. Once Shonto hobbled
back to retrieve a hundred. The others paid no attention to
the errant bills.

Nearby, the meadowlark burst into song. Vince whirled
about. "Sounds like a real bird," Jigger said.

"Indians. They're coming at us from both sides."

"What'll we do?" Jigger asked again.

Ramah groaned and Sandy started toward him. "Wilcox!"
Vince shouted.

"He's dying."

"So what else is new?"

"I'm scared," Penny said.

"Don't worry, sweetheart, we'll be at home plate before
you know it. Grandpa, bring the mule over here. I want you to
lead him out. Jigger, you get over on that side, and you knock
him off if they start firing. I'm sorry about that, Grandpa, but
we've got to show them we mean business."

"He's going to get your share of the money back," Sandy
told Shonto.

Vince glared. "We'll see that your folks get it, Grandpa.
You got folks, haven't you?"

Grim-faced, Shonto nodded. He had been certain he had
the money—and freedom. The girl was right. They had no
honor. They would kill him with no more compunction than
shooting a jackrabbit. If he could signal the girl, and get the
idea across to her of jumping the kids . . . well, by golly, they
might get away with it. Again, they might not. But at this point,
they had better die fighting than meekly accept death.

Vince continued, "Get over here with me, Wilcox. Jigger,
forget about Grandpa. I've decided to knock off Wilcox first."

Shonto raised his voice. "No, you don't, son. I ain't got
much time left but the girl's got years comin' up."

"No!" Sandy cried out, taken back by Shonto's offer. Their
eyes met briefly. His had a message. Puzzled at first, she then
got it. She gave no hint she understood.

To Vince she said, "Have you stopped to think that we're only good to you alive? Dead, they'll be all over you."

"She's right," Jigger said.

Vince was amused. It was a geek show watching people squirm. "We need you, Grandpa, to show us how to get out of here. But we don't need Wilcox for one damn thing."

"I'm awful scared," Penny repeated. "All those Indians out there."

The coyote barkings sounded nearer all the time, now about thirty or forty feet distant, and the meadowlark, about the same.

"They're getting ready to attack," Jigger said. "They're going to pile in here and kill us all. Everybody, including them." He indicated Sandy and Shonto.

"Let 'em pile in. I'll knock them off fast as they come. Nobody can outshoot Vince Roberts."

Stepping to the edge of the ruins, he shouted into the night, "Listen, you bastards out there, we've got two hostages —and we're going to execute them if you don't let us through. Okay, we're heading out—but one shot from you—only one shot—and they're dead. You got that?"

He stared out over the moonlit landscape, eerie and myste-rious as only forgotten canyons can be. In the distance, the river still rushed, foamed and thundered. High up, the whine of a wind imprisoned in the sheer canyon walls rose and fell. But on the canyon floor there were only fitful gusts occasionally, and at this moment, not a leaf moved. Neither an animal that the eye could see, nor a human being.

Only the faint echo of his own voice came back to taunt him.

"Go to hell!" he yelled, and turned back to the others. "I gave them warning. Penny, did you hear? I warned them. You heard me. I warned them."

Fall flat at the first shot, Sandy told herself. Watch his gun hand. If he tries to kill you, grab his legs, upset him. Do any-

*thing, do something. Don't freeze, don't panic. Don't die
quietly.*

Tonalea said, "Come in, Davis." When there was no answer to his repeated calls, he grew concerned. "I can't raise
her," he said to Yazzie. Both were tense. Zero hour was only
seconds away.

Tachee came in. "I can't draw them out. I'm only twenty
feet away."

"Hold it there," Tonalea instructed.

Once again Tonalea said, "Come in, Davis."

The number one officer came over. "Major, I'm at the
command post on orders of Davis. She's taken over my assignment. She said the captain ordered the switch."

Tonalea exploded. "You get up there and tell Davis—"

"I can't, Major. She's advancing on the target. She's very
close. Maybe ten feet away."

"What's she got in mind?"

"She didn't say."

"Keep me posted."

"Yes, sir."

Tonalea turned to Yazzie. "I don't like it."

"She knows what she's doing," Yazzie answered. "I'd put
my money on it."

"She should have advised us."

Ten minutes gone. None to go.

Only a few feet from the rubble, Davis wormed her way beneath a stunted growth of tough little cedars and came to rest.
Now that she was within whispering distance, she tried to quiet
her labored breathing. With a struggle, she contained a persist-
ent desire to cough.

The gun was cold in her hand. There was none of the comfortable, confident feeling there should be between a weapon
and a person. In four years, except on the gun range, she had
never fired it. She had hoped she never would.

Then she discovered that it was not the gun that was cold. It was her hand.

Careful not to shake the cedars, she squirmed about until she had a keyhole view of the scene. The principal subject, Vincent Roberts, stood slightly behind Sandra Wilcox on the far side of a mule. His voice had had the maturity and depth of one far older than his years. Underlying the words, in the very woof of the voice, was a foreboding, sinister quality. There was no question he would murder the hostages and no question he would kill anyone who got in his way. She had been prepared for that since learning he had used a six-year-old as a target. Yet hearing the voice and seeing the slayer—this was more terrifying than knowing what he had done.

The old prospector, Shonto, held the reins preparatory to leading the mule. The boy they called Jigger was on the side opposite Vince, and the girl called Penny was set to follow the mule. Again, Officer Ramah was missing, and she concluded he had been slain.

Taking a deep breath, she moved along the ground, flat with it, veering sharply to her left. By the time the signal was given, she must be on a dead line with Vincent Roberts.

An old chant came to her. *Soon it would be the land of the dawning, the pollen of the dawning. Soon all would be beautiful again, all would be restored in beauty.*

We're Navajos, Larry. We're The People, The Dineh.

Nathaniel Smith stood on the tower's rim, which was a foot wide, staring down into pitch darkness. In the hope he might see what lay below, he took his time in letting his eyes adjust. Eventually, they did—with the help of faint moonlight seeping in where chunks of masonry had fallen away. He saw that the tower was like a square silo. If there had been floors or ladders, they were long gone. The descent would be straight to the bottom.

The roof, which had consisted of poles probably covered with brush, had disappeared. The masonry, though, appeared in amazingly good condition. With his pick, he tapped the stonework. He didn't dare pound it for fear those below might hear but he satisfied himself that he could depend on it to hold a nylon rope which he carried over his shoulder. He would go down the rope hand over hand.

Finding a crevice, he took from a shirt pocket several nuts —small, six-sided, metal objects with holes in the centers. He tried them for size, then forced one into the crevice. First, however, he ran the rope through the hole. He tested the nut by lowering his body a few feet down into the tower, all the time holding to the rim but putting increasing weight on the rope.

For added safety, he ran the rope through an opening near the top, where a stone had fallen out, and over the rim itself. He worked fast, conscious of the time factor. Once his heart skipped several beats when he sensed movement below. Then he heard the twitter of a bird. He made a mental note to swing away from the wall as he descended. He would avoid disturbing a nest, and frightening a bird that might cry out and arouse suspicion in those below.

He was finishing when Aguilar joined him. They conferred briefly in whispers. They assumed that once they were at the bottom of the tower, they would find access to the second floor of the cliff house and from there they could work their way to the first.

Still whispering, Nathaniel Smith held the radio close to his lips to advise Chinle they were descending and should be in position within a few minutes.

30.

Still prone, Tachee waited. He was tense and a little nervous. It was the waiting that gnawed at his guts. He liked to rush headlong into situations. He was disappointed, too, that Vincent Roberts had not fallen for the coyote cries.

Tachee was on a dead line with the boy called Jigger. When the signal was given to move, his job would be to take

Jigger out of the action. The number one man, who was now Davis, had been assigned to Roberts, and the officers in the rear room to the high school girl. The timing had to be split second, and no matter how well the officers executed the operation, there could be casualties.

Major Tonalea had emphasized that no subject was to be fired upon until that subject had been given an opportunity to surrender. Tachee would follow the major's instructions, although he thought that was an excellent way to get himself killed.

At long last, Tonalea's voice, a whisper over the radio, came over, clear, cool, precise. Everyone was at his post. They were to move as soon as Tachee activated the operation.

Tachee lifted his head slightly and bellowed into the night. "We are the Navajo Tribal Police. Come out with your hands behind your necks. Everybody. This is the only warning we are giving you. All right?"

Without a moment's hesitation, Vince fired in his direction. The bullet bit a branch off a shrub a foot away. Tachee swore. Firing in the dark at only the sound of a voice, Vince had scored a near hit.

Jigger and Penny froze. Sandy and Shonto dropped flat to the ground.

Davis answered Vince's blast from a crouching position in the open. She had anticipated his quick reaction, and had her sight set upon him. He was in full moonlight with his attention riveted on Tachee's location. He was waiting for a telltale movement in the brush.

The officer on the far left echoed her fire. But at that instant, the mule panicked and Vince ducked out of the way, and both their shots missed.

Turning, Vince plowed a bullet a few feet from Davis, and for a second, she was stunned. In a flash, he got off another in the direction of the officer.

All the time, Vince was yelling instructions to Jigger and Penny. Davis, firing again, failed to catch a word. An enormous cloud blacked out the moonlight, and the people in the ruins became only indistinguishable forms moving about. Calmly, Davis waited. An officer on her left fired a flare but it fizzled.

The mule broke into harsh, loud braying and, subdued by the uproar, let Penny lead him. She got him turned about so Vince could use him as a shield.

From the rear room, the two officers who had descended from the rim triggered a couple of quick shots. Hidden behind the stone work of the door opening, they showed only half their bodies for the seconds required to take aim and fire. By now Vince was flat with the back wall and out of their range unless they exposed themselves.

Using her Saturday Night Special each time they darted out was Penny, who stood alongside Vince. A bad shot, she nevertheless kept them pinned down.

At any time Tachee could have dropped Jigger, but he had a hunch. Jigger stood rigid, petrified. Tachee yelled for him to throw him his gun. Vince screamed at him. Jigger cried out, "I can't! I can't!" He tossed the weapon into the brush where Tachee was hiding. Then he backed slowly to the rear wall. He sank down and sat in a stupor. Only a few feet away, Frank Ramah lay, still unconscious.

Suddenly the scene was theatrically lighted. The helicopter was high overhead. It had stayed out of sight until the ground command post advised Tonalea and Yazzie that Sandy and Shonto had fallen flat. Its searchlight moved in to focus a powerful spot on Vince and Penny.

With the two protected by the mule from a frontal attack, and the officers in the rear pinned down, Davis and the others held their fire. So did Vince and Penny. Quickly, Vince reloaded.

From overhead, Tonalea said in Navajo over the loudspeaker, "Hold your fire until we get them in the open."

Yazzie carried a rifle with telescopic lenses. An expert marksman, he doubted if he could use it. The turbulence was great, and the innocent people below were grouped too closely together. The copter might lurch at the time he triggered a shot.

In scrambling backward for the protection of the wall, Vince had dropped the moneybag he had been clutching under his left arm. On hitting the ground, it had burst open and the bills spilled out. Twenties, fifties, hundreds. A few floated lazily about, and more rose to join them as the mule and Vince shuffled around.

Quietly, Davis worked her way up the gentle but rocky rise to the ruins. She was raked by sharp edges, her clothing torn, her skin cut in long, knifelike slashes. She clawed at the ground to pull herself up. The rocks slipped under her boots.

Meantime, Shonto lay where he had fallen. If he was going to get a bullet in the back, he didn't want to know about it.

Heading for the back room, Sandy crawled slowly, praying no one would notice her. The abdominal pain was excruciating. Every movement sent a shriek exploding in her brain. For a moment, as she passed before Vince, he stood tall and threatening above her.

God help me. Don't let him look down.

Breathing hard, he talked calmly to Penny. "Watch the door, and give those bastards a blast every time they show their faces. Watch 'em. They may try to storm us."

"How am I doing, Vince?"

"We've got to get out of here. Where's Wilcox?"

"She's here. On the ground."

Sandy's heart stopped. *Make a run for the door. No, don't, he'll bring you down. You'll never reach it. Hold it where you are. See what happens.*

"Okay, Wilcox, on your feet, damn quick, before we let you have it."

Hold it. Don't panic. Play along.

Penny dropped to her knees. "Please, please. You've got to get up . . . do what Vince says . . ."

Sandy was halfway up, ready to run. *Not yet. Stall, stall.*

From above, Tonalea barked, "The girl's bent over Wilcox. She's doing something to her. Kill the mule! Open fire on the mule!"

They had to remove Vince's shield, and get him in the open.

Shonto heard. He rose fast as a teen-ager, desperation smothering the arthritic pain. He was waving his hands in front of Sam and crying out, "No! No!"

Tonalea shouted, "Hold your fire until we get the old guy out of the way."

Shonto turned and struck Sam a hard blow on the rump which took him by surprise. He leaped, screamed, and panicked. Whirling about, he exposed Vince and Penny.

The second he did, Vince opened fire, blasting in all directions. Shonto dropped again to the ground. Tachee worked his way stealthily to Vince's blind side. The plan now was to draw Vince's fire in one direction while Tachee and his men moved in from another.

"You coming with us, Wilcox?" Vince yelled.

He was under constant attack but was crouched low and a small target. Again, he reloaded, his fingers working unbelievably fast.

Don't panic. They'll bring him down any minute now.

When Sandy didn't answer, he shouted at Penny, "Let her have it. We don't need her. We don't need anybody."

Penny hesitated. "Come on," he yelled. "Give it to her. We've got to get going."

Penny rose and stood above Sandy, the gun aimed straight for Sandy's head. It was not more than six feet away.

Don't worry. She won't kill you. Not Penny.

But Penny would. *I do what Vince tells me to do.*

Davis fired, and the Saturday Night Special dropped from Penny's hand. Screaming, Penny grabbed her shoulder and doubled up. The mule jumped in fright and his rump knocked her flat. Still shrieking, she was back on her feet, looking about wildly for the weapon.

Vince turned on Sandy, who was running for the door. Before he could get off a shot, Nathaniel Smith, crouching low, emerged with a .357 magnum exploding. Aguilar stepped out of the doorway to cover him and Sandy. Smith grabbed Penny who, despite her wound, fought like a baby tiger.

Vince caught a slug in his left thigh. For only a second, he hesitated. "Damn you!" he yelled, and continued firing.

Smith was still wrestling with Penny when Vince felled him with a shot in his right arm. He dropped the magnum and, letting go of the girl, staggered to the back room. Aguilar retreated with him.

"We're going to make a run for it," Vince told Penny. "We'll grab Grandpa. Can you make it?"

"I don't know, Vince." She was moaning and sobbing.

"Come on, sweetheart."

"We can't leave Jigger."

"Jigger!" he yelled. "Jigger!"

From above, Tonalea and Yazzie could not believe what they saw below. They could not believe it then or afterward.

Bent low, Davis was running up the rise toward Vince. In the open, she exposed herself not only to his fire but to the cross fire of her fellow officers.

Tonalea said, "Hold your fire. Everyone. Davis, what're you doing? Get down, get down! Davis! Davis! Don't you hear me? Tachee, try to draw subject's fire."

She got entangled in a tamarisk but yanked herself free. She fell but in seconds was back on her feet. With one hand on the rubble, she swung her body over what remained of the front wall.

Vince saw her coming. For a second, he was nonplussed. He suspected a trap. Frantically, he glanced around, thinking someone else was moving in on him. He saw Tachee standing upright, shouting at him, then firing. He answered the shot, turned back to Davis.

Rising to her full height, she walked toward him. He yelled to Penny to clear out.

He grazed Davis' right side, but the impact failed to stop her. He screamed in agony as he caught a slug in the chest. Dropping, he rose an instant and his .38 exploded twice.

Davis crumpled and slowly went down, sinking to her
knees. She uttered no sound. For a long moment, she sat there,
then toppled. As a child in the womb, she lay drawn up.

Penny fell sobbing over Vince, who lay stretched out in the
money he had coveted and killed for.

As in a nightmare, Sandy walked unsteadily toward Shonto
to help him up.

The number one man, who had left the command post the
moment Davis fell, glanced at her, then said into the radio,
"Major, Officer Davis is dead."

Jigger stood over Penny and Vince. "He was a great guy.
A great guy."

Tachee said, "Come on, boy. You too, girl. You're both
under arrest."

Other officers hurried about. One picked up the bills. The
paramedic concentrated on Frank Ramah, still unconscious,
then treated Penny and Nathaniel Smith.

Shonto put his arms about Sam's neck and mumbled. Then
he led Sam out of the ruins and disappeared into the night.

The thunder of the river persisted. The meadowlark, si-
lenced temporarily, resumed its age-old song.

In Chinle, Tonalea sat in shock and grief.

Yazzie said, "You never know what someone will do until
they're actually under fire."

"Not Davis," Tonalea said. "Not Davis."

31.

Ramona Davis was buried up near Mexican Hat on a high,
dark mesa close to the turquoise sky she loved. Puffy white
clouds floated gracefully, clouds that in her childhood she
thought bore Changing Woman on her missions about the
world.

She was buried in a blanket with her cradleboard. In accord with an ancient custom, she could take with her any possession she wished. On her last visit home, she had told her mother that if she should die, she wanted the cradleboard. She had laughed. "Don't let them lose the squirrel's tail."

In accord with custom, too, there was no funeral and no graveside services. Only the white trader, who had volunteered to bury her, was at the grave. Some distance away stood four members of her clan. Her mother remained with friends in her hogan.

When the trader had finished, he broke the shovel handle over a rock and left both parts on the ground. The shovel would never be used again.

In time, Major Tonalea and Captain Yazzie went to Mexican Hat.

"She was one hell of a woman," Yazzie said. "I wish I knew what happened."

Tonalea shook his head. "She had a problem, I know. I was always going to talk to her about it. We put things off, and friends die, and we wish then . . ."

They saw her mother. Though shrunken and wrinkled, she stood regal, and her patrician face reflected the wisdom of the years. If there were tears inside, she did not put them on display. She said little. Her daughter's life told it all. What more could be said about a daughter who had lived the corn-pollen way, who had never forgotten her mother or her people, who had died heroically?

Larry came when the family and clan members gathered to divide Ramona's possessions. Not that he asked for or expected anything. He looked haggard and they said he was working too hard. He wore sunglasses and gave as an excuse that he had an eye infection. His voice was husky at times, and not true, but no one thought anything about it.

Many will grieve but there will be no shame.

32.

The sun drenched the canyon rim where Shonto stood with Sam by his side. To the south were sand dunes, to the east, the mountains. A land primeval, scarcely touched. Yet.

"Good old Sam," he said, rubbing an ear.

He took an old buckskin tobacco pouch out of a torn hip pocket. It was yellowish with age and smelled strongly. Next he reached into the saddlebag and extracted a one-hundred-dollar bill. With a rusty knife, he cut the bill in half. He tossed one half away, and shook the makings into the other. Carefully he rolled the bill until he had a cigarette.

33.

The next day, Bill paced restlessly outside the little hospital in Chinle. On Captain Yazzie's orders, he had been released from custody and informed no charges would be filed against him.

When Sandy emerged, she was still in pain. A Navajo doctor had treated and bandaged her arm and found she had suffered severe contusions of the abdomen but no apparent serious injuries.

"Don't give me one of your bear hugs," she said. "Treat me like a lady for a change."

He kissed her gently.

"Not like that much of a lady," she protested, and showed him exactly the degree she had in mind.

Heading for Kayenta in his Mustang, she found comfort in the old familiar scenes, and some of the long night slipped away. She put it out of mind by talking, and he listened, knowing that she needed to escape memories that would fade with time but nevertheless haunt her for years to come.

"She was a stranger," Sandy said. "A stranger. I wish we could thank her—let her know . . ."

He said thoughtfully, "You know, I think she did—know, I mean."

She looked at him questioningly, but he didn't elaborate. "I phoned Skeet. He's going to charge his friends admission to talk with me."

"Good idea."

Her boy Skeet—*shi' ash kii Skeet*. She liked the sound of that. He would always be her boy Skeet. He would be waiting, scuffing his shoes in the dust. He would rush her like a puppy, throw his arms around her and hug her. One minute he would cry, thinking how near she had come to dying, and the next, laugh when she kidded him.

"Pull over here," she said abruptly. "I want to talk to you."

"Now?"

"Now."

Mystified, he parked the car well off the highway. It was a quiet spot, not a hogan in sight. Everywhere she looked were the mesas and mountains and desert that she loved. No matter where she went in the years to come, they would always be with her, and The Dineh would always be her people. She thought: nothing, not even time, obliterates the growing-up years.

She got out of the car and he followed. She stood looking at a hawk wheeling in the sky.

"Have you phoned Boston?" she asked without preamble.

He was taken by surprise. "I—I—well, we had called it off, Sandy."

"You can call her at the next pay phone we come to. I'll get the change."

"She'll be at work."

"Doesn't she have a phone at work?"

"Yes, but—"

"After that, we'll find a minister."

"Say, what is this?"

"A shotgun wedding—as soon as I find the shotgun."

"What about—what about—?"

"Strip mining? I'll fight it until hell freezes over—and you'll go on doing it. Bill, we don't have to agree on everything. Just because we're married doesn't mean we have to be carbon copies, does it? We're thinking people, I hope. For heaven's sake, Bill, we don't have to be twins."

He thought that over. "We're going to have an awful lot of fights."

"And we'll kiss and make up and make love and it'll be better than ever. I'm putting a new sentence in the wedding ceremony."

"Without asking me? I mean, I haven't even accepted your proposal yet."

"It's the bride's prerogative."

"Who said so?"

"You want to make something of it?"

"What is it?"

"An old Navajo saying somewhat Anglo-cized. 'As long as the rivers shall run and the grass shall grow, I shall love you.' "

"Good. I'm glad you consulted me."

As long as the rivers shall run and the grass shall grow . . .

ADDENDA

Ronald Hardin, alias Jigger Hardin, was given an indeterminate sentence in Los Angeles County juvenile court, Los Angeles, for complicity in the slaying of six-year-old Louis Mercado. He was turned over to the California Youth Authority which could hold him until he was twenty-three or release him earlier.

Georgia Thompson, alias Penny Thompson, was found guilty in U. S. District Court, Phoenix, Arizona, of assault with intent to kill. She was sentenced to serve time in a federal juvenile facility until the age of twenty-one.

Charlie Begay was buried near his hogan. His classmates asked to name their school after him.

Officer Frank Ramah, after four months in an Albuquerque, New Mexico, hospital, recovered and resumed his duties.

The Navajo Tribal Police forwarded $397,000 to J. C. Berchtol's employer, Pina and Fanta of New York City. Accompanying the money was a note explaining that this was the amount recovered at the crash scene.

Shonto disappeared and those who knew him assumed he had died in some lonely spot.

Sandra Wilcox and William Delaney were married in the Presbyterian Mission Church at Ganado, Arizona. Rinni Sky was the bridesmaid. Skeet Wilcox gave the bride away.